Bloodstone

SPARROWHAWK BOOK 1

Kathryn Hoff

Copyright © 2019 by Kathryn Hoff.

All rights reserved. No part of this publication may be reproduced, distributed or transmitted in any form or by any means, including photocopying, recording, or other electronic or mechanical methods, without the prior written permission of the author, except in the case of brief quotations embodied in critical reviews and certain other noncommercial uses permitted by copyright law.

Cover Design by JD&D Design. © 2019 by Kathryn Hoff.

Book Layout © 2017 BookDesignTemplates.com

Bloodstone/ Kathryn Hoff. —1st ed.

For Ari

CHAPTER 1

The lure of brandy and a beautiful woman

THE SELKID COLONISTS ON SANTERRO made a brandy that, according to the traders' database, was famed throughout the outer sectors as *an exhilarating, carefree immersion in silken texture and enticing flavor.*

Or as my half-brother Kojo said: "Quick high, tastes good, headache manageable."

We ordered enough to fill the cargo holds of our little space hauler *Sparrowhawk*.

Judging by the level of inebriation on Santerro's streets, the brandy lived up to its reputation. Selkids the size and shape of walruses lolled happily next to tipsy Terrans, flippers and hands alike in their grip on their precious bottles.

"You know, Patch," Kojo said as we dodged boisterous tipplers, "maybe we should stay here another night. We could see the sights, enjoy the famous Santerro hospitality." He pushed his black curls from his face, flashing his cocky grin.

I'd learned to distrust *that* smile a long time ago.

"You mean enjoy the hospitality of the casinos." I shoved him toward the spaceport. "Forget it. We leave tonight, as planned. Go oversee loading while I buy the rest of the provisions."

With a regretful look toward the glittering lights promising food, drink, and other delights, Kojo strolled toward the docks. I shook my head as he left, wishing the ancestors had endowed my half-brother with more caution. He was twenty-eight—eight years older than me—but sometimes I felt like Kojo's scolding auntie instead of his younger sister.

Recharged power modules, jump cells, food staples, air and water filters, engine lubricant—I'd almost fulfilled my list when my datacon buzzed with a message from Kojo: *Delays in loading—new inspection procedures. Found some passengers.*

Damn. New inspections, just what we didn't need. And passengers? Zub blast him, we'd said no passengers this trip.

By the time I got to the spaceport, the gates to the docks were mobbed. Queues snaked out into the street with luggage-toting Selkids vying for position with Terran traders and their crates of merchandise and freighter crews staggering back from shore leave with bellies full of brandy and pockets crammed with extra bottles. And among the screeches, howls, and grumbles, one topic prevailed: complaints about the new inspectors.

Even with my height, I had to climb onto a crate to peer over the crowd. I spotted Kojo in queue, halfway to one of the five inspection stations. He was chatting up a pretty woman. *Of course.* With his handsome brown face and winning smile, Kojo never failed to find someone to flirt with.

Looking beyond Kojo, my stomach sank. No wonder there were delays. The inspection stations weren't staffed with easy-going, bribable Selkids, but by Gavoran Corridor Patrol officers. The Patrol employed only Gavs: Terrans' Neanderthal cousins, sober and dedicated to enforcing the Settlement Authority's tech restrictions. They were stopping everyone going to the docks, scanning identity implants and scrutinizing baggage, searching for items on the Settlement Authority's lengthy list of regulated technology.

And somewhere among the docks beyond the inspectors, past the grand passenger ships and freighters, lost among the independent haulers and ragged shuttles, berthed in one of the cheap slips with low-capacity lifters, was *Sparrowhawk*.

"Burzing Neanderthals," said the bleary Terran to my left. "They don't give a damn about holding everyone up. I don't mind Selkids—flippers out all the time for a little sweetener, sure, but at least they keep the traffic moving. But Gavs—they won't even take a decent bribe."

I shot him a glare. Apparently, he was too drunk to notice my own half-Gav features.

At least I had the advantage of Gavoran size. I'd just begun to push my way toward Kojo when shouts came from behind.

"Runaway slave! Halt!"

I froze, craning my neck to see what was going on.

A young Gav girl, furred forearm bearing a slave brand, dodged between torsos in a desperate dash toward the docks.

"Stop her!" Two burly Gavs in the black vests of Clan Enforcers pounded after her. Massive shoulders and long arms, forward-thrusting heads covered with sleek pelts instead of hair, they shoved the waiting crowds aside with the bluster born of centuries of Gavs' technological domination.

A bystander snatched at the girl, but she darted behind a trio of mountainous Selkids. Terrans sympathetic to the plight of Gav slaves clucked their tongues at the enforcers or cheered the runaway, but none risked breaking the Selkid laws of non-interference between races.

My heart ached for her. With the Corridor Patrol at the gate, she'd need a miracle to make it onto a ship willing to take her to a Terran world where she could claim asylum. And if she were caught, her future would be grim.

Maybe I could improve her chances.

I turned my back on the pursuit and stepped to the right, leaving a clear path on my left for the girl to dash through. As soon as she passed, I stepped left and quick-turned.

The foremost enforcer barreled into me. Swinging my bag of ration packs and Prestoseal into his knees, I shrieked in Terran, "Watch where you're going!"

We fell in a tangle. As the second enforcer stumbled over us, I caught his ankle. He was on his feet in a moment, but by then the girl was out of sight, lost in the crowd.

The enforcer grabbed my arm, pulling me to my feet. "Filthy Terran! Interfering with Gavoran clan matters is a violation."

"What are you talking about?" I snatched my arm away.

"Burzing gorillas. *You* ran into *me*! Go harass one of your own kind."

The enforcer paused, staring at my mismatched features. Terran father and Gavoran mother—my face fit nowhere. To Terrans, my heavy brow ridge—not quite hidden by my yellow beret—and receding chin suggested brutish stupidity. To Gavorans, I was embarrassingly ugly: prominent Terran nose, ears too big, and bushy orange hair instead of a neat Gav pelt.

For a moment, my heart beat fast. Would he arrest me out of sheer anger? Out of suspicion? Did I face hours in a detention cell while a Selkid official considered the size of the bribe he'd need to confirm my identity as a free Terran?

With a snarl, the enforcer pushed past me to comb through the crowds at the next queue.

I breathed again. *Ancestors, grant her courage.*

It was only then, after the excitement was over, that I noticed blood dripping onto my left wrist. *Damn!* The collision had torn the graft that hid my old slave brand.

I snatched the scarf from my neck and stuffed it into my sleeve to hide the blood. Somehow, I'd have to get past the Gav inspectors without them noticing.

At the inspection station at the head of Kojo's queue, the Selkid keeping order shrieked like a clash of tin pots. His translator plug barked out, "Next in line!"

The line shuffled forward.

"Excuse me, sorry, pardon me." I threaded my way through the scores of people, crates, boxes, and cases, earning more than a few Terran and Selkid curses. Reaching Kojo, I inserted myself into line, sparking more grumbles from the people behind.

After a single glance, Kojo's newest friend turned away to fuss with her many pieces of luggage. I could almost read her thought: whatever I was to Kojo, I was *not* competition.

"Patch. About time you showed up," Kojo said. "Most of the cargo's loaded, there's just the special-handling bits to go through inspection."

"What passengers? We agreed we'd just haul cargo this trip."

"I had a bit of luck," he said. "Wrangled a charter, a couple of Terrans in a hurry to leave tonight. They won't be any trouble. I already settled the terms."

There was that smile again, the one that beguiled the ladies and the gamblers in all the ports in the outer sectors.

"You settled terms without me?" *Blast him.* Papa's will had named Kojo *Sparrowhawk*'s captain but Papa had made *me* the business partner. Kojo might have inherited Papa's good looks, swagger, and charm, but *not* Papa's business savvy.

"Next in line!" The people in the queue jostled and shifted. The pretty woman shoved her six suitcases ahead one pace.

I pulled out my datacon and opened the contract file—there was no telling what Kojo might have agreed to. *Destination: Palermo. Charter party: Miranda Tai, Terran. Fare: 3200 standard credits.*

I raised my brow at Kojo. Thirty-two hundred was a good price—maybe *too* good?

The duration clause made me pause. "Seven standard days? It's only four days to Palermo...Oh." *Destination subject to amendment by charter party.*

The damn fool. Thirty-two hundred credits were not enough to take *Sparrow* into a war zone or some pirate's lair—not to mention the other complications a snooping passenger might pose.

"Absolutely not," I hissed. "No side trips. We're up to our retros in debt—we need to get home and sell the cargo."

Kojo put on his most innocent, let's-be-reasonable face. "She's not going anywhere dangerous, just a Terran ag planet. Someplace called Oakdale, sector 204."

"Ridiculous. Who'd charter a whole ship for an ag planet on the back side of nowhere?"

"Next in line!" The queue scuffed forward.

Kojo leaned closer. "Mzee Tai overheard Hiram yarning in the saloon about knowing the currents and backways. She's willing to pay for privacy: leave tonight, no other passengers, and no checkpoints."

A smuggler. *Ancestors, give me strength.* "Kojo, that's the last thing we need!"

"Hush, Patch. It's not what you're thinking. She's not asking for cargo space, just a couple of cabins. She only wants to get away without leaving a trail. Nothing that will interfere with our other business. And look."

He opened his hand to give me a glimpse of a finger-sized rhollium ingot, the Selkid emperor's glyph imprinted on the top. "She paid an extra five thousand sovereigns. We need the money, don't we?"

Every dracham, but I didn't give him the satisfaction of admitting it out loud.

"Next in line!" Waiting travelers shuffled and grumbled.

It *was* tempting. Thirty-two hundred standard credits, plus five thousand sovereigns. The risk seemed small, but who knew why the lady needed to travel on the sly?

Kojo nudged me, nodding at the blood spots on my left sleeve. "What's wrong?"

"Nothing." I stuffed the scarf more tightly against the oozing wound. "This passenger. Is she pretty?"

Kojo ran his fingers through his curls. "Not bad. Why?"

"Because you only brought us to Santerro because the brandy trader was Terran, female, and pretty."

"So? We got a good deal on the brandy, didn't we? I've been doing this a lot longer than you, Patch. I've got a feel for people—"

"You mean women."

"—and trust me, Miranda's all right. The best thing we can do for the next few weeks is take on business as usual. This is a good job. Simple."

Simple? I hadn't missed the fact that Kojo was already calling Mzee Tai by her first name.

"Next in line!" We were getting closer now, only three parties between us and the inspectors.

I shook my head. "You'll have to give back her money, I'm not going to sign the contract. We should stick to the plan. Go home, sell the brandy, get ready for the next job."

Kojo took a breath. "We can't. I told you, I already agreed the terms."

"But the contract isn't final without *my* imprint."

He smiled his lopsided grin and pointed at my datacon.

I scrolled to the end of the charter, only to find—unbelievably—my own imprint as business manager. "You stole my access codes?"

"She was in a hurry."

"Next in line!"

Damn! If we hadn't been standing right in front of a brace of Selkid port officials and a Corridor Patrol squad, I would have knocked him on his backside—then broken all his fingers and knocked him on his backside again.

"You burzing idiot! Zub's pitchfork, this is too much."

But Kojo wasn't listening. His gaze paused on someone in line behind us. He caught my eye and rubbed the side of his nose, our private signal for *be ready*.

Stifling my anger, I glanced around.

A few places behind us in the queue, an aging Terran was nearly swallowed up among a group of Selkid merchants. The man peered around with the vacant smile of a nervous traveler, asking the people near him, *Am I in the right line? Why's it taking so long?*

I faced front again. Ahead on the docks, just beyond the inspection point, our engineer Archer bobbed and bounced, checking crates of supplies against a manifest. He was easy to pick out. As tall as me and reed-thin, his brown hair was even bushier than mine—birds could nest in it.

"Next in line!"

Reckoning with Kojo would have to wait.

The pretty Terran ahead of us struggled to heft her luggage to the inspection counter. Kojo obligingly stepped up to lend her a hand, earning a bright smile.

Behind us, there was a kerfuffle. Selkid squawks mixed with Terran cries. "Help! We need some help here!"

The old man had fallen.

A Selkid official waddled over, shoving people aside as his translator plug shrieked questions. The dazed old man struggled to get up.

Sharp words and Selkid howls were exchanged as the people in the queue jostled to protect—or improve—their place in line. The old man looked in danger of being trampled.

Abandoning Kojo, I pushed my way to the fallen man's side. "Mzee, are you hurt?"

The old man blinked rheumy eyes at me. "Thank you, missy. I'm all right, I think. Just a little shook, is all. Standing so long made my bum leg give out." His skin was the color of cheap whiskey and as worn and weathered as leather. He waved a half-empty bottle of brandy.

The Selkids helped him up, brushing him off and honking at his tipsiness. I offered my blood-blotted left arm for support, and he folded it under his, his fingers clutching mine.

"Much obliged, missy." The top of his head barely reached my shoulder. He leaned heavily on me as he limped forward, wheezing thanks as the official waved us to the head of the queue.

Kojo was already beyond the inspection station, chatting with the pretty woman and carrying a heavy gray duffel down the dock.

More important, Archer was far down the dock, pushing a handcart of crates that wouldn't appear on our manifest.

The Corridor Patrol inspector turned to us. "Identification?"

The old man and I turned our right shoulders so the Gav could pass his scanner over the implants. I kept my left arm linked with the old man. As long as the Gav officer didn't see the grafted-over slave brand on my injured left arm, I'd be all right—my shoulder implant listing me as Terran wasn't some black market override, but a genuine replacement, granted when Papa had smuggled me into Terran sectors and claimed asylum for me.

The Gavoran stumbled over our names. "Hiram Willows, Terran. Pachita Babatunji, Terran. Any luggage?"

The Patrol officer rooted through my bag, pawing through my purchases. After checking the tariff stamp on the old man's bottle, he passed us through.

I walked onto the docks arm in arm with Hiram, who'd been *Sparrowhawk*'s pilot since before I was born.

Hiram patted my hand and whispered, "All clear, missy. The lad's got the goods."

CHAPTER 2

Cargo and contraband

HIRAM AND I PAUSED at the top of *Sparrowhawk*'s gangway to enjoy the view. The cargo hold was nearly filled with crates of brandy, neatly stacked and lashed to the battens, inspection seals and tariff stamps all properly on display.

Hiram sighed. "Ah! Now *that's* a lovely sight."

I quickly counted crates. One hundred fifty-four. "Archer? What about the other crates?"

Archer popped out from behind a rack with a sheepish smile and even more twitches and jitters than usual. "Hey, Patch. Kojo put some in the small holds above, to balance the load." We'd hired Archer two months before, when Papa's worsening health forced Kojo to move from engineer to captain. At twenty-two, Archer was a couple of years older than me and just as tall, but he had the eager-to-please smile of a puppy begging for a *good boy* and a pat on the head.

Ancestors, give me patience. "Archer, I meant the *other* crates."

"Oh, those! They're in the vault." He grinned. "The razzle-dazzle worked."

I skirted the walls of brandy and peered into the vault. Crammed within were eight crates of premium Santerro brandy that had slipped past the tariff assessor—worth more on their own than the twelve score crates of middling stuff that had been duly declared and stamped.

I pasted a kiss on Archer's cheek, making his pale skin blush pink. "That's for hustling the extra cases in."

I kissed Hiram's bald spot, too. "And that's for the fancy acting."

"Aw, missy. It's nothing like the old days. Your pa and I had some rare old times when we was no older than you are now." Hiram was a second father to us, Papa's longtime bunkmate as well as crewmate. He never intruded, but was always ready to offer a word of comfort or advice, and an inexhaustible supply of yarns.

I eyed Hiram's half-full brandy bottle. "Kojo will want to lift off pronto. Maybe I better keep that for you." I held out a hand.

He took a lingering look at the bottle before handing it to me. "Good idea, missy. Never can tell when someone might need a jolt."

"All the provisions loaded?" I asked Archer. "Jump cells and power mods stowed?"

"Forty cells, but somebody must have let them get warm—they tested a little low. You should complain to the supplier. It would be bad to run out of juice in the middle of a jump."

So it would, but I wouldn't complain. Bottom prices meant bottom quality. Forty cells should still be more than enough to get to sector 204 and then home to Palermo.

Kojo traipsed in. "Why are you all standing around? The passengers are on their way. Launch in half an hour. Archer, secure the hatch. Patch, what are you doing, drinking before a launch? Better put that bottle away and get changed, I want to make a good impression. Hiram..."

Hiram crossed his arms and raised his chin.

Whatever orders Kojo had been about to give, he reconsidered. "Yes, well. I'll get started on the prelaunch checks. See you in the wheelhouse." He trotted up the aft steps toward the upper decks.

My teeth were grinding. "*Captain* Kojo is getting awfully high-handed with the orders. Does he think we've never left port before?"

Hiram chuckled. "He's growing into hisself, missy. Don't take it to heart. You just keep a firm hand on the business side. He'll settle in time."

"If I don't throttle him first."

Sparrowhawk was an old Selkid military cutter turned oligarch's private transport and then converted into a pirate's raider before being reborn under Papa's command as a hauler. She was a solid ship, for all her age, with a lot of power in her engines. Papa had remodeled *Sparrow*'s barracks as holds that could be reconfigured for passengers as needed, and in the process had built in plenty of well-hidden caches. Over the years, Papa and Hiram had added homey comforts, like a salon with couches and a long dining table. They'd also installed some extra touches for eluding raiders—or inconvenient Corridor Patrol cruisers.

A quick check of the stateroom and its adjoining passenger cabin proved them tidy, their blankets and towels clean and ready for use. Furnished in soothing beige, the cabins were softly lit to give the illusion of luxury and hide the threadbare patches in the carpet.

But one item in the stateroom was new. In the luggage locker sat a gray duffel—the one Kojo had carried away from the inspection station, even though he hadn't had it the minute before.

Yes, I thought sourly, the razzle-dazzle had worked just fine. Kojo had used the diversion we'd set up for the premium brandy to sneak the passengers' goods past the inspectors.

Damn the man.

I didn't have time to corner Kojo about the duffel or forging my imprint. After checking the stowage of the crates in the small holds, I climbed the aft steps to my cabin—an awkward little 'tween-decks space with room for an elevated bunk, now stowed, over a locker that served as table and business office. It had seemed spacious when I was seven years old.

The first thing I did was change my access codes. *Burzing Kojo*, imprinting my name on a contract he knew I wouldn't want.

After transferring credits for docking fees, I contacted Vell, the local agent for the Selkid Trading Cartel.

"Ah, Mzee Patch," his translator plug screeched. "Wouldn't you like to visit my office to do our business in person?" His squinty grin multiplied the creases in his face.

I manufactured a smile. "Sorry, Vell. We're on a schedule." Given Vell's roving flippers, I preferred to deal with him remotely—ideally from another sector.

I keyed in the required payment for the Cartel's cut of our haulage.

Vell squawked, "Next time, you must visit me. Yes, payment received. Do you confirm?"

"Cutter *Sparrowhawk* confirms agreement with the Cartel's trading articles." I put my imprint on the agreement.

"Fine. That squares me. Smooth sailing and easy berths."

A ping on my datacon told me he'd activated our ship's transponder. A flash from that would alert other Cartel members—and potential pirates—that *Sparrowhawk* traveled under the Cartel's protection.

I found a med kit and smoothed a clear skin seal over the torn graft on my left forearm. The slave brand had been burned in deep when I was a baby. One of the first things Papa had done after taking me from Gavora at the age of seven was to get the brand grafted over.

The Gavoran aristos claimed the clans were sacred, established by the blessed Sages in the dawn of history when they'd seeded Earth's Neanderthals onto the planet Gavora. *Crap.* As far as I was concerned, there was nothing sacred about slavery and the Sages were nothing more than myths concocted by aristos to justify keeping the lower castes subservient.

I'd had to renew the graft from time to time as I'd grown, but I'd hoped the current one would survive my latest—hopefully my last—growth spurt. Unfortunately, that little clash with the Clan Enforcer had ripped it open. I'd have to keep my sleeves down until I could get a more permanent fix. *More expense.*

I donned a dark blue jacket and matching beret. With a glance in the mirror, I yanked my hat a little lower on my forehead, letting my orange hair frizz out in back. Ready to meet the clients.

At the passenger hatch, Hiram was withdrawing the gangway.

"They're already boarded," Hiram whispered. "Best keep an eye on the boy—the lady has the kind of looks he likes."

As if *I* could do anything about Kojo's romantic adventures. I hurried to the cabins.

Hiram was right—Miranda Tai was a petite Terran with long-lashed eyes, a tawny complexion, and smooth, black hair pulled into an elegant bun. When I arrived at the stateroom, she had Kojo's hand in hers.

A tall, tan man with military-straight posture knelt among a jumble of suitcases and packs, checking the seal on the gray duffel.

Kojo nodded to the man. "Your property hasn't been disturbed, Mzee Grimbold."

Grimbold flashed a smile under his ginger mustache. "Just checking, Captain. Can't be too careful. The damn Settlement Authority with its damn restrictions. Nothing more than a Gav tool to keep Terrans from expanding."

"We appreciate your helping us, Captain Babatunji," Miranda cooed. "The hydroverter will make a huge difference to our future." Her smile made little dimples in her cheeks.

Kojo patted the client's hand. "I understand perfectly. We always try to stay on the right side of the law, but a hydroverter's harmless."

So *that's* what was in the duffel. I relaxed a little. Hydroverters might be illegal without an extensive—and expensive—environmental justification to the Settlement Authority, but they were a necessity on ag planets and not nearly as sensitive as some other items.

Grimbold stood and brushed the dust from his trousers. The butt of a stun pistol peeped out from under his jacket.

I stepped forward. "Welcome aboard. I'm Patch, the ship's business manager and steward. If everything's in order, Mzee?" I presented my datacon for payment.

Miranda's smile froze. She looked back to Kojo as if to reassure herself that the captain, at least, was truly Terran, before transferring thirty-two hundred credits for seven standard days' charter of *Sparrowhawk*.

That would help to refill our slender assets.

Kojo grinned. "If that's all settled, I'll tell the crew we're ready to depart."

After stowing their luggage in the cabin lockers, I led the passengers to the salon. Decorated in warm colors, the salon was equipped with plush couches for relaxing and watching the ether and entertainment consoles to help pass the time. A dining table and chairs were bolted down—we wanted no flying furniture when we hit the occasional bout of turbulence.

Large viewscreens—bracketed by curtains to give the illusion of windows—relayed the scene around us. At the moment, the only things to be seen were the featureless sides of the cargo haulers flanking *Sparrow*. Once we were underway, the salon's telescanner would let the passengers track the ship's progress toward the next beacon.

Hiram's voice came over the com, "All hands, secure for departure."

Grimbold sprawled on a couch. "How about a little drink to start us off?"

"Of course." I went to the narrow galley at the salon's side, but I knew better than to pour drinks yet.

The docking clamps released with a loud *clang*. With a low rumble, and a jerk as our grav generator adjusted, the port's lifters propelled *Sparrowhawk* into space.

There was a heart-stopping hiccup and moment of weightlessness. Grimbold stiffened. Then, with a jolt, *Sparrow*'s engines roared to life and the ship sailed out of the atmosphere.

As I served the passengers some wine, the glare of the planet's lights gave way to muted darkness and the slivers of Santerro's moons. A Selkid cargo transport smoothly passed us, heading for the jump gate, and a trim Gavoran corvette sped by on its way toward the planet.

In the background swirled the dark haze of ether—currents of energy and subatomic particles left from some primordial galactic collision. Its whorls of color blocked all but the brightest stars.

"How lovely," Miranda murmured, taking the wine goblet. She was a fit woman in her middle thirties. Her jacket and trousers were practical, faded, and comfortably worn; her hands showed calluses and healing scrapes. She might have been the owner of a farm or small business, but she spoke in educated tones and moved with elegance and assurance.

She turned to me brightly. "I say, I'm quite impressed that you should be the ship's business manager. One doesn't see many Gavorans running an enterprise with Terrans."

My jaw tensed. "I consider myself Terran. The captain is my half-brother."

"Oh, dear!" Miranda's perfect teeth glistened in a fleeting smile. "I *do* apologize."

Grimbold kept his eyes on me. "Right. No offense." The man was younger than Miranda, and a bit of a dandy. His clothes were casual, clean, and new, his ginger mustache neatly trimmed.

I forced a friendly smile. I'd lived all my life with prejudice from both Terrans and Gavs. And I had to admit, I had mixed feelings about both my races.

I realized I was rubbing the graft scar under my sleeve and put my hand down.

Kojo's voice came over the com node. "Patch, report to the engine room, *now*."

In the passage between the cargo hold and engine room, Kojo confronted Archer, posture stiff, hands on hips.

As soon as Archer saw me over Kojo's shoulder, he rushed to say, "It's my fault, Patch. I didn't think you'd mind." He shifted from foot to foot.

"Mind what?" What could shy, nervous Archer have done to get Kojo riled up?

Archer waved his hands and stepped aside to reveal a man—a Gavoran.

I took an involuntary step back, my stomach cold. A Gav on my ship? Outside of Gavoran jurisdiction, I was legally Terran, but Gav laws still saw me as a runaway slave.

But this Gavoran was no Clan Enforcer. Head hanging, eyes cast down, he stood stoically, as if waiting for a blow. His clan badge had been torn from his tunic, but he could only be a slave.

"He's a runaway, Patch." Archer jiggled some more.

Kojo snapped, "You mean he's a stowaway." He stabbed a finger at me. "Did you know about this?"

"No." As if *I* was the one bringing contraband aboard without checking.

Archer jittered. "I told you, it's my fault. I saw the security patrol looking for a runaway at the dock, so when I saw him slip up the cargo ramp, I didn't say anything. I didn't have a chance to tell you, but I didn't think you'd mind."

Damn. The last thing we needed was another stranger aboard.

Sparrow shuddered. Archer dashed into the engine room just as Hiram's voice came through the com with a sharp, "Archer, what are you doing? Mind the balance, lad."

Kojo growled, "Figure it out, Patch." He shook his head as he passed me, muttering, "Simple. Why can't it just be simple?"

The Gav had the sturdy frame typical of his race, with wide shoulders and long, muscular arms. His eyes peered from under a prominent brow ridge, and a light brown pelt covered his sloped forehead and crown. He was not much older than me, but his tunic and trousers had seen a lot of wear and his hands were calloused from labor. A cloth was tied awkwardly around his furred forearm—no doubt it hid his brand. His left wrist was marred by a jagged wound, still healing.

He murmured in Gavoran. "Please, Mzee, I only ask to work. I will do anything, for no pay, only for a little food and passage away from Santerro." He rubbed his hands together, a Gav nervous habit I'd worked hard to break myself of.

"Speak Terran," I ordered. I avoided my mother's tongue—I still had a telltale slave accent. "What's your name?"

"Fandar, Mzee. Cactus Clan."

A coincidence—Cactus was my own maternal clan. "What's your job?"

"The mines, Mzee. I ran away from the mines." He hung his head.

Archer peeked out of the engine room like a naughty puppy, unsure whether he was about to be stroked or kicked.

I backed Archer against the console and whispered, "Do you know what the fine is for carrying a runaway?"

He crossed his arms and pouted. "Why shouldn't we help him? He can get asylum on any Terran world."

I poked a finger into his chest. "We won't be in Terran space for days. If the Patrol catches us, the fine is coming out of *your* pay."

A ping signaled a need for power adjustments. Archer turned away, twisted dials, and grumbled, "Fine. I haven't been paid in weeks anyway."

I turned to the Gavoran. "You don't talk like a miner."

"I was a house servant. A daughter of the house, she became…sympathetic. My masters sent me away."

I cringed internally. Sending an educated man to the mines was a deliberate cruelty—one a pampered house servant was unlikely to survive. The wound on his wrist might well be self-inflicted.

Fandar whispered, "I heard rumors that Terrans would not send me back. Please, take me with you."

Archer turned his puppy-soft eyes on me. "You won't send him back, will you?"

I sighed. "All right, Fandar. As it happens, our course doesn't take us through any checkpoints. Oakdale's a Terran colony, you can ask for asylum there. Don't make trouble. And stay away from the passengers and the cargo."

"I will do as Archer tells me."

As I left, Archer reassured Fandar, "I told you she'd come around. She may be half Gav, but she's really more Terran, if you see what I mean."

Ancestors! I was the youngest member of the crew, but since Papa died, I felt like the only adult.

CHAPTER 3

Runaways

I CLIMBED THE STEEP COMPANIONWAY to the command deck and found Kojo in the small cabin behind the ship's wheelhouse that we glorified with the title of wardroom. Its small table and two chairs served as captain's dining table and office and its bunks provided sleeping quarters for him and Hiram.

Kojo lounged on his bunk, Hiram's cat Tinker curled into an orange-and-white ball at his feet.

"The stowaway's name is Fandar," I said. "Archer saw him slip aboard but kept his mouth shut. I said he could go with us to Oakdale." The scanner showed our vector toward the distant jump gate.

Kojo rubbed his temples. "Zub's beard. Archer takes a lot of liberties for a new hand."

"He must be hanging around you and Hiram too much—he's learning to be sly." I scooched Tinker to the side so I could perch on the bunk.

"I oughta fire him at the next port," Kojo grumbled.

It was an empty threat. Archer was the best engineer we could get for the wages we paid—*when* we paid. Archer knew engines cold, and could have gotten a better job but for his shyness and odd twitches.

"I ought to fire *you* next port," I said. "Agreeing to contracts without me? Forging my imprint? And what about Miranda and that duffel?"

Kojo teased Tinker's tail, earning an annoyed squint from the cat. "Nothing to make a fuss about, Patch. Just a hydroverter."

"You're as bad as Archer. If we're taking on trouble, don't you think I'm entitled to know what it is? *Before* my name goes on the contract?" With a pang, I remembered Papa's failure to tell me about the huge risk we were already taking.

Kojo waved a hand. "It was a lot of money and I had to decide on the spot. If you don't like gambles, we should have sold out after Dad died."

That's what it always came down to. I wanted to keep the business going a lot more than Kojo did, and he knew it. It gave him the upper hand in every argument.

I took a breath—getting mad with Kojo never helped. "We've been through that. Once we sell the brandy, I'll pay the suppliers and Hiram and Archer, and the interest on that damn loan from Branson. That will put us on a smoother course."

"Just make sure we have enough credit left to resupply for the delivery to Ordalo."

I calculated in my head, weighing the upfront expense of a voyage to the distant port of Kriti against the eventual profit. "I hope the payment's worth the risk," I said. "I wish Papa had talked to me before he struck that deal."

"I guess he got sick too fast." Through the viewscreen, a fine Cartel hauler smoothly outdistanced us.

Tinker stretched, arching her orange-and-white back. She extended first one set of toes, then the other. Jumping to the deck, she waited at the door. Kojo took the hint and opened the door just enough to let her slip out.

He blew out a breath. "Patch, don't fuss, but the Selkid Trading Cartel offered berths to both me and Hiram as pilots. Hiram promised he'd stay long enough to make the delivery to Ordalo, but after that, I expect he'll take the Cartel berth, especially if we can't keep up his pay. And without Hiram..."

My stomach dropped. Losing Hiram would mean losing one more tie with Papa. And without Hiram's skill and knowledge of shortcuts and backroads, we'd have a tougher time keeping the business going.

Kojo put a comforting hand on my arm. "Maybe it's for the best. We could sell *Sparrow*, pay off everyone, have a clean slate. Everything simple."

"We can't sell *Sparrow*. She still has Papa's spirit in her." I blinked back tears, looking around the dim cabin where Papa had spent his last days, where I'd nursed him while Kojo and Hiram struggled to get us to a port with a Terran med center. "I know you don't believe in spirits, but for me they're real."

"We may not have much choice. If we've got to sell out, we'll split whatever's left after paying our debts. You can find a job with the traders on Palermo or somewhere else where nobody gives a damn who your parents were." Kojo touched my hand. "Think about it—if we weren't tied down by *Sparrow* and all that debt, you could be really free. Go anywhere, make a new start."

I forced my hands out of tight fists. "I don't need a fresh start. *Sparrow* is the only home I want. Papa made a go of it and so can we. Kojo, promise me! Don't make any decisions until we finish Ordalo's job. We'll see where we stand then."

Kojo turned to watch the swirling ether. "Sure, Patch. That's the important thing—we'll deliver the goods. After that, we'll see what comes."

The ether glowed a lovely blue that evening, with a few of the brighter stars shining through. The soft light from the viewscreens helped to disguise the shabby carpet and couches.

We still had a few hours of sublight travel before we reached the first jump gate of our journey. Kojo had dressed to impress in one of Papa's best jackets, and he'd shaved again. He sat at the head of the table, with Miranda in the honored seat at his right. She wore a black blouse and a flowing gold scarf that set off her bronze skin and dark hair.

I eyed her tidy bun and pulled my hat lower to control my curls.

As *Sparrow* trembled in the ether currents, Kojo patted Miranda's hand. "Don't worry, the ride will smooth out once we get to the jump gate."

"We're *so* grateful for your help today." She bit her lip prettily. "I know I asked to avoid checkpoints, but is the route safe?"

Kojo pointed to the swirls of ether on the viewscreen. "Sure. As long as we're in Selkid space, we should be safe from pirates. No one likes paying protection fees, but the Selkid Trading Cartel is very efficient at controlling bandits."

Her brows knitted. "What about the Corridor Patrol? I'd prefer our route not be tracked."

"We'll use the outlying jump gates and bypass the big hubs. We'll have one long passage at sublight—we'll use a current that runs through the mining sector—to avoid the checkpoint between Selkid sectors and Terran space. Trust me, you'll be safe enough from ether currents, pirates, *and* the Patrol."

Miranda fiddled with her napkin. "I know it's wrong to circumvent the authorities, but it's ridiculous to restrict something as beneficial as a hydroverter."

Kojo was practically purring. "We couldn't agree more. Some rules are meant to be bent."

All that honey made me want to gag.

"Burzing gorillas," Grimbold mumbled.

I glowered at him until he shrugged.

"No offense," he said. "I just can't stand that self-righteous Gav crap about looking after us 'lesser' races. Just an excuse to keep us from settling more planets."

I reminded myself that Grimbold would be aboard for only a few days. Glancing at his soft, manicured fingers, I asked, "Will you be farming on Oakdale?"

Grimbold helped himself to more pilaf. "Old friends there. They'll help us get set up."

Miranda reached out to take her companion's hand. "In fact, Grim and I are running away, going to Oakdale to begin a new life together. That's why we need the hydroverter and why we wanted to take a, well, less public route."

"Running away? Together?" Kojo's shoulders drooped.

Miranda smiled shyly. "You see, I'm from one of the outer settlements. My parents arranged a marriage for me to an older man. A *much* older man." She turned to Grimbold with a shining smile. "But Grim and I are in love, and we couldn't bear to be apart."

"Right. Couldn't stand by and see the lady sold off like that, could I?" Grimbold lifted his chin to look stalwart, almost noble. He patted Miranda's hand before picking up a spoon.

It was a scene straight out of a romance entertainment—a third-rate one. Kojo turned his head to me so they wouldn't see his rolling eyes.

I covered my mouth with my napkin and managed not to giggle as I choked out, "Best wishes on your marriage."

Grimbold was eyeing *Sparrow*'s structure. "Selkid ship, cutter class. Old military design. How'd you come to have her?"

Kojo grinned. "Our dad won her on a bet from some Selkid oligarch. I've been on this ship since I was nine years old, as cabin boy, engineer, pilot, and now captain and owner."

In fact, Papa had captured *Sparrowhawk* in a furious battle with a gunrunner, back in his days as a privateer. I hoped Papa was rollicking about in the afterlife with the same flair he'd enjoyed in life.

I nudged Kojo's ankle. "*Sparrowhawk* belongs to *both* of us. She's named for a bird from back on Earth, one that's small but fierce."

"I think it's adorable," Miranda said.

Kojo winked at me and squared his shoulders. "You know, Miranda, as captain, I can marry you two aboard *Sparrowhawk*. Give you a romantic tale to tell your friends on Oakdale."

"Great idea!" I said. "The pilot and I could be witnesses."

Miranda's eyes widened. "Oh, I didn't think of that! I didn't realize that old custom was still valid."

Grim cleared his throat. "Thanks all the same, but we wouldn't want to disappoint our chums on Oakdale. Would we, dear?"

Miranda tittered and touched her napkin to her lips.

The engine room during sublight sailing was a noisy place. The steady throb of the propulsion drivers was punctuated by whistles and snorts from the maneuvering rockets and pings from the monitors showing status changes and power drains. Four freezer bays for jump cells lined one side of the room; the six bays for power modules were ranked on the other. Between them, two bolted-down swivel chairs faced consoles and monitors, viewscreen and scanner. Within easy reach were the controls for the propulsion balance and maneuvering rockets, and the trigger for a thruster burst that could launch the ship off a planet even without the help of lifters or ease her down gently to the surface. A cubby tucked into the corner housed a bunk for quiet times.

The place smelled of lube and Prestoclean—Archer kept the place fastidiously clean and polished. I found Archer's compulsion for neat surroundings ironic, since his clothes were always a mess and his face was rarely clean.

I'd come to see if Archer needed help shifting the heavy jump cells out of cold storage, forgetting for a moment that Fandar was there to help with the heavy lifting.

Archer spritzed some Prestoclean onto the panel of gauges and wiped it down. "Fandar's doing all right, Patch," he said. "He's still learning, but he won't be any trouble. Today I told him all about the differences between Gav engines and ours."

Fandar, shoulders slumped and heavy brow knitted, turned away with a resigned sigh. I almost pitied him: Archer could talk about engines for hours without needing a response or noticing any sign of boredom.

Fandar was handsome, for a Gavoran. His light brown fur set off intelligent eyes and a wide, thin-lipped mouth. I could see how an aristo daughter might be attracted.

"I'm glad you're settling in." I pointed to his improvised bandage. "You haven't tried to burn the brand off yourself, have you? Do you want me to look at it?"

"Oh, no, Mzee. I simply don't wish to see the mark of servitude." He self-consciously touched the bandage. "Please, Mzee, what is your clan?"

"Don't worry. I was raised by my Terran father. I don't have anything to do with the clans." I still wasn't comfortable with a Gav on my ship. I'd spent years avoiding them, fearful that somehow I'd be dragged to Gavoran sectors and forced back into slavery. Even a poor runaway made me nervous.

"Your Terran is very good," I said.

"My masters required me to learn. There were Terrans also where...where I was before." He turned away, perhaps reluctant to speak of his home.

"Any good gossip about our passengers?" Archer asked.

I laughed. "They *said* they're runaways themselves. They're eloping so she can avoid an arranged marriage." For a moment, I imagined eloping with a lover—stolen kisses, a romantic rendezvous, and sailing away in *Sparrow* to live happily ever after.

Archer jiggled a foot. "Good for her! See, Fandar? Everyone has a right to choose for themselves."

Fandar accepted this bit of encouragement with a stony face.

"Fandar's already chosen for himself," I said. "The penalties on runaways are so severe—what made you take the risk?"

Fandar rubbed his hands. "Please understand, I did nothing dishonorable in my masters' home. My misfortune was that the daughter became attached to me. At the mines, I did my best, but it was a place of bad luck, terrible accidents. The miners said evil spirits were at work." Fandar shuddered at the memory. "But the leader of my work crew was kind and took me for her companion."

I nodded. In the matriarchal Gav society, it was the females who chose their lovers. A young, educated house servant would be a nice change from rugged miners.

"For a time, she protected me from the other miners and the worst of the work. But then…she died." He bent his head, stroking the puckered skin of the scar on his wrist. "I thought to end my pain. I awakened in the medical center."

How terrible. To decide to die, only to be dragged back to life to face punishment.

Archer was riveted. "Did they send you back to the mines?"

"I know it is shameful to abandon my duty, but I could not bear to go back. I had heard rumors that Terrans might help runaway slaves. I escaped the hospital and hid in a transport to Santerro. And then"—he smiled widely—"the blessed Sages favored me by sending this ship to me, and kind Archer, who told me the captain and mistress of the ship would not betray my trust."

Archer grinned and bobbed his head at this. I'd have to have a talk with that man. He had the softest heart in the outer sectors, but *this* time he'd been way too generous with my and Kojo's ship.

"And the ancestors granted my prayers that the crew of this ship be generous! Gratitude to you, Mzee Patch, and to my new friend Archer! And to the ancestors. I will work very hard, Mzee Patch."

"Just make sure you stay out of the passengers' sight," I said.

Kojo's voice came over the com, "All hands, approaching gate. Secure for jump."

CHAPTER 4

Suspicious behavior

I JOINED KOJO IN THE WHEELHOUSE while we took our place among the cargo haulers lined up to make the jump.

Arching over the ships was the spidery gantry of the jump gate: part beacon to guide ships through the ether, part relay station to speed communications across vast stretches of space, and most important, a gateway to the faster-than-light star corridors to other star systems.

"Anything going on?" I shooed Tinker off the watch station seat and took her place. The hailer crackled with chatter among the waiting ships, punctuated by announcements relayed by the beacon to traffic entering and leaving the gate.

Tinker sniffed my feet to see if I'd been anywhere interesting. Satisfied, she stretched elegantly, forelegs extended, chest to the deck, hindquarters high, before settling into a good licking session.

Kojo stretched as well, less elegantly. "Nothing unusual. Typical Patrol alerts, usual complaints from the Cartel ships."

"What's our course?"

Kojo pointed to the charts. "The lady wants backroads. From here, we'll make a quick jump to this gate, then this, and this." He tapped the lines between jump gates that indicated star corridors. "We'll pick up the current that passes the Lazuna mines. Once we cross into Terran space, we'll hit the jump gate near Ringgold. From there, we'll make two jumps to the ag sector, then sublight to Oakdale."

"That should be off track enough." I tapped my fingers on the console, counting the drain on jump cells and power mods. "Five jumps and two legs at sublight. Archer said the cells tested light. I hope we have enough to get back to Palermo—restocking in a remote place like Oakdale would be expensive." I wished we were going straight home. I'd been looking forward to having a few days to relax.

A ping from the console signaled our turn to enter the jump gate.

Kojo maneuvered *Sparrow* into position within the gateway's arch. Blue lights on the gantry turned a deep red to indicate proper alignment.

A message came in. *Destination gate?*

Kojo keyed in the code for the least used of the five connecting star corridors.

Destination gate confirmed.

I had no idea how the gates worked—nobody did. Gavorans had built and placed the gateways and beacons millennia ago, under the direction of the Sages and using Sage components, to enable the far-flung races to communicate and travel beyond their own isolated star systems. But the Sages had been gone for five thousand years. Without them, we'd lost all knowledge of how the corridors carried ships and messages between gates at faster-than-light speeds.

"Archer, engage jump cells."

Archer responded by com. "Jump cells engaged."

Kojo unlatched the jump activator. "Activating jump."

The gateway and all the ships waiting nearby blurred and disappeared. All hails and chatter ceased, no outside communication being possible within the star corridor. The ether haze grew slightly darker, but otherwise, the view was largely unchanged. And yet, somehow, at the end of a few hours or days, we would alight at another gate in another star system, ready to repeat the process.

Tinker twitched her ears and scooted out, called by some urgent cat business.

Kojo kept an eye on the scanner showing our position in the corridor. Once inside the star corridors, there was little for the pilot to do other than monitor power usage and ship functions.

I relaxed, enjoying the stars and companionship. I used to sit with Papa that way. Kojo's high-handedness and devil-may-care attitude might get on my nerves, but those were the same traits that had made Papa a daring captain. My eyes got teary.

"I miss Dad, too," Kojo said.

I sniffed. "Papa would be proud of you. The ship's running well, we've got a good crew, and we've got cargo and passengers." I rubbed my arm under my sleeve.

"Huh. The ship needs rehauling, the crew hasn't been paid, and we're up to our ears in debt. And stop that—if you keep scratching, you'll open up that scar. If that happens, you might as well have a brand all over again."

I forced my hand down. "It tore open on Santerro and I had to put a skin seal on it. I'll try to be less conspicuous. Especially now that we have a Gavoran aboard."

"Damnit. Does he know you're from a slave clan?"

"Fandar knows I'm a hybrid, but I've never even told Archer anything about my clan."

"I hope not. What made him run?"

"Fandar said it was a bad-luck place, lots of accidents. At first, he was under the wing of the crew leader, who took him for her lover. But she died and Fandar tried to kill himself. When that failed, he lit out to take his chances."

"Good for him."

I glanced at Kojo, twisting my hair and thinking. "Something seemed off, though."

"What?"

I focused on the glowing ether, trying to remember what had bothered me. "He thanked the blessed Sages, but it's the upper castes who worship the Sages. In ancient times, it was the Sages who dictated that some clans would be slaves forever. We venerated our ancestors, but we'd never pray to the Sages."

"He was a house slave—maybe he got taken to the masters' religious services."

My mother and I had been a house slaves, too, and we'd been taken to Sage temples, but we'd resented every moment of it. And now that I thought about it..."He said he was afraid of evil spirits."

"What's wrong with that? *You* believe in spirits."

I looked at Kojo seriously. "Spirits aren't evil. They're just family who lend us wisdom and courage to face whatever life brings."

Kojo grunted. "Maybe in the mines things are different. If I was stuck there, you can bet I'd be seeing ghosts behind every rock."

Maybe. But no slave I'd ever known had blamed the spirits for unsafe conditions the masters had created.

We were quiet for a few minutes.

"Sorry about Miranda," I said. "Her being tied up with Grimbold."

Kojo grinned. "How'd you like that romantic story?"

I chuckled. "Not even close to believable. She's too old for anyone to be arranging a marriage for her. And if he's a farmer, then I'm a Selkid geisha."

Kojo laughed. "Con man, more like. Somehow, they got their hands on a hydroverter, and they know they can sell it on the ag planets. I'll bet the only reason they're traveling together is because they don't trust one another. Miranda must have dreamed up that elaborate cover story—he doesn't seem like the romantic type."

"I thought Grimbold would choke when you offered to marry them!"

He shook his head. "Amateurs. They should just keep it simple."

I glanced at him. Passengers who lied and were smuggling tech. A runaway slave to keep out of sight. And that risky delivery to Ordalo. At the moment, keeping it simple was the one thing we *couldn't* do.

I pulled my bunk down that evening, but sleep didn't come. The more I thought about the weeks ahead, the more I worried. The business was teetering, propped up by goodwill from suppliers, hopes for the future, and loans whose interest grew like cancer. And Kojo—I knew he was tempted by the Cartel's offer. He loved handling the helm and the engines, but he was utterly bored by the day-to-day business of buying and selling and meeting expenses.

The future of our ship, our home, our livelihood…even our ability to stay together as a family rested on a good sale for the brandy, and on reaching the rendezvous with Ordalo in two months' time.

Ordalo.

I didn't mind a bit of off-the-books transport. Favors for friends didn't bother me, or a little extra income from carrying some item on the Settlement Authority's restricted list. But the commission for Ordalo was something far out of our league. *Sparrow* was smuggling a microbial synthreactor, able to analyze dust and rock and to use available elements to synthesize microbes that could foster plant growth. A synthreactor could turn a wasteland into farmland, a barren planet into a colony site, and a poor but peaceful sector of space into a war zone.

The Settlement Authority—dominated by Gavs, of course—kept a strict control on synthreactors, tightly limiting who could use one and where. That made this one worth more than all the brandy and everything else on the ship—and extremely illegal to transport.

Papa had broken the synthreactor into five pieces and scattered them through the ship, some hiding innocuously in plain sight, some shielded deep within the bulkheads. We had to carry the damn thing for *weeks* until Ordalo could take delivery in a distant pirate haven at the fringe of the uncharted region known as the Gloom.

Just thinking about it made me sweat.

Twice in the long, sorrow-filled nights since Papa's passing, I'd seen him in my dreams—not as the daring ship's captain I wanted to remember, but as an old man who gazed on me with worry and sadness. He hadn't spoken. He hadn't given me the answers I craved.

Aboard ship, I couldn't light a candle to my ancestors like I would in a planetside shrine, but I figured the ship was enough of a connection for Papa to find me. To reach my mother, I took from my private locker a tattered bit of cloth, the remnants of the scarf my mother had tucked around my neck the night she smuggled me out of the masters' house to Papa. She'd paid dearly—that act of defiance got her sent to a noxious factory and an early death. Sometimes, just touching the scrap of fabric and reciting the ritual prayer helped me find a little peace of mind.

Beloved ancestors, help me find the wisdom to choose what is best, the strength to do what I must, and the courage to face what may come. Mother, thank you for my life and freedom. Papa, thank you for your care, but please, help me understand.

I wondered sleepily if a Terran prayer might have a better chance of reaching Papa's spirit, but I had no idea how Terrans prayed. All Gavorans were spiritual, in one way or another, but Papa had worshipped nothing and no one, and he'd certainly never taught me any prayers.

I went to sleep, still holding the scarf.

"Be careful."

Papa stood next to my bunk, in his usual jacket, looking well and hearty—not like he had in his last terrible days of fever. He seemed to shine with an inner light.

"Be careful," he repeated. "Lies. Don't trust them."

I reached my hand toward him, but he was gone. The tiny cabin was empty and dark.

I felt the familiar ache of grief, tempered with anger. Papa had come, as I asked. I should be grateful. But all he'd given me was a warning I didn't need.

Why, Papa? You told Kojo about the synthreactor, why not me? Didn't you trust me? Surely he knew the peril he'd left us in, the weeks of danger we faced to smuggle the synthreactor through Corridor Patrol checkpoints to a pirate lair?

I shook off my resentment and concentrated on being thankful. I'd been a child among slaves, for whom ancestral spirits were a constant, comforting presence. Kojo scoffed at my "ghost stories," but I took heart knowing Papa still watched over us.

I said a brief prayer thanking Papa for his visit, but I asked him, if he could, to be more helpful next time.

On the second day of the voyage we reached a gate in a quiet Selkid sector. While we waited in the queue for the jump gate, I joined Hiram in the wheelhouse to pick up messages from the beacon.

I kissed the bald spot on his head. "Kojo told me," I whispered.

Hiram raised his brows. "Did he, now?"

"I'm not surprised the Cartel would offer you a berth. You're the canniest pilot in the outer sectors. I just want you to know how grateful I am that you've helped to see us through the rough time after Papa passed on. But you don't need to worry about us—we'll be on better footing once the money comes in for the brandy and that job for Ordalo. I'll miss you like crazy, though."

He cleared his throat and shuffled his feet. "Ah, well, nothing's decided yet, one way or the other. I'll stick with *Sparrowhawk* yet awhile."

"Whatever you decide, you'll always be family."

I forwarded one message to Kojo and another to Archer. All mine were from creditors looking to collect. I went to my cabin-office to check the accounts—had the interest on Branson's loan really stacked up so much?

Kojo popped in, his black curls tousled.

"Trouble," he said.

Sparrow moved into position in the jump gates. Blue lights turned to red, then disappeared as we slid into the star corridor.

Kojo leaned against a bulkhead, arms crossed. "Got a broadcast from the Cartel to all its members. The Corridor Patrol is stopping and searching ships in Selkid sectors."

Ancestors! If the Patrol tracked the microbial synthreactor to us, we'd lose our ship and our licenses, not to mention spending a few years on a penal colony.

Kojo must have seen the panic on my face. "Don't worry, the Patrol's not looking for us. Not specifically, anyway. The

Cartel said some treasure was stolen from a Gav temple on a Selkid world. The Gav priesthood is raising hell to track the thieves down. It's got the Cartel all riled up—Patrol searches interfere with business."

I breathed again. "Sage temples have all kinds of treasures. What are they looking for?"

"Some sort of icon or idol, taken by a Terran female by name of Patil and a high-ranking Gav male called Balan."

I shook my head. "That can't be right. No Gavoran aristo would steal from one of their own temples."

Kojo shrugged. "That's what the message said. The idol is supposed to be in a heavy metal case. The Patrol is scanning or opening anything that might contain it."

Like a few unstamped brandy crates in our vault. I *really* didn't want the Patrol opening our cargo, sussing out the lack of tariff stamps and maybe even finding the synthreactor.

"We're already bypassing hubs and checkpoints," I said. "Short of sailing sublight all the way to Oakdale, is there anything else we can do to avoid the Patrol?"

"Not really. But the Cartel is offering a reward of ten thousand sovereigns in rhollium for finding the loot and turning it in to them. I think we should check the passengers' luggage."

"Why? They went through the inspection point on Santerro—if they were wanted, the Patrol would have picked them up there."

"What about that stowaway? *He* didn't go through any inspection."

I shook my head. "Fandar's just a slave. I saw his hands—he's been doing manual labor, and he's got that slash on his wrist. He didn't bring anything with him, either, not even a change of clothes, much less a Sage icon. Miranda and Grim brought some luggage aboard, but except for the hydroverter, they didn't have anything heavy."

Kojo rubbed his jaw, avoiding my eyes.

I knew *that* sheepish expression. "Kojo? You *did* check to see that it was really a hydroverter in the duffel, didn't you?"

"Zub's pitchfork. When somebody admits to you straight out they're carrying restricted tech, you can generally believe them."

Kojo. Letting a pretty face distract him—he should have known better.

His eyes lit up. "Look, I just want to check. If we find the loot, we could put the Cartel in debt to *us* for a change. And I *know* that female is slippery. Just think, we could turn her and Grim and the goods over to the Cartel, keep the fare, forget about Oakdale, and claim ten thousand sovereigns on top!"

I had to laugh. "You're dreaming."

Kojo stood. "I'll chat up the passengers while you search their cabins. Who knows? We could get lucky."

"Grimbold's armed," I warned.

"We can fix that." Kojo opened his jacket to show me a stun pistol stuck into his belt.

For once, Kojo had thought ahead.

CHAPTER 5

A search for treasure

GRIM HAD LEFT HIS BLANKETS in a rumpled pile on his bunk. With distaste, I rummaged through them enough to be sure nothing was hidden. His suitcase and pack held only clothing, mostly new, and a shaving kit.

In Miranda's stateroom, only one of the bunks held wrinkled blankets and there was no lingering scent of Grim's aftershave on the sheets. Not much romance for an "eloping" couple, then. Miranda's suitcases held only clothes and toiletries—not many. I repacked them and returned the luggage to the locker.

That left the gray duffel.

I pulled it out and hefted it. It had a padlock, but I'd borrowed a bolt cutter from Archer, so that was no trouble.

Inside the duffel was a bulky bundle—a thick coat wrapped around a neat metal case with an intricate lock.

Damn. Definitely *not* a hydroverter.

I brought the case to the salon and laid it carefully on the table.

"What are you doing?" Miranda demanded.

Grim's hand moved, but Kojo already had his stunner out. "Hands in the air, Mzee Grimbold. That doesn't look like any hydroverter."

Grim froze. "What is this? A holdup?"

"Sit still while Patch checks you out."

I pulled Grim's weapon from its holster. It was a new, military-grade stunner, built for range and accuracy. I held it up for Kojo to see, then stuck it in my belt.

Kojo whistled. "Nice!"

I finished patting Grim down. When I got to his tender parts, he growled, "Watch it, sister."

"Don't worry. I haven't crippled a man yet." I confiscated a knife from his boot and moved to Miranda.

"Why are you doing this?" Miranda cried.

"I don't like being lied to," Kojo said. "At the gate, we got an alert that the Corridor Patrol is stopping ships in this sector and searching them for some treasure stolen from a Sage temple. There's a reward for turning it in—and a prison sentence for transporting it."

Miranda had no weapons and only one item of interest—a wallet clipped to her belt, the kind that holds rhollium ingots. It was heavy.

She hissed when I opened it. Inside were nine finger-sized five-thousand-sovereign ingots, and space where a tenth ingot had been. I showed it to Kojo and stuck it into my pocket.

"*Very* nice." He grinned at her. "Don't worry, Miranda. We're moderately honest. If that case doesn't hold Gav loot, you'll get your rhollium back."

Miranda looked at Kojo appealingly. "Captain, let me explain. We're not thieves."

"You're not a couple, either," I said. "At least not a couple that sleeps together."

Kojo shot me an amused glance.

"You're looking for treasure from a Sage temple?" Grim smoothed his mustache and nodded to Miranda. "We've got nothing like that. You might as well show them, honey."

Miranda sat up straight. "Very well. The item in the case is obviously not a hydroverter, but neither is it anything belonging to the Gavorans. It is simply a piece of stone artwork. Perhaps...Kojo, perhaps I could just speak to you alone for a moment?"

"No. Open it."

Miranda clenched her hands. "Very well. But you must understand—the item in the case is irreplaceable. It must not be touched. Will you please listen, before I open the case, so you will understand its importance?"

Kojo looked at me and scratched his ear, signaling he was willing to go along. I nodded.

"All right," Kojo said. "You've got two minutes."

Miranda sat up, no longer the simpering sweetheart. "I admit I...misled you about my background. I am an archeologist from Evergreen University, in the central sectors.

I've been working on an ancient site on an uninhabited planet. In that metal case is an artifact from an extinct civilization, a stone tablet covered in symbols. It is certainly *not* from a Sage temple, nor is it anything belonging to the Gavorans. If some sort of Gavoran goods are missing, I assure you, that has nothing to do with me."

She stroked the case. "This artifact is thousands of years old. It has no value in monetary terms, but it is invaluable to understanding our history. We need to take the artifact to Evergreen for it to be researched properly and to translate the symbols."

Whatever I expected, it was nothing like that. Kojo raised an eyebrow at me. I touched the back of my hand to signal I wasn't convinced.

"So why the story about the hydroverter?" I asked. "Why smuggle it out of Santerro? Why not just book passage on an ordinary transport?"

"Because I told her not to." Grimbold spoke with crisp authority. "The professor hired me to provide security. There are thieves who specialize in rarities like this. On Santerro, I received solid information that Selkid interests have targeted this tablet. I know the Selkid Trading Cartel runs that sector and I know how deep they are into smuggling and other illegal business. We didn't dare run it through the Selkid officials at the docks—I know for a fact the Cartel pays them to skim off anything interesting or valuable."

Kojo nodded. "True enough."

"So," Miranda said, "we invented a plausible reason to avoid passing it through the inspection." For a moment, she fluttered her lashes like the old Miranda. "We couldn't have done it without your help, Captain."

Kojo chuckled. "That'll teach me to trust a pretty woman."

Humph. I doubted the lesson would last long.

"As for the transports," Grim continued, "once we stepped onto a Selkid ship, we'd be sitting ducks. I went out of my way to find a Terran-crewed ship, one that had a certain reputation for flexibility."

Kojo and I exchanged a glance. Half the traders in the Selkid frontier sectors knew *Sparrowhawk* was available for just about any job that paid well.

"You could have just hired more guards," I said.

Grim shook his head. "Bringing in more guards would just be more people who could leak our location. You can't trust anybody out here. On our own, we're less conspicuous. I figured that by using out-of-the-way ports like Oakdale, we could throw the thieves off our track."

Like Kojo said, as smugglers, they were a pair of amateurs.

Kojo rubbed his chin. "Go ahead, then. Open the case."

Carefully, Miranda turned the case to face her.

The case was sturdy rather than elegant, the hardware strong and well-made. As Miranda manipulated the combination, she said, "Remember, you must not touch the artifact. The oils in your skin could damage the surface."

She lifted the lid, her effort showing how heavy the thick panels were.

The padding inside the case was custom cut to snugly hold a dark stone block. It was a precise hexagon, so wide it barely fit into the case. Graceful symbols were deeply incised into its surface.

Kojo let out a deep breath. "It's just a stone." He leaned closer. "Is that writing?"

He started to reach toward it, until Miranda hissed, "No!"

It was strange. I also felt the urge to touch the artifact, to run my fingers across the odd symbols. It had an eerie beauty. The mounded face had looked black at first, but on closer view it was an amalgam of very deep browns, reds, and purples. The subtle colors seemed to move, swirling over the surface.

The incisions on the tablet were so deep that no light reflected from them at all. The letters, if that's what they were, didn't follow lines across or down, but seemed to radiate in a whorl from a central point, like a galaxy, except that, oddly, it was hard to pinpoint the center. It was as if any point you chose might be the center of a different galaxy. I would have liked to pick the tablet up to see it more closely.

I felt the others watching me and realized I had drawn close to the thing. I forced my hand down from where I'd been rubbing the itching skin seal on my arm.

Home.

I pulled back, startled. It wasn't quite a voice—there were no words, only a strong longing. I even looked around to see if Papa's spirit was visiting.

Miranda watched me narrowly. Kojo stared at me, too, with a puzzled frown.

I grinned sheepishly at my brother. "It really is fascinating."

"Does that look like Gav writing to you?" Kojo asked. "Or like something from a Sage temple?"

"Definitely not," I said.

Kojo rubbed his chin. "It doesn't look old. It's not cracked or corroded or anything."

"Indeed. One of many fascinating aspects of the artifact." Miranda closed the case and relocked it. "I hope that satisfies your curiosity."

Kojo winked at me and bowed to Miranda. "Thank you for clearing this up. My sincere apologies for the inconvenience. I guess you're not the ones the Corridor Patrol is looking for."

At Kojo's nod, I gave Miranda back her rhollium-filled wallet, but I kept the stunner, telling Grim I'd give it back at the end of the voyage.

Miranda smiled graciously. "Please don't be concerned, Captain Babatunji. I quite understand your need for caution. However, I would like to continue to travel to Oakdale without any...publicity. Do you think there is any danger the Corridor Patrol will search *this* ship?"

"I doubt it. The jump gates we're using aren't very busy. Once we're past the third jump, we'll sail off-corridor, then two jumps in Terran space. No promises, but our chances of avoiding the Patrol are pretty good."

"Thank you, Captain. I knew I could count on you." Her smile made dimples.

Kojo pulled me into the wardroom. "What do you think?"

"It's beautiful. I've never seen anything like it."

Kojo slapped my shoulder. "The Patrol, idiot. Could that rock be something looted from a Gav temple? Some kind of icon?"

"I don't think so. The Sage temples I've seen have lots of fancy art, ornate metalwork, jewels. Not that sort of thing at all." And how bitterly I'd resented being forced to attend Sage worship and seeing all that useless wealth on display. "Besides, how could a couple of Terrans pull off a robbery of a Sage temple?"

"Even if they had a Gav to help them?"

I shook my head. "It doesn't make sense. Not all Gavorans worship the Sages, but they all worship *something*. Even a slave wouldn't turn something sacred over to Terrans."

Kojo rubbed his chin. "Hmm. You're probably right, but Miranda's pretty slick and Grimbold's a burzing liar if I ever saw one."

I twisted a lock of hair. "Maybe we should divert to a Cartel outpost just to make sure."

Kojo nodded slowly. "Maybe even lie low for a while, until the Patrol finds whatever it's looking for?"

"The passengers won't like it."

"I'll tell them we need repairs or something. Captain's prerogative." He flashed his wolfish grin.

That night I wakened in the early hours from a nightmare about fighting the currents in some desperate effort to get home— only, home wasn't the friendly inns of Palermo, but some distant, peaceful place I'd never been.

Unable to get back to sleep, I brought a couple mugs of ale to the engine room.

Archer was wide awake, squirting Prestolube into the engines' orifices and wiping specks from the console. A streak of lube marred his forehead.

"Ah, thanks. You're an angel." He took a long draught.

I settled into the second chair, sipping my ale.

On a pallet in the sleeping cubby, Fandar snored heavily, a furred lump.

"How's he doing?" I asked.

Archer waggled his hand. "Not so good. He's not really interested in how engines work. I even caught him skiving off toward the forward cabins. I guess he's just killing time till we get to Oakdale." He tapped both feet. "He talks to himself a lot. When I asked him about it, he said he was praying. Is that a Gav habit? Praying all the time?"

"Not that I ever saw. Maybe he's still grieving for his lover."

Archer snorted. "I doubt it. Do you know he has a kid?"

I shrugged. "Gavs start young. Females are expected to provide a child to the clan as soon as they reach adulthood."

"Well, when I asked if he missed his baby, he didn't even seem to understand what I was talking about. Can you believe that?"

"It's different with them. Gav children are raised by their mother and her clan. Men don't help raise their children, it's just the clan and the maternal line that counts."

"That's *awful*. When I have kids, I want to be with them every day. Don't you?" His eyebrows drew together, like he really wanted to know. "I mean, assuming you want kids."

"Sure. I'd like to have a baby some day." I smiled at the thought of teaching a sturdy little girl the ins and outs of trading, the way Papa had taught me. Or a little boy, or one of each. Making *Sparrow* a real home, teaching them to pilot and sharing with them the wonders of all the different worlds we visited.

"Did your father help raise you?" I'd never asked Archer about his family.

"Sure! Me and all my brothers and sisters."

"Uh, *all* your brothers and sisters?"

"Two of each. I'm the second youngest of five."

"Wow." I tried to imagine a room full of five little Archers in assorted sizes, all with halos of curly hair, all bouncing and jiggling. It was frightening. "You must miss them."

"Sure, I miss them. I call them, whenever we're in port. But I like it here, too." He looked around the orderly consoles and propulsion coils. "It's quiet."

"Quiet? Not when we're at sublight."

"I don't mean sound. I mean everything in its place and acting like it should. Predictable." He wiped a bit of dust from a console. "Not like people. Take those passengers—they lied once. They might lie again."

"Don't worry. I'm no hatchling."

He raised one eyebrow. "Maybe not, but you don't always notice things about people, either."

I grinned at him—that was funny, coming from someone so shy he rarely stepped out of the engine room and who never noticed the dirt on his own face.

For all his odd ways, I liked having Archer aboard. It was sort of like having another brother. One who, unlike my actual brother, had to follow my orders.

"Hold on," he said, glancing at the scanner. "The gate's coming up."

With a long slide that ended with a bang, *Sparrow* dropped out of the star corridor.

This jump gate was busier, with three ships already waiting in the queue. None were big haulers, just transports no larger than *Sparrow* shuttling between Selkid mining colonies.

After swapping in fresh jump cells and returning the spent cells to cold storage, I climbed to the command deck, nearly running into Kojo coming out of the wardroom.

"What's the news?" I asked.

"Somebody got lucky, just not us. Some freighter captain turned the goods over to the Cartel and claimed the reward."

"Look on the bright side. The Cartel will hand the loot over to the Patrol and the searches will stop. Everyone can go back to business as usual."

Kojo stretched and yawned. "I guess Miranda's on the level after all—we might as well go on to Oakdale. Get some sleep. We'll be at the next gate in a few hours, and after that, the sailing is going to get a lot rougher."

With the familiar slide and bump, *Sparrow* came to rest at the jump gate at the end of the third jump. Hiram steered us away from the few waiting ships to begin the sublight leg of our journey. The engines whined and hiccupped and roared to life as *Sparrow* turned her stern to the gate and headed into the ether.

Soon we were rumbling along the swift current used by Selkid supply ships heading for the Lazuna mines. The scanner showed warning blips all around as the current barreled between eddies and gravity sources, dense ether pockets and radiation hazards. Hiram adjusted course constantly to remain in the safe part of the stream, and with every course change, there was that momentary feeling of falling or accelerating as the grav generator adjusted.

I pulled the jump cells from the engine room to put them back into cold storage—we were draining them faster than I'd planned.

"Check the scanner," Archer said. "We're not alone. See that ship, just at the edge of scanner range? It's been behind us since we left the jump gate."

I peered at the blips. "That's not a Selkid ship."

Archer bobbed. "Terran hull with some funny add-ons. Why was it hanging around the gate if it wasn't waiting to jump?"

There could be a dozen innocent explanations, but I didn't like the way it kept pace with us. "Maybe it's just going to the mines. Stay sharp."

I climbed to the wheelhouse. "Hiram?"

"Yeah, I see it. That damn oddball shadow. Been ducking in and out of scanner range."

I moved Tinker to my lap and took her place at the watch station. "Transponder?"

"I flashed him. No burzing response. Kojo's gone to the gun turret, just in case."

Not a Cartel member, then, even though we were still squarely in Selkid space. That was bad.

With a whistle, a hail blasted through the ship.

"Ahoy, *Sparrowhawk,* heave to. No need for arms, just a talk. You've got something we want to buy, fair terms." The accents were Terran, from outlier sectors.

They knew our ship's name but didn't identify their own.

Very bad. A freebooter.

Kojo called from the turret, "Rabbit, Hiram."

Grimbold squawked something into the salon's com about being sensible and making a deal. I shouted into the com, "Pirates don't make deals. Shut up and strap in."

Hiram pinged the engine room. "More power, lad! We're gonna run."

As the ship shuddered into acceleration, Tinker yowled and ran for the sanctuary of her snug sleeping cubby—she knew what that roar from the engines meant.

I was shaking, and not just from the engines' vibration. "You think somebody found out about the synthreactor?"

"You know any other reason somebody'd waylay us, missy?"

"How far are we from a beacon?" I hated to cry to the Patrol for rescue, but it would be better than being boarded by a pirate.

"Too burzing far. They waited until we were all alone to jump us."

Kojo called from the turret. "Hiram? They're gaining on us. Head for the lanes to Lazuna, see if we can lose them in the traffic."

Ancestors! That damn synthreactor was going to get us killed.

CHAPTER 6

Duck and hide

IF PIRATES WERE AFTER US, Archer would need help in the engine room.

I ran down the steps, running straight into Fandar.

"What are you doing here?" I demanded.

He looked upward in confusion. "Archer sent me for power modules."

"Not this way—this leads to the passenger quarters. Modules are in cold storage." I led the way and helped him load extra modules on the handcart and wheel them to the engine room. Archer set me to keeping the propulsion drives balanced while he tittered and twitched, fine-tuned the maneuvering rockets, adjusted the coils, and complained that the propulsion cylinders needed reaming.

"Are we in danger?" Fandar asked. "Perhaps we should call to the Corridor Patrol for help."

"Are you space-happy? If the Patrol found you, they'd send you right back to the mines." And probably arrest all of us for helping him. "Besides, we're outside the corridors now. There's no Patrol anywhere nearer than the gate."

He looked down. "Ah, I do not like the life of a runaway."

Sparrow shook and shuddered. Hiram sped through the current like a fish swimming down a rapid, dodging hazards while using the faster streams to add to our speed.

The com node squawked. "Who's driving this rig?" Grim shouted from the salon. "We're shaking to bits up here!"

"You all just sit tight," Hiram drawled back. "Just part of the ride."

Fandar rushed to the head and came back clutching his stomach. "At least the mine stayed still," he mumbled.

I kept an eye on the scanner while helping swap power mods. Our shadow had the hull of a Terran clipper-class passenger transport, but it had odd projections on the thrusters. The gun turret had a suspiciously Gavoran silhouette.

"That's bad," Archer said. "See that energy signature? They've grafted on a Gav propulsion. Chances are, they can outlast us."

I called the turret. "Kojo? Archer says we can't outdistance them like this. We may have to fight."

"Bad idea," Kojo responded. "Those are Gav guns, they've got more range. Keep accelerating."

The viewscreen lit up with a silent flash. A moment later, *Sparrow* jolted.

Archer hustled to keep the stabilizing rockets aligned. "What was that?"

I helped Fandar back to his feet. "Concussive charge. They're trying to knock out our propulsion."

"Whatever Kojo has in mind, he'd better do it fast," Archer muttered.

A few shots flashed from our gun turret. The raider was out of our range, but now they'd know *Sparrow* was ready for a fight.

I called to Kojo, "If you need space, I can arm a couple drones with grenades. *That* would slow them down."

"Do it."

I turned toward the cargo hold. "Fandar, help me."

Sparrow bucked and swayed as Hiram took evasive action. Our grav generator—not the best quality even when it was new—was having trouble keeping up, giving us a bruising jolt at every course change.

The ship shook again as another concussion wave hit us, followed by a dull vibration as Kojo trained the guns on the raider.

In the cargo hold, Fandar helped me push a heavy drone—designed for delivering bulky cargo—into the launch bay. He hooked on its mooring lines while I took three grenades from the ship's magazine. I set them to detonate on remote signal, threw them into the drone's payload, and slammed the hatch shut.

Fandar shoved the drone in the launch airlock and sealed the airlock hatch.

From the drone console, I opened the airlock to the ether and punched the launch control. With a soft tremor, the drone departed the airlock.

"Drone launched," I called on the com node.

Hiram answered, "Give 'em hell, missy."

Fandar was already pulling another drone from the locker. From the drone console, I snaked the drone into the raider's path. It helped—the raider began to concentrate its guns on the drone, and not on *Sparrow*. Still, it was getting closer.

I was used to using drones to deliver goods in space, to the delicate process of guiding a drone into a customer's airlock or a station's grapplers. But usually we were in a nice stable orbit at the time, not tearing through ether eddies. And usually no one was firing on us.

Fandar positioned the second drone in the launch bay. He was proving surprisingly useful. "The drones are not effective," he said. "The brigands will detonate them before the drone reaches it."

"They're mostly for diversion." I threw three more grenades into the payload.

Sparrow rocked as another concussive detonated nearby.

There was a flash as the first drone exploded, too far from our pursuer to damage it.

I slapped the launch control and set the second drone on a twisting, turning path toward the raider. I hit the com. "Second drone away. Kojo, I hope your plan kicks in before we use all the drones."

"Soon, Patch. Archer, keep accelerating."

There was a flash as the second drone detonated—close enough to the raider to give them a good shaking, but not close enough to stop them.

Hiram broke in. "Kojo, I got the Lazuna lanes in sight. There's a big carrier a-coming. Time to earn your pay, boy."

"Good. Patch, secure the hold and get to the engine room. Archer, prepare escape thrusters, half bore, three second burst. Time to duck and hide. We're going to join the traffic in the shipping lanes."

Archer's reply was a disbelieving shriek. "Shipping lanes? You're going to hide in the *shipping lanes*?"

Hiram snapped back, "Do it, boy."

I sent Fandar back to the engine room while I secured the drones and grenades.

The Lazuna system was a mining hub where every moon and large asteroid sprouted a Selkid excavator and every planet had a dozen refineries to feed the huge carriers of concentrated ore.

Sparrow's engines chugged steadily, accelerating us toward a stable, high-velocity ether current dedicated to ore carriers traveling from Lazuna toward the central sectors. Blips on the scanner pulsed with warnings to stay away.

Archer shifted settings, readying the engines for a massive thrust. If our speed wasn't nearly that of the current at the point of entry, the sheering forces would tear the ship apart.

Kojo went ship-wide, telling all hands to strap in for a rapid course change.

Fandar buckled himself into the engineer's bunk. I took the second chair at the propulsion console. *Ancestors, give me courage. And please spare a little wisdom for Kojo.*

Kojo announced, "All hands, brace. Thrusters in three, two, one—now!"

Archer slapped the thruster controls.

Sparrow surged forward.

The three seconds of half-bore thrust felt like three minutes being crushed under a load of bricks. By the time the thrusters cut out, my head was reeling.

Kojo screamed, "Maneuvering!"

Thanks to a thick Gavoran skull, I recovered quicker than Archer. I worked the controls until Archer swore and told me to let him do it.

Still accelerating, we approached the current sweeping away from Lazuna. *Sparrowhawk* shook and slewed as we passed through the eddies spawned to the edge of the current. One long slide, our grav generator slow to adjust as usual...

Then, quiet. The current had us.

A long ore carrier traveled in the current's stable center— dozens of ore-filled carriages, each carriage large enough to house a small town, strung together for the journey to the central sectors. Far too big to withstand the stresses of a jump, the carriers plied the dedicated shipping lanes, accelerating to breathtaking sublight speeds, stopping for nothing and no one until they reached their destination.

Kojo edged *Sparrow* closer, close enough to see every scratch and seam on the long carriage.

Faster and closer we went, until the carriage seemed to stand still beside us.

No pirate would be crazy enough to follow us there.

"Cut propulsion."

Sparrow trembled as Kojo brought her closer to the giant carrier's flank. With delicate touches, Kojo tucked us next to the carrier's belly.

The carrier was steady as a rock. Carried along by the current, we could ride there at rest as easily as orbiting a planet. But the carrier was no planet, she was a ship in transit. She'd need to slow and leave the current as she approached Lazuna. If we were anywhere near her when she fired retros, it would mean certain destruction.

Of course, I didn't say any of that to the passengers when I went to check on them.

"Why the hell are we standing still?" Grim asked. From the salon's viewscreen, filled with a close view of the carrier's side, we might have been parked on a Lazuna dock.

"Lying low," I said, serving a hasty meal. "Making sure whoever was following us loses interest."

"We should have just stopped and talked to them," Grim groused.

Amateurs. Since when were pirates happy with just talking?

I brought a ration pack to Kojo in the wheelhouse. "Nice sailing. Even if anyone thought to look in here, they'd never find us." Facing forward, we seemed to be at rest next to the behemoth, no more noticeable than a minnow next to a whale.

The scanner and out-facing screens told a different story—our speed was far greater than would be advisable in any other region of space. Kojo watched the controls tautly for any tiny turbulence that would have us hitting the carrier or straying too far from her side.

"We don't dare stay here long," Kojo said. He pulled up the charts. "This lane is taking us away from the Terran sectors again. If we pull out up ahead, and decel to a safe speed, we can hit the jump gate near Chuchan. It'll take at least five jumps to get to Oakdale. It's roundabout, but it still avoids the checkpoint."

"Five more jumps? We'll need to buy more jump cells." I mentally toted up the expense of cells bought in a high-markup outlying colony like Oakdale rather than a major trade hub. "This job isn't turning out to be as profitable as I had hoped. I'd like to get my hands on whoever was chasing us."

Kojo grinned wolfishly. "Whoever it was, our transponder must have transmitted enough of that oddball config that the Cartel will identify them. It may take days for a sublight message to reach a beacon, but I hope the Selkids give him hell."

Tinker jumped to my lap and used her tongue to smooth out her ruffled fur.

I chucked her under the chin, thinking. "That was no random freebooter, Kojo. They called us by name."

"Yeah." Kojo ran a hand through his black curls, making them stand on end. "Maybe somebody on Ordalo's end let something slip. We might need to get to Kriti a little quicker than we planned."

"I dreamed of Papa the other night. He said someone was lying."

"You and your dreams. We already knew that. No need for Dad to come visit from wherever he is."

"Mmm." I stroked the cat.

Kojo narrowed his eyes at me. "What's on your mind? You don't think that freebooter had anything to do with the passengers, do you?"

"True. But that stone tablet was really interesting."

The com sounded. "Pardon me for disturbing you," Miranda said, "but I would like to speak to the captain as soon as possible. We have to change course."

Kojo rolled his eyes and shook his head.

"The captain's busy," I answered. "I'll join you in a moment."

Miranda paced the salon. "I can't help but feel unsafe." The blank side of the ore carriage filled the viewscreen, giving the illusion of standing safely still.

Grim shrugged. "Honey, be reasonable. Patch here says it wasn't a Cartel ship. Probably just some brigand taking his chances. Once we get to Oakdale, we'll sit tight until Galactic can come get us."

"Galactic?" I asked.

Miranda shot a look at Grimbold before answering me. "Galactic Conglomerate sponsored the dig. I've decided to ask them for help to ensure the artifact gets to safety. But, Grim, if whoever was chasing us followed us from Santerro, might they not realize we're heading to Oakdale? I'm certain it would be safer to change to another destination."

With a slight rumble, *Sparrow* left the carrier's minuscule slipstream. I held my breath. Slowly, smoothly, the carrier drifted farther away. The passengers didn't even notice. As soon as we passed out of the shipping lane, the engines rumbled on, firing retros to slow us down to a safer speed.

I pulled up the charts, rubbed my chin Kojo-style and said, as if reluctant, "We're still in the heart of Selkid mining sectors. Most of the gateways lead to corridors that go deeper into Selkid territory, or to Gavoran sectors."

"No!" Miranda said sharply. "We must find a Terran colony."

"All right, that narrows the possibilities. The nearest gate is in the Chuchan system. From there we can jump to the checkpoint at the entrance to the Terran sectors." I knew how to negotiate—present least acceptable choices first, so the client thinks it's her choice to take the way you want to go.

"Not the checkpoint." Miranda smiled apologetically. "There must be another way."

I traced the route Kojo had plotted. "There's a more roundabout way. It will take more jumps, but we could get you to the Avon system without hitting the checkpoint. You'd be as safe there as on Oakdale." That would take only four jumps instead of five, and the price for jump cells in a trading center like Avon would be far better than Oakdale.

Grim scowled, but Miranda smiled. "Excellent."

"The captain won't like it," I lied. "And there will be an extra expense." I eyed the wallet attached to her belt.

"Of course." Miranda reached into the wallet and took out a five-thousand-sovereign ingot.

I made no move to take it.

With a sigh, she took out another.

Grim muttered, "Highway robbery."

I took the ten thousand sovereigns. That would compensate us nicely. "I'll talk to the captain."

The rest of that night and following day were tough on both passengers and crew. Our hours in the shipping lanes had carried us far from the friendly current we'd been riding. After leaving the ore carrier's side, Kojo navigated at sublight through the swirls of ether, latching onto stray currents and skirting gravity wells to cross the system. When he tired,

Hiram took over, grinding us through the turbid ether toward the Chuchan jump gate. *Sparrow* shook and rattled with every eddy and course change.

I cheered the passengers as best I could with entertainment suggestions and light meals they had no appetite for. Grim and Miranda snapped at one another in the close confines of the salon. Just as well they weren't eloping lovers—the honeymoon would have ended already.

I took refuge in the engine room to give Archer a break. Traveling sublight wasn't like the smooth jump corridors, the engineer had to constantly adjust power loads and maneuvering rockets. Even so, Archer was right—compared to dealing with bored, turbulence-sick passengers, the engine room was quiet.

While Archer snoozed in the bunk, I balanced power loads and babied the rockets. Fandar sat at the console with the engine specs pulled up in front of him, but he stared at nothing, lost in thought or memory.

Fandar was a well-built man, showing that he'd had a better childhood than most slaves. He was even attractive, for a Gavoran.

My success rate with Terran men was spotty—some were spooked by advances from a large, strange-looking woman. But Gav men preferred to be seduced. Since I'd been smuggled out of Gavoran territory at the age of seven, I'd had very little to do with Gavs. I'd certainly never invited one to my bed. But here was a lonely runaway from my own clan, one who might welcome a friend—even a cross-blood.

I knew how to make the right signals: a long, smoldering gaze into the man's eyes. A gentle touch, sidle closer, a slow stroke of the pelt on the arm or thigh.

I opened my mouth to say something encouraging, but then I noticed his lips moving in some silent prayer and remembered the scar on his wrist. Fandar was too troubled. Once we got to Avon, it would be best if he sought out his own kind. I hoped he wouldn't become one of the aimless refugees that haunted the Terran frontier towns.

Even so, when I got to my bunk that night, I let myself dwell on the possibilities of a Gavoran lover. I dreamily imagined snuggling against the warm fur of his chest, feeling his brawny arms around me. His fingers would entwine my curls. His hands would stroke my cheek. His breath would warm my neck. His sinewy thighs would rub mine.

I was surrounded by swirling dark shapes.

Home. Take me to my home. Peace and joy await.

I wakened with a start, almost sure someone was speaking to me.

But I was in my narrow bunk in my cabin, with only darkness for company.

On the morning of the fifth day after leaving Santerro, we reached the relative calm of the Chuchan gate. We joined the ships waiting to jump as a convoy of colonists took priority. Ship after ship of colonists arrived through the gate, then milled around to organize themselves before leaving again, one after another.

The chatter from the merchant ships waiting in the queue crackled with complaints: burzing colonists, burzing

Settlement Authority restrictions on new colonies, burzing Gavoran control of terraforming technology, and the burzing Corridor Patrol being a burzing nuisance.

In my little cabin, I went through the messages we'd picked up at the beacon: invoices and offers for cut-rate supplies.

I hadn't been sleeping well. Maybe it was just the turbulence of sublight travel, but the ancient tablet had invaded my dreams again. *Bring me to my home. Peace and joy.* In my dreams, the tablet's shifting colors became confused with swirling whorls of ether. Under my caress, its smooth surface felt warm and pulsing with life.

Even when I was awake and working, the tablet niggled in the back of my mind. I would have loved to see it more closely, to watch the colors swirling over its surface and to touch those strange markings.

Why not? Miranda was watching a program in the salon. I could slip into her stateroom, open the locker, lever open the case...

Kojo sidled into my cabin, brow creased. "We picked up some gossip from the pilots in the queue. The Patrol has stepped up the search, expanded it to Terran sectors."

"I thought somebody turned the loot in to the Cartel?"

"That was a dud. Some low-life tried to con the Cartel out of the reward money." Kojo stroked his chin. "You looked at that stone dingus pretty close. How sure are you it's not Gav?"

"Very sure."

The jump gate gantry filled the viewscreen as *Sparrow* entered the gate for its turn to jump. The lights flared red, and the screen blurred as we entered the dead calm of the star corridor.

Kojo nodded. "I think you're right. The best thing to do is keep lying low, stay away from the Patrol." He flashed his cocky grin. "I'm sure everything will be fine by the time we get to Avon."

It was then the shouting started.

CHAPTER 7

Liars and thieves

FANDAR, WIELDING A STEEL LEVER, had Grimbold backed into the corner of Miranda's stateroom. Grimbold yelled, "Help! Somebody help!"

Some bodyguard.

I shouldered my way in. "What's going on? Fandar, what are you doing here?"

Grim pointed. "He was forcing the locker! I caught him in the act." One of the luggage lockers—*the* locker—gaped open.

Damn! Fandar must be mad.

I blocked the door. "Fandar, don't be a fool. There's no place to go."

Miranda peeked over my shoulder. "What's happening?"

"Get back." I kept my bulk between her and the madman.

Fandar directed his hate-filled glare, not at me or Grim, but at Miranda. He pointed with the tip of the lever. "*She!* She is a thief and a liar." He repeated his charge in Gavoran, using terms that were brutally insulting.

That made me pause. No slave would dare speak that way, not even about a Terran.

There was movement behind me.

In a voice as cold as space, Kojo said, "Out of the way, Patch." He pointed a stun pistol at Fandar. "Drop it, or I'll stun you and shove your body down the recycling chute."

"Wait." I spoke quietly to Fandar. "On this ship, the captain is law. If you threaten me or any of the passengers, he will kill you. No one will ever know your end. But if you have something to say, we'll listen." I held out my hand.

He hesitated, his gaze darting between the damaged locker and the stunner. "You will listen?"

"I swear."

After a tense moment, he handed me the lever.

"Oh, dear god," Miranda cried, still crowding the passageway. "Balan? Is it you? Kojo, he's a madman!"

"And you!" Fandar cried, pointing at Miranda. "You have lied again and again. Her name is Jamila Patil, and she has stolen the relic!"

Patil? Balan? "Wait. *You're* the ones the Patrol is looking for? You stole objects from a Sage temple?" *Ancestors!*

"Damn!" Grim peered at Fandar. He turned to me. "He must have followed us. He's working with the antiquities thieves!"

"No!" Fandar cried. "I am no thief. *She* is the thief!"

Kojo shouted, "Quiet! Everyone into the salon. Now!"

"Be careful," Miranda said. "The man is mentally ill. He could be dangerous."

As they herded everyone into the salon, Kojo muttered, "You should have let me shoot him."

I shook my head. "That won't keep the Patrol off our trail. We need to find out what's going on."

In the salon, Kojo ordered the three of them to sit at the table, hands visible. "What's your real name?" he snapped at Miranda.

She sighed. "Professor Jamila Patil. I am from Evergreen University, as I told you. I adopted an alternate name solely for security purposes."

"How'd you get through the checkpoint?" I asked.

"Grim provided an implant override."

Grim winced. Through clenched teeth, he said, "Thanks, honey." Implant modification could earn them both three years in a penal colony.

Kojo pointed at Fandar. "And you?"

Fandar thumped his chest with his fist—a Gav male's expression of strength. "My name is Balan, of Wind Clan."

He whipped the dirty bandage from his arm to reveal pristine brown fur. Clearly, he'd never borne a slave's brand.

Ancestors! Wind Clan was among the highest-ranked aristo clans.

I held my gaze steady, but inside, I was shaken. As a slave's child, my mother had schooled me never to confront an aristo, never to speak unless spoken to. Eyes down, always subservient, never threatening—forgetting would earn me a slap from the chief house slave or a beating from whatever master I'd offended. For a week, I'd been ordering Fandar—Balan—around. If he knew my true heritage…

I'm no slave. Not anymore.

Balan sat proudly, head high, dark eyes glinting from under his brow ridge. "I am a scholar from the College of Religion on Gavora. I was one of two Gavorans on the research team at the Cazar archeological site."

An archeologist—which explained why an aristo would have calloused hands. I turned to Miranda—Jamila. "Is that right?"

She nodded.

Balan stiffened. "I assure you I am telling the truth. Duty has demanded I board this ship under false pretenses, but I will not have my word doubted by a"—he looked me up and down—"an ugly fuzzhead cross-breed!"

"Watch your language," Kojo snarled.

So much for my fantasies about a Gav lover. He must have been bursting the past week, forced to act like a slave.

I grinned at Balan. "You've already admitted to lying, and this particular ugly cross-breed is the one deciding what will happen to you. Why would Gavorans join a Terran dig?"

"The site is a ruined city built by the Cazar, allies of the blessed Sages during the Corridor Wars."

Kojo's head jerked up. "Wars in the corridors?"

"Five thousand years ago," Jamila said. "The Gavoran myths talk about ancient wars among the advanced races to control the star corridors. The myths equate the Sages with the benign deity and their enemies with forces of evil, rather like Terran tales of angels and devils."

"They are not myths," Balan said. "They are our sacred histories." Although still dressed in a torn work tunic, he'd reverted to the bearing and attitude of an aristo.

Jamila waved a hand. "Certainly, there is a factual basis. The purpose of the dig was to find out more about the Cazar culture."

Balan leaned forward intently. "I was mapping the temple ruin with my clan sister Deprata. Something strange happened—we both had dreams, Deprata and I, that we were being called to a particular place in the ruins."

Strange dreams? I didn't like the sound of that.

"It was Deprata who first found the crypt. The relic was there, in the place to which our dreams led us." Balan paused, breathing heavily, his eyes staring at nothing. "It called to us," he said quietly. "The relic houses a living soul. It called to us."

Jamila shook her head sadly. "I told you. He's delusional."

Grim snorted. "Why are you listening to this crap?"

"We could not help ourselves," Balan said. "The relic demanded to be fed."

"Fed? Fed with what?" Kojo asked.

"With blood."

"Blood?" I felt a sudden chill. Could there really be an evil spirit in the tablet? Could spirits even *be* evil?

Home! Peace and joy await.

I'd been having some strange dreams, but nothing like Balan described. Maybe Jamila was right about him being delusional.

Balan spread his hands palm upward, as if in prayer. "On the surface of the relic, there are channels containing small openings. Deprata and I felt driven to allow some of our blood to enter the channels, as if the being inside were starving and only we could help it." He stroked the healing scar on his wrist.

Kojo rolled his eyes at me. "Why's it got to be complicated?"

Jamila said, "We found Balan and Deprata at the bottom of a crypt, bleeding all over the relic. It was madness. They had both torn open veins in their arms. Balan was unconscious, Deprata was nearly dead. We thought they must have made a suicide pact. We brought them up to the camp and treated them as best we could. After a day, they were both recovering, but Balan kept raving about the spirit in the relic needing to be fed, and about going to Nakana, the mythological home of the Sages."

"We spoke the truth," Balan said.

Jamila shook her head. "They were recovering. But the next day, Deprata wasn't in her bed. We found her in the crypt. She had opened her vein again and this time, she'd bled to death."

It made no sense. Spirits didn't harm us. Everything I'd been taught as a child affirmed that spirits were loving and friendly, lending us wisdom and strength and courage.

Jamila covered her eyes with her fingers, as if to block out the sight. "It was completely senseless. Balan was still weak and raving about the relic. As soon as we could, we sent him to the nearest medical facility, on Santerro."

"And you took the relic!" Balan cried.

Jamila snapped, "Of course I did! It's an incredible archeological find. It has to be studied."

Balan half rose from his chair. "You are lying. You are stealing it for yourself, to sell it to outlaws!"

"Sit down." Kojo waved the stunner and Balan subsided.

"What I want to know," Grim asked, "is what that Neanderthal is doing here? We were careful. We chose a ship that was listed as having a Terran captain and a Terran crew." He stared pointedly at me.

"He stowed away," I answered. "We didn't know he was on the ship until after we were underway. He said he was a runaway slave." I realized I was touching my injured graft and put my hand down.

"And you believed him?"

I shrugged. "Worn clothes, calloused hands. He told a plausible story."

Kojo slapped the table. "Enough! What none of you have explained is why the Corridor Patrol is looking for you."

Balan replied stiffly. "I am no thief. As soon as I could, I reported the find of the artifact to my superior in the College of Religion."

Jamila tapped her fingers nervously. "You mean Lyden?"

"Of course. I sent her images of the relic and the inscriptions. No doubt, when she spoke to the Terrans on the site, she learned that Professor Patil had absconded with the relic. Mzee Lyden must have enlisted the Corridor Patrol's aid to recover it." Balan smirked at Jamila. "You will have to answer for your crime."

I rubbed my forehead. This *was* getting complicated. If Jamila and Balan were the fugitives the Corridor Patrol was looking for, then the "treasure" stolen from a "temple" must be the tablet. The Cartel must have jumbled the facts: If a Gav priestess was looking for the relic, they'd naturally assumed it must have been stolen from a Sage temple.

But that left more questions. "Balan, why did the alert name *you* as a thief along with *her*? And why were you pretending to be a runaway?"

Balan glowered. "I was recovering in the medical center when I realized the relic was being taken through Santerro's port. Weak though I was, I left my bed and followed Professor Patil. I saw your captain take the bag with the relic into your ship. There was no time to tell Mzee Lyden what had happened. I hid on the dock, looking for a way to get on the ship, when I saw your strange engineer. Everyone knows Terrans will assist slaves to betray their masters, so I presented myself to him as a runaway." He sneered. "He is a simpleton, easy to fool."

I sneered back. "At least he's not a liar."

"It's ridiculous," Grim said. "Balan's probably trying to steal it himself. He's hiding something—how could you know we were on Santerro? How did you know the relic was in the locker?"

Balan looked at Grim with disdain. "It calls me," he said. "I hear it in my dreams, and when I am awake. It has fed on my blood. It knows me. It calls me. It needs me."

Home.

I felt cold. "Needs you for what?"

He answered as if it were the most reasonable thing possible. "To take it to Nakana. There we will find a beautiful new home, filled with peace and joy. It is the will of the blessed Sages."

"The man's a lunatic," Grim said.

I tried to tamp down panic. Home? Peace and joy? Was the tablet causing me to have the same sort of hallucination? Was I going as mad as Balan?

Balan turned to Kojo. "I assure you, Captain, I am perfectly sane. You need only contact the Corridor Patrol. They will verify my identity and take these criminals into custody."

Kojo snapped, "Good idea. As of now, all three of you are under ship's arrest. I'm turning you over to the Corridor Patrol at the first opportunity." A bluff—the last thing we wanted was the Patrol rooting through our cargo hold.

Balan smiled. He placed a hand on the metal case as if claiming it.

Jamila pulled the case out of Balan's reach. "Captain, you mustn't let the Patrol have it. That could be terribly dangerous."

"Dangerous how? And try to make it the truth this time."

"Gavorans," Jamila said. "Something in the artifact affects their sanity."

My stomach took a dive. "That's ridiculous," I said, maybe a little too fast.

Kojo eyed me sidelong.

"Through touch," Jamila clarified, glancing at me. "It seems to work in part through touch. I've handled it without ill effect, but you can see that Balan...I'd better tell you from the beginning. But first, please put the artifact back in my stateroom. I'm afraid, with a Gavoran so near..."

Kojo nodded to me. "Vault."

The case felt heavier than before, as I took it down the aft steps to the vault in the cargo hold.

Home!

"Not now," I mumbled, lashing the case between crates of premium brandy. Silly of me to talk to a rock. Maybe I *was* cracking up.

CHAPTER 8

Blood and madness

WHEN I GOT BACK TO THE SALON, Jamila had begun her story. "...but there were no Gavorans on site until this season. Balan and Deprata's focus was the temple, to study the Cazar's connection with the Sages. I had no idea they were being drawn into some mystical obsession—not until we found them, half-dead at the bottom of the crypt." She grimaced. "It was terrible, blood everywhere. Of course, our first concern was to give them medical help."

"We told them the relic spoke to us," Balan said, "but Terrans are blind to all but the most base of the senses. They thought us insane."

Like Kojo, who never really believed in my visions of Papa.

I'd heard the relic speak, but only a little whining to go home, not any strange bloodlust. Did my half-Terran blood make me so different from Balan?

Jamila searched our faces for understanding. "While Deprata and Balan raved about blood and finding Nakana, I was worrying about disease vectors and food contaminants. After all, it seemed mad to think the stone would speak to them. Then Deprata died by her own hand before we could transfer them to Santerro." She looked with sympathy to Balan. "I am sorry, Balan. I know you cared for her."

He nodded with dignity.

"We sent Balan to Santerro that day," Jamila said. "It was only then I was able to pay attention to the artifact and the inscriptions on the crypt. As soon as I examined it, I realized the tablet was not made by the Cazar—it's from another culture entirely. It may already have been ancient when it came to the Cazar city, rather like the Caesars in ancient Rome on Earth collecting even more ancient Egyptian art."

"It is a gift from the Sages," Balan said.

Jamila bit her lip, then nodded. "It's possible. The Cazar *were* Sage allies, that's why the Gavorans were with us. The inscriptions describe the artifact as a gift from the Cazar deity—something both sacred and dangerous. They called it the *bloodstone*. According to the inscriptions, from time to time the artifact demanded to be fed and the Cazar would open the crypt with great ceremony and provide the artifact with blood from a living being."

I kept my face blank.

Jamila looked at us, as if expecting a reaction. "Well! That changed things, don't you see? The fact that Balan and Deprata had experienced a call for blood—so similar to that described in the inscription—suggested the artifact itself was psychoactive. Somehow, Deprata and Balan had been caught in the artifact's blood cult. The more I thought about it, the more it seemed possible there was something about the bloodstone that affects the Gavorans, as it did the Cazar, but not Terrans."

"That doesn't make sense," I said. "Gavorans are Neanderthals from Earth, practically cousins to Terrans. How could the tablet tell the difference?"

"It is obvious," Balan said. "The sacred relic can distinguish ally from enemy. The Cazar and the Gavorans were allies of the blessed Sages, chosen to exercise dominion over lesser races. Terrans are the dregs, the ones the Sages deemed unworthy when they delivered our ancestors from Earth."

Grim murmured, "Dregs, huh? Thanks, buddy."

Jamila shook her head. "Balan has a point. Sage technology is the common factor between the Cazar and the Gavorans. The Sages were advanced enough to terraform planets and to seed Neanderthals onto Gavora. Perhaps the bloodstone was programmed to issue a telepathic message—and could somehow distinguish allies from non-allies even if they were closely related. Something genetic, or tuned into brain waves, maybe. I don't know how—that's one of the reasons we need to study the artifact."

I rubbed my forehead, trying to follow this mix of science and mythology. I knew, of course, the tale about the Sages rescuing the peaceful Neanderthals from the hell that Earth must have been. In doing so, the Sages no doubt saved them from the Terrans' aggressive ancestors who were spreading over the planet, crowding out all competitors, driving even large carnivores to extinction.

"So," I said, "you took the tablet because…?"

"Because it drove both Deprata and Balan to madness, and Deprata to her death. The only safe, responsible thing to do was to get it to Terran scientists as soon as possible. I would never have set foot on this ship if I'd known Balan was aboard, or that a member of the crew was part Gavoran. Patch, you haven't been hearing voices, have you?"

"Of course not," I lied. At least, I wasn't feeling any urge to sacrifice my lifeblood to a stone relic.

"Thank the stars for that. So you see, it could be disastrous if the artifact fell into Gavoran hands—whether the Corridor Patrol, the College of Religion or any other Gavoran agency."

Grim added, "And it's true that some Selkid collector had heard about it—the sort who doesn't care about archeology. He just wants it because it's a one-of-a-kind object."

"Unacceptable," Balan said. "This is a gift from the Sages to the Gavoran people."

It didn't sound like much of a gift to me. "Balan, is the stone still asking you for blood?" I absently scratched my arm.

"No. My blood, and Deprata's, has sated it for now."

That was a relief.

Jamila listened with a worried frown. "The inscription said it needed to be fed periodically, but I was unable to translate the time references. Who knows when it might activate again?"

Damn. We might as well be sailing with an armed grenade in the vault.

Jamila continued, "The temple inscriptions suggest the crypt was somehow protective, so I used some of the metal from the crypt to line the case, hoping it would act as an insulator. My goal was, and still is, to get the artifact to a place where Terran scientists can study it without endangering any more lives."

"You could just destroy it," Kojo said. "In fact, we could dump it right now."

"No!" For once, Jamila, Balan, and Grimbold were united.

I felt the same. "As long as that raider and the Patrol are looking for it," I said, "jettisoning it won't protect us."

"It would keep anybody else from going crazy over it," Kojo snapped. "Jamila, you're an archeologist. It makes sense that you want it, or some collector. And if the Gavs think a Terran is pilfering some sacred object, it makes sense that *they* want it, and set the Corridor Patrol to looking for it. But what I really want to know is, who was shooting at us? No Selkid collector is *that* obsessed."

Jamila looked troubled. "Surely it was just some outlaw who happened upon us?"

I shook my head. "That raider targeted *Sparrowhawk* specifically, called us out by name. And they took a huge chance by accosting us in Selkid sectors—the Cartel is very touchy about poachers."

"We've got to land somewhere soon," Kojo said. "We need to know who's after us."

"Maybe *you've* got enemies," Grim said. "Could be nothing to do with us at all."

Kojo's hands tightened into fists. "Except they knew where to find us." Kojo loomed over the table, smiling wolfishly at Jamila, Balan, and Grimbold in turn. "So, which of you told someone we'd be traveling off-corridor to Oakdale?"

Grim laughed. "That's ridiculous! Why would any of us do that? We'd be risking our own lives!"

I glanced at Balan. "Gavorans risk their lives for something they think is right."

"It was not I," Balan said. "I would have reported your destination to Mzee Lyden if I had known of it, but I had no chance."

Jamila pointed at Grim. "It had to be you. Balan would have told the Gavorans—only *you* would go to some pirate."

Grim looked around but saw only hostile faces. He straightened, chin firm. "They're not pirates. They're agents for Rampart Militech."

Kojo's eyebrows went up. "*Rampart?* The mercenaries?"

"Patriots," Grimbold snapped. "Defenders of Terran interests. All Rampart wants is the artifact. If you'd stopped when they hailed you, Captain, everything would have been fine. My friends would have boarded the ship, paid us off, and left quietly. But when you skedaddled...maybe they thought I was double-crossing them. They're suspicious people."

Kojo ran a hand through his hair. "Of course we ran! In Selkid sectors, if a ship doesn't show a Cartel signal, you assume the worst."

Grim spread his hands, in a *why-can't-we-all-get-along* gesture. "It's not too late. Why should we let her sell it to Galactic rather than people who put Terran interests first?"

I turned to Jamila. "You're *selling* it to Galactic? You said you were taking it to the university to be studied."

She waved a hand. "Indirectly. But I couldn't trust the university—Gavorans control Evergreen's directorate. Galactic has some rights as the dig's sponsor, and it's strong enough to resist any Gavoran demands."

Balan sniffed. "Fools."

Kojo shook his head, his expression confused. "But why would Galactic *or* Rampart care so much about an old stone?"

"Are you kidding?" Grim pointed at Balan. "Something that psychologically affects *them* but not *us?* Any Terran military force would pay a fortune for it."

"Is that what you told them? This is a weapon?" Jamila frowned in disgust. "You're an idiot."

As far as I was concerned, Jamila and Grim deserved each other.

I stood. "If this tablet is a weapon for Terrans to use against Gavorans, it's going out the airlock right now." Kojo looked thoughtful, but nodded once.

Balan stepped in front of me, fists clenched. "No!"

I looked at Balan. "Why not? You should be the first to want to see it destroyed."

Jamila touched Balan's arm. "Tell them. You raved about it for days on Santerro."

Balan's lips compressed into a thin line. "The relic is much more than this fool imagines. The relic is a map. A map to Nakana."

Kojo narrowed his eyes. "So? Nice for the religious folks, I guess."

Jamila leaned forward, eyes alight. "Religious value, of course, and tremendous archeological value. But what about the technology? The Sages invented the beacons and the jump gates and *all* the terraforming technology we have today. If this artifact shows the way to the Sage homeworld, think of what else they might have left behind, just waiting for someone to uncover it."

"Oh." A cold chill crept over me, as I finally understood.

Grim glared at Balan. "The damn Gavs have kept Terrans in line for centuries, hoarding the bits of terraforming tech the Sages left behind, technology even they don't understand. They dole it out in drips to other races and keep the best for themselves. Out of every ten promising new worlds, the burzing Settlement Authority lets Gavs develop eight for themselves."

Balan glared back. "We *protect* the civilized systems from Terrans' unbridled greed. The Sages left the star corridors in our care, and their technology under our dominion. It is our sacred duty to see it is used wisely."

"And we have to stand for it," Grim said, "because otherwise the gorillas will close the jump gates to us. But now—now we've got a shot at grabbing some of that tech for ourselves."

It was true. The Sages had left in Gavoran hands all the hydroverters, microbial synthreactors, and other tech needed to change a barren moon or planet to a habitable one. In theory, all the space-capable species were represented when the Settlement Authority handed out terraforming technology, but everyone knew it was the Gavs who dominated, using their control over the jump gates as leverage.

Kojo whistled. "An ancient Sage colony, maybe with tech to unscramble? That would be worth a lot."

Worth enough to kill for.

Kojo and I exchanged a look.

"We need to hide," I said.

CHAPTER 9

Change course and lie low

THE SALON'S VIEWSCREENS showed only the star corridor's monotony of muddy ether swirls.

I brought the charts onto the screen, checking the systems that could be accessed from the next jump gate.

Home!

I shook my head at the tablet's annoying intrusion. "Do you know where Nakana is, Balan?"

"I have seen the system in my visions. I believe I can find it, with guidance from the relic. But I will not tell *you*."

Kojo frowned. "You saw a map in a vision? Sounds like a fairy tale."

Jamila bit her lip. "Not a fairy tale. While he and Deprata were ill, Balan mentioned certain facts and places, things that have puzzled archeologists for years. An undiscovered Sage colony would make sense of those anomalies."

"All right," Kojo said, "maybe we don't dump it out the airlock, but I don't want Grim's friends at Rampart to get hold of it, either."

Balan sniffed. "You have been duped into helping these criminals. The only reasonable course is to surrender to the Corridor Patrol as soon as possible."

"Even if it means endangering your people?" Jamila turned desperate eyes to Kojo. "If I can get to some Terran colony, I can contact Galactic Conglomerate and turn the tablet over to them. I'm sure they'll be generous to anyone who assists me." She glanced at Balan. "They have the means to finance an expedition and I will make it a condition that they include participation from responsible Gavoran interests."

Grim patted the air in calming motions. "Listen, Captain. I'm sure you don't want the Neanderthals monopolizing new tech any more than I do. Find someplace quiet to hole up and let me contact Rampart. They'll make it worth your while." He turned to Jamila. "Play your cards right, honey, and you'll be rich, too. Rampart Militech will need a translator, won't they? An archeology expert? You could write your own ticket. Everyone will be happy."

She harrumphed and turned her back on him.

Kojo turned to me. "Any ideas?"

"From what Jamila says, it's too dangerous for the Gavs, and for damn sure I don't want a bunch of Terran vigilantes like Rampart to make a weapon out of it. For us, the most important thing is to find some quiet place to resupply before we're power-stranded."

"Right," Kojo said. "The first port we get to, all of you are off the ship."

"You can't just drop us anywhere you want," Grim objected. "Your contract says we choose the destination."

I stepped up to him, eye to eye. "In the first place, you're not the client, *she* is. And the contract also says the captain has the right to take any action, including terminating the voyage, to preserve the safety of the ship and crew."

"I'm exercising my prerogative as captain," Kojo said. "All three of you and that burzing rock are off my ship at the first reasonable port."

"And," I said, "there's a cost. We've racked up a lot of extra expenses on this run because of you."

Jamila stiffened. "You can't blame me for marauding pirates!"

"Sure I can. Grimbold's the one who set them on us, and you brought him aboard. You lied about your identity, you tricked us into carrying fugitives, and you brought aboard a dangerous item, all in violation of your contract. Ten thousand sovereigns ought to do it. Rhollium, not credits."

"That's extortion."

"Call it what you want," I said. "The Cartel would pay us that much to turn you in."

"You wouldn't!"

Kojo wasn't the only one who could bluff. "Try me. Ten thousand sovereigns rhollium."

After Balan gave his word of honor as a member of Wind Clan to keep the peace, I let him use a small cabin that was half-filled with brandy crates. It would be more comfortable than the pallet in the engine room and now that I knew he wasn't a runaway slave, I fully intended to bill him for passage.

As for Jamila and Grimbold, I told Jamila that if she caused any trouble, I'd dump the tablet into space. I told Grim I'd shoot him.

After tucking two more of Jamila's beautiful little ingots away in a bulkhead cache, I climbed to the wheelhouse and took the seat at the watch station.

Kojo slumped at the helm, staring into the featureless ether of the corridor. "So Miranda and our stowaway really are the thieves the Patrol's looking for."

"And the Cartel. Can we get back to Selkid space, collect the Cartel reward?"

Kojo shook his head. "We're stuck in this corridor for another day. Once we reach the gate, there's a small Terran colony, Calista, within sublight range. The best we can do is to shed these passengers there and let the Cartel know where they are."

"And hope the Cartel doesn't think we deliberately held out on them, carrying something valuable without cutting them in. It might be best to lie low for a while."

"Agreed."

Tinker rubbed my ankles. I lifted her onto my lap, and she squirmed to make herself comfortable.

Kojo tapped his fingers on the console. "What about that stowaway—Fandar or Balan, whatever his name is? Do you think we should lock him up?"

"No. Balan's Wind Clan—that's an aristo clan with strong ties to the military. He could make serious trouble for us."

"Another burzing complication. Are you worried? We're outside Gav jurisdiction, and under Terran law, you're free."

"True, but in his eyes, I'm still a slave. We can't trust him."

Kojo snorted. "Trust him? I'd like to launch him into cold space. He's a lunatic. Talking rocks!"

I took a deep breath. "Kojo, Balan's not crazy. I've heard the tablet, too. Like a voice in my head." And I hoped my brother wouldn't decide I needed to be locked up, too.

"Don't mess with me, Patch."

"I'm serious. This isn't like Gavoran spirits—those are family and loved ones who give comfort and advice. The tablet's voice is different, demanding."

He looked at me, probably checking to see if I was joshing. I guess he saw the worry on my face.

"For true? You heard the same thing that Balan did?"

"Nothing about blood. Just the part where it wants to go home."

"Huh. Who doesn't?"

That made me smile. "Its home. Very insistent, like a whining baby."

Kojo gazed at me for a minute, brow creased. Finally, he turned back to the scanner. "With a whining baby, if you don't give it something, it just gets worse. Where's its home, then?"

"I don't know. Home is peaceful."

"So's death. How bad is it, this whining baby?"

"Just an annoyance, and it's less of one since I locked the case in the vault." I was getting used to it, like the drone of the engines. "The point is, Balan isn't crazy—he's being perfectly reasonable, even brave, in acting on what he hears. And unless

I'm hallucinating the same thing, what he hears isn't just a delusion."

Kojo frowned at me. "Do you feel an urge to hurt yourself in any way?"

"None."

"Would you tell me if you did?"

"Of course I would. I have a very healthy desire to live."

Kojo stared at the ether haze. Finally, he nodded. "Fair enough. We won't lock him up. But stay away from the vault. And promise me—*promise me*—you'll tell me if the voices you hear want anything different."

"I promise—if in return, *you'll* promise *me* that once the heat's off, we'll go home."

Kojo gave me his lopsided grin. "Straight home to Palermo, I promise."

With all the disruption, mealtimes had become erratic. I put something together for Jamila and Grim, but when I took a tray to Balan's cabin, he wasn't there.

I found him standing before the vault, his hand resting on the door. His eyes were closed, as if deep in meditation or prayer.

"Balan, you shouldn't be in the cargo hold."

He blinked his eyes open and stared at the vault dreamily, as if he could see through the door.

"It was alone for so very long. Perhaps it has been calling for centuries, seeking someone to care for it, to return it to Nakana."

I began to worry. "Is it asking you for more blood?"

"No. Not yet."

That wasn't very reassuring.

I made him leave, then reset the lock on the door to the hold.

Archer watched me from the passage. "You should stay away from him. He's a liar—he made me feel sorry for him, pretending to be a slave, when he's really just another aristo."

"Don't be too hard on him. He was just trying to protect the tablet. And don't forget he helped with the drones when that raider was shooting at us."

Archer's right hand and left foot tapped out a little rhythm of their own. "That doesn't make him our friend. But maybe you have another reason to go easy on him. I suppose he's kind of good-looking, for a Gav."

"Don't be ridiculous," I said, but Archer had already ducked back into the engine room.

That night, I lay in my bunk making a mental list of the supplies we needed. Jump cells, power modules. If the Calista population liked brandy, we could get what we needed without dipping into our cash. Some fresh food, whatever the Calista farms produced, would be good. Once the passengers were gone, we could all relax a bit. It would be nice to have *Sparrow* to ourselves again.

"Danger."

Papa's voice was so clear, I startled awake, looking around for him. My little cabin was dark and empty, desk stowed and lockers closed. The only decoration was an image of Papa and Hiram, taken in their young mercenary days, cocky and grinning and ready for anything.

I lay back down, but the uneasy feeling lingered. Finally, I dressed and went to the wheelhouse.

"Can't sleep?" Kojo asked.

"Something's wrong."

Kojo looked at me questioningly.

"I dreamed of Papa again. I think something bad is ahead." Tinker batted at my ankles and I picked her up for comfort.

Kojo looked at me skeptically. "Any idea what?" he asked.

"He didn't say." I closed my eyes and let the feelings wash over me, trying to pin down something definite. Now that I was among lights and company, the feeling of unease eluded me.

"People," I said finally. "Danger from people."

"Ain't it always? Where? Calista? Palermo?"

"I can't tell."

Kojo sighed. "Well, whoever it is, we don't have many options about where to go. Once we get to Calista, that thing and these passengers won't be our problem. Next time, tell Dad to be more helpful. And give him my love."

I rumpled his hair and went back to bed, but I didn't sleep. There were too many problems looming. All I wanted, at that moment, was to go home.

The next morning, as we neared the jump gate to the Calista system, Kojo and I met with Jamila in the wardroom.

"From this gate," Kojo said, "we have a day's sublight journey to the planet Calista. You'll disembark there. That fake implant should get you past the port gate and I'll escort you and the dingus to the local sheriff."

"Won't the sheriff just turn me over to the Patrol? Balan will go running to them as soon as the hatch opens."

"I'll keep Grimbold and Balan aboard," I said, "and ask the port officials to take custody of Balan. I'll take my time explaining about him stowing away and hiding his identity and tell them he's hearing voices and needs medical care. By the time he convinces anyone that you should be arrested, you'll have had time to call Galactic."

She turned melting eyes on Kojo. "I suppose that's the best I can hope for. Kojo, I am so very grateful for all you've done."

"Just wish I could do more." Kojo touched her hand and returned her smoldering gaze.

I herded Jamila back to the salon before Kojo could make any foolish promises.

To celebrate the end of the voyage, I made as fine a luncheon as I could, and was graciously thanked by Jamila. I brought a plate to Balan's cabin, together with a bill for his passage. He disdainfully keyed his payment into my datacon, with a grimace like something smelled bad.

As we neared the Calista gate, I daydreamed about getting home to Palermo and using Jamila's rhollium to pay the crew and some of Branson's loan. There would be time to relax a little before beginning the journey to meet Ordalo. Once we were ready to sail, it wouldn't be too hard to find some cargo and passengers to Kriti—there were always some lowlifes with ready cash who wanted to head out to the fringe sectors.

In the interim, the crew would enjoy the pleasures of Palermo. Kojo would seek out some gambling den and spin yarns with other captains over chinko. Hiram would haunt a homey bar with a soulful balladeer and find some brawny space lad for companionship. Archer would comb the shops for the complex games and wailing music he favored. And I would find endless fascination in watching the people from faraway places. Maybe I would even find some rugged wayfarer interested in a dalliance with a big, odd-looking, curly-haired lass.

The voice of the tablet had become a background rustle in my mind, easy to ignore. I wished it well, hoping it would find peace, whether with Terran scientists or in the unknown world of Nakana. Some part of me would miss the strange voice from the relic, but it would make a fine tale to tell when we got home.

Home.

The familiar slide and bump told me that *Sparrow* had arrived at the jump gate. Only a day's sublight journey to go before we would land on Calista.

I had a notion to go and say a farewell to the artifact. I started toward the cargo hold, but just then, Hiram called on the com. "Kojo, Patch, we got trouble!"

Ahead of us—a ship of unmistakable Gavoran design, sleek and powerful, with the insignia of the Corridor Patrol.

Waiting.

CHAPTER 10

Prepare to be boarded

KOJO STARED THROUGH THE CANOPY at the sleek ship. "Patrol vessel, corvette class. Complement of twenty or so."

It was fast and beautiful and filled with people who would gladly put us in the brig.

A hail reverberated throughout the com nodes. "This is the Corridor Patrol cruiser *Betanda*. Selkid cutter, heave to and submit to search. Prepare to be boarded."

"Outpowered and outgunned, boy," Hiram murmured.

Kojo nodded once and hit the com. "This is Captain Kojo Babatunji of the cutter *Sparrowhawk*, registered in Palermo. Permission to board granted. Always happy to cooperate with the Patrol." He ordered Archer to power down and the passengers to wait in the salon.

My stomach churned as the cruiser's grapplers reached for *Sparrow*.

Kojo patted my shoulder. "Let's go meet the boarding party. And don't worry, Patch. It'll be fine."

Kojo. You can't be a gambler if you're not willing to bluff.

On the way to the passenger hatch, I checked the salon. Balan paced between the couches and rubbed his hands; Jamila and Grimbold sat in a corner, conferring in whispers.

While *Betanda* married her passenger hatch to *Sparrow*'s, I tried to quell my nerves. Surely, once they had the tablet, the Patrol wouldn't bother with anything more than a cursory check for contraband? I didn't think they'd care about the lack of stamps on the brandy—the Patrol cared about smuggled tech, not Selkid taxes. A standard search might find the hidden caches of rhollium ingots, but not the synthreactor components. Unless...

Unless they were suspicious enough to bring on sophisticated imaging equipment. Or to put enough pressure on Hiram—or me or Kojo—to talk.

And then there was me. Under Gavoran law, I was contraband, too. In theory, as long as I was outside Gav space, my Terran implant should be enough to protect me. Still, any Gavoran seeing the raw scar over my damaged brand would know I'd been born a slave. And any technicality that provided an excuse to drag me into Gav sectors would have me back in slavery for the rest of my days.

First to step through the hatch was a tall Gavoran who identified himself as Gurin, captain of *Betanda*. Other officers—all Gavs, of course—followed and immediately moved into *Sparrow* to search her.

Gurin wore the badge of Cloud Clan, one of the lesser warrior clans. His gray-streaked pelt, wary eyes, and a puckered scar on his neck suggested a lengthy and varied experience.

Kojo bowed formally. "Welcome aboard *Sparrowhawk*, Captain Gurin. I'm Captain Kojo Babatunji. This is the ship's business manager and steward, Pachita Babatunji."

Gurin's gaze passed Kojo and aimed straight at my face. I stared back at him with friendly interest, as no slave would dare. We presented our shoulders to an officer to check our implants.

"We're glad to see you," Kojo said. "We had a terrible scare, had to run from pirates. Barely escaped."

"Where are you sailing from, Captain?" Gurin's tone was polite, even bored.

"Our last port of call was Santerro and our cargo is Santerro brandy. We're carrying two Terran passengers, plus a Gavoran male who came aboard as a stowaway."

Gurin scowled. "Assisting runaway slaves is prohibited."

My fists clenched, but Kojo just shrugged. "He's not a slave. You'll have to talk to him about the reasons why he boarded our ship."

"We will. The names of your passengers?"

Without hesitating, Kojo said, "Miranda Tai, traveling with a man named Grimbold. The Gav gave his name as Fandar when we found him hiding in the engine room."

Gurin checked his datacon. "The registry confirms the charter. Departure from Santerro seven standard days ago. Destination"—he paused, glowering—"Palermo in sector 184. You are far off course, Captain."

Kojo spread his hands engagingly. "Like I said, we had to run from brigands, sail the currents. Too bad there weren't any Patrol vessels around *then*. We could have used some protection."

One of the officers stepped up and reported in Gavoran, "All secure, Captain."

I had to look twice to believe my eyes. The officer was a truly ugly man. His ears stuck out like flaps, his nose jutted like a beak, and his square chin thrust forward. His long arms extended from thin shoulders and his wrists and hands were nearly hairless. His head was covered with curly, reddish-brown hair—clipped short, but darker than typical Gav coloring and definitely hair and not fur. A scar near his left eye did nothing to improve his looks.

A hybrid.

"Three passengers, two Terran and one Gavoran, in the salon." It was odd to hear the upper-caste Gav accent coming from his misshapen face. "Two Terran crew members. And, Captain, the female Terran's implant has been modified—she admits to being the fugitive Patil, and the Gavoran admits to being Balan of Wind Clan."

Gurin grinned. "Excellent, Sergeant Danto. Relay to base that we have intercepted the fugitives without resistance."

Gurin turned a stern face to Kojo and switched to Terran. "Captain, you are carrying wanted fugitives. All the checkpoints have broadcast alerts about Patil and Balan."

"Fugitives?" Kojo made a good imitation of astonishment. "Captain, if they're wanted, we had no way of knowing it. We had to sail off-corridor. We didn't pass any checkpoints or pick up any Patrol broadcasts."

"Nevertheless, this ship and its crew will remain under arrest until your complicity in the matter can be determined." Gurin stalked toward the salon. Danto gave me a hard stare before turning to follow him.

Kojo nudged me and whispered, "Let's see her talk her way out of *this*."

As Gurin entered the salon, Jamila leaped to her feet. "Are you the one in charge? Thank the stars! I demand protection." She pointed at Balan. "That man has been stalking me, making wild accusations."

With a low growl, Balan stepped forward. "Lies. She is a thief. She has taken the sacred relic!"

Grimbold shoved himself in front of Balan, as if Jamila needed his protection. "Back down, buddy. Leave the lady alone." He turned his head to Gurin. "He's a lunatic. Escaped from a hospital on Santerro and hid on board, just to harass my boss."

The half-blood sergeant pulled Balan and Grim apart and shoved them onto the couches.

Gurin frowned at Jamila. "You are Jamila Patil?"

She raised her chin. "That's right. Professor of Archeology, Evergreen University. I—"

"Quiet. And you, you are Balan of Wind Clan?"

Balan replied in Gavoran. "Of course. Member of the College of Religion. Mzee Lyden will vouch for me."

"Mzee Lyden has reported stolen a sacred temple object and has named you as complicit in its theft."

Balan drew himself up. "I am a man of honor. I simply followed the faithless Terrans who were stealing it. I want only to protect the relic."

Gurin switched back to Terran. "Professor Patil, you are under arrest on suspicion of theft."

Jamila held out a hand in supplication. "Captain Gurin, I'm afraid you've been misled. Balan is ill—delusional. He was working with me on the dig until he needed to be hospitalized after a suicide attempt." She pointed to the healing scar on Balan's wrist. "You can confirm that with the Santerro medical center. I'm transporting an artifact from the dig to Evergreen for study. I'm afraid, in his confused state, Balan came to believe the artifact is some sort of Gavoran religious relic and made accusations to his superiors. In fact, the artifact is not of Gavoran origin, nor from any Gavoran settlement. It is legitimately in my custody."

"You must not believe her," Balan insisted, rubbing his hands together. "I am perfectly well."

Sergeant Danto's hard policeman's gaze had not left Jamila. "You have illegally modified your implant."

Jamila looked down shyly. "Well, yes. That was necessary. My bodyguard learned on Santerro that antiquities thieves were interested in the artifact. I'm sure *you* know how corrupt the Selkid Cartel is! Our very lives were in danger. I tried to throw them off our trail with a temporary identity override and by switching destinations. Even with all our precautions, the ship was attacked. It was terrifying! But now you're here. I'm *so* glad to be under your protection!"

She was good—I almost believed her myself.

Gurin shook his head and focused on Balan. "What exactly is this object?" he asked.

"A relic, left for us by the blessed Sages."

Jamila smiled sadly and spread her hands. "It's simply a stone tablet, found among ruins in a Selkid sector."

Gurin grunted. "The proper authorities will adjudicate. My orders are to take you into custody. Where is this object?"

Balan pointed to me. "*She* locked it in the ship's vault."

"Sergeant Danto, verify its security and post a guard. Captain Babatunji, your ship will remain in custody, linked to *Betanda*, as we proceed to the nearest checkpoint."

I led Sergeant Danto down the forward steps to the cargo hold. He wore the badge of Star Clan, a military clan that ranked even higher than Balan's Wind Clan. Despite his homely appearance—or maybe because of it—his arrogant attitude seemed to dare anyone to cause trouble.

Ancestors! Wind Clan, Cloud Clan, and now Star Clan? My ship was suddenly crawling with burzing Gavoran aristos. I made sure not to let my hand stray toward my itching scar.

I worked the combination on the vault door and allowed the sergeant to peer inside.

Home. Bring me home.

Sergeant Danto showed no sign of hearing anything.

Danto's face was like a jigsaw puzzle put together with the wrong pieces. His thick brow ridge and sloped forehead were pure Gav, but his nose stuck out as much as Archer's. It had a little crook in it—no wonder, the thing was a standing temptation to be punched. He'd trimmed his beard to mimic Gav fur, but it wasn't long enough to hide the squareness of his chin and its little cleft, so unlike the subtle, receding jaw of a true Gavoran.

I'd never actually seen another hybrid. Did I look as odd as he did? No wonder people stared at me.

I pointed to Jamila's metal case, atop the crates of the premium brandy. "The artifact is in there. I don't have the combination to open it."

"Have you seen the object within?"

"The lady showed it to us a few days ago." I shrugged. "It's some kind of carved stone." I lowered my voice. "Watch out for Balan. He's obsessed with the thing, hears voices. He needs medical help."

Unimpressed, the sergeant told me to relock the vault.

Soon, Gavs guarded the vault and prowled *Sparrow*'s passages. Two officers herded Balan into *Betanda*, despite his loud protests that the blessed Sages wanted him to be near the relic. I expected they would give him a good grilling, and maybe a major sedative.

A Corridor Patrol pilot relieved Hiram. Her sour expression showed what she thought about taking the helm of an old Selkid hauler. Maybe sailing *Sparrow* was punishment duty.

While Hiram stood over the new pilot, giving her advice she didn't need, I pulled Kojo into the wardroom. "Did you see that sergeant?" I asked. "He's a hybrid."

"Yeah. Could you tell anything about him?"

"Star Clan. That's the most influential military clan. His matriarch would have the clout to get him accepted to the Patrol, but I'll bet he had to fight his way to promotion."

"Does he know you're a hybrid?"

"He didn't say anything, but he must have noticed. Even with my hair showing, he would see I'm not all Terran."

"Well, nothing we can do about it." Kojo gazed resentfully at the Patrol's handsome ship filling the viewscreen. "Whatever comes, we'll have to play it out."

As I helped Archer restock the engine room bays, he jittered and asked, "What's going to happen? I've never been arrested before."

"It's the ship that's been arrested. And maybe Jamila and Grimbold. They'll take *Sparrow* in tow to the nearest checkpoint that has a magistrate." I shrugged. "Don't worry, they won't do anything to the crew. You might as well enjoy the downtime and let the Patrol take us where they want."

He put a wiry arm over my broad shoulder. "But what about you? Will *you* be all right?"

"Sure," I lied. "They won't do anything to me, either." Unless the magistrate found us complicit in a crime. Then they might confiscate *Sparrow* and our licenses and send me and Kojo to a penal colony—or worse, in my case.

Archer hung his head and waggled his fingers. "I feel like this is my fault. Maybe if I hadn't let that rat Balan aboard..."

"Stop it," I snapped. "We are where we are. Worrying won't help. Go grease a flange or something. Or clean up—your hair will get caught in the coils if you don't tie it back."

His head hung lower.

Stupid. Why should I take my worries out on Archer? The truth was that I was worried sick.

I patted his shoulder. "I'm sorry. We're all on edge. Let's just do what we can to get through this." I kissed his cheek and headed for my cabin.

I didn't get far—Jamila awaited me in the passage. "Oh, Patch. Could you help me with the bunk? Those goons took it apart searching—god knows for what—and I can't seem to get it right."

She pulled me into her stateroom and slammed the door in the guard's face.

"I need your help," she whispered. "We must get the artifact away from the Gavorans. If I can distract the guard at the cargo hold, you and Grim can place the tablet in a drone. It would only take a moment. Send it into orbit around some convenient planet where we can recover it later."

"Forget it."

With a strained smile, Jamila laid a hand on my arm as if we were old friends. "Please, Patch. We can't let the Gavorans take it. Think of the damage it could do, the lives it could ruin! There's no real risk. They haven't opened the case yet—it could be empty for all they know." She touched her belt wallet. "I'll make it worth your while."

I pulled my arm away. "The Patrol's scanners would see a drone the moment it launched. This won't work."

Jamila's eyes grew hard. "Find a way." She grabbed my left wrist and snatched at my sleeve, forcing it up above my forearm. The skin was red under the skin seal. "You touch it when you're stressed. You were born into a slave clan. I'm sure the Patrol would like to know. All they need to do is pull a few strings, and you'll find yourself back in Gavoran jurisdiction facing Clan Enforcers."

I pulled my sleeve down. "Don't be ridiculous. I'm legally Terran, on a Terran-registered ship, traveling in a Terran sector. And *Betanda*'s scanners would certainly pick up anything leaving the ship. It's a crazy idea. Forget it."

I slammed the door behind me and retreated to my cabin, smiling at the dour guards as if everything was under control.

In my cabin, I took a deep breath. If ever there were a time for prayer, this was it. *Beloved ancestors, I pray for wisdom to choose what is best, strength to do what I must, and courage to face what may come.*

A Gavoran pilot sat at *Sparrow*'s helm and Gavs guarded her passages. A Patrol ship was dragging *Sparrowhawk* to a place I didn't want to go, where a Gavoran magistrate would decide whether we were criminals.

I felt like *Sparrow* was no longer my ship at all.

CHAPTER 11

Arrested

BETANDA SPED US THROUGH the three jumps toward the sector 102 checkpoint. At each gateway, Gurin exercised the Patrol's priority rights, inserting our joined ships at the head of the jump queues, earning grumbled curses for the Corridor Patrol and *Sparrowhawk*.

And with every ship we passed, word would spread at jump speed: *Sparrowhawk* was in custody, caught with fugitives in her cabins and stolen treasure in her vault. Ignominiously towed, in full view of every ship waiting by every gate.

It was a disaster.

The best case for me and Kojo would be to convince the magistrate we were innocent dupes, unknowingly carrying criminals and their loot. That might keep us out of a penal sentence, but throughout the outer sectors *Sparrow* would be a laughingstock or damned as jinxed. It would take years to repair our reputation. And if our suppliers didn't extend credit, or customers didn't trust us? We might be forced to sell *Sparrowhawk*, break up our crew. Break up our family.

The worst case? Ship confiscated, years in a penal colony. Ordalo gunning for us when we failed to deliver the synthreactor. The Cartel seeking revenge for holding out on them.

And in my case, perhaps even extradition to face Gavoran clan justice—whatever rock-bottom work they could find for a troublesome slave, like the dangerous factory that had killed my mother.

Kojo had tried to reassure me that Gavs had no right to ignore my Terran status, as long as I stayed out of Gav sectors. But what if they found the synthreactor? That was made from Sage tech, nominally under Gav control. That might be enough of a reason to take me back to Gavoran territory for trial. And why would any of the Terran authorities care enough about a half-blood smuggler to stand up for me? The thought made me sick with fear.

By the second morning, we'd arrived at the checkpoint, a sector base for the Corridor Patrol. A sprinkling of ships cruised nearby, each pausing within the checkpoint's field long enough to be recognized and cleared before proceeding on its way, a few being selected for a routine board-and-search.

I pulled up the messages the beacon had relayed to us. There were a lot of them, mostly from suppliers demanding immediate payment. Word was out and already the vultures were circling.

Sergeant Danto appeared at my door. "The case from the vault. You must bring it to the salon." He dogged my steps the whole way.

In the salon, Jamila sat on the couch beside Kojo, watching the ships come and go. If she was nervous, she did a good job of hiding it.

Balan, now wearing a blue tunic and pants borrowed from some checkpoint worker, paced between the couch and the galley. His eyes brightened when I placed the case on the table.

Gurin strode in and announced, "Mzee Lyden of the College of Religion."

Balan rushed to the door to greet the newcomer. Jamila raised her eyes to the ceiling as if casting blame on the heavens.

A slight Gavoran woman, old enough to be my great-grandmother, entered. Her pelt was gray and scant, but her dark eyes were sharp and she carried herself with an imperiousness that dominated. She wore a long robe of deep red bearing the badge of River Clan—a clan with ties to the more mystical religious houses.

"Hello, Lyden," Jamila murmured. "And Mya. How nice."

I hadn't even noticed the young Gav woman behind Lyden. She was younger than me, barely out of school, wearing the same type of robe and badge as Lyden. She peered about curiously, like a student on a field trip.

Lyden ignored Kojo's bow but stared at me for a moment, her lips compressed into a thin, disapproving line. Mya anxiously drew her to a chair.

The priestess turned to Jamila. "The relic. Show it to me." Her face might be lined with wrinkles and her pelt may have grayed with the years, but her voice was still strong.

Jamila leaned forward earnestly. "Lyden, we need to be careful. You know what happened to Deprata. Now Balan is out of his mind over it."

Balan harrumphed. "I am perfectly well."

Jamila ignored him. "Surely the most important thing is to get the artifact to a safe place where it can be studied? We can build a safe environment for it, just as the Cazar built the crypt to contain its power. Then our peoples can decide, together, what to do with it."

That sounded reasonable to me. I hoped Lyden would agree.

Gurin glowered. "Mzee Lyden, is this truly a dispute over the ownership of an archeological artifact? The Patrol was led to believe a precious relic was stolen…"

"Don't be a fool," Lyden hissed. "The thing is vital to Gavoran interests. Show it to me." Mya solicitously laid a hand on Lyden's arm.

"You mustn't touch it," Jamila warned. "It seems to cause the greatest harm through direct contact."

She opened the case.

Lyden made a quick intake of breath. Gazing at the relic, she bent toward it.

"It's exquisite," Mya said, peering over her shoulder.

I rose on my toes, eager to see the tablet again. A solid chunk of stone, yet its smooth, undulating surface seemed to ripple as I watched. It seemed darker than I remembered, the swirls of color on its changeable surface less active.

Home.

Balan stared, his lips moving soundlessly. A Patrol guard behind me gasped.

Lyden tentatively reached out a hand.

"No!" Balan hissed. Lyden drew back with a start.

Jamila closed the case and locked it. "I lined the case with metal from the crypt, which seems to have a shielding effect. Although"—she glanced at Balan—"even that doesn't seem to help when someone has been directly in contact with it. Taking the artifact to Gavora would be a dreadful mistake."

Lyden narrowed her eyes. "I have in mind another course of action."

I sighed. Time for the damned thing to go, if not to its home, at least somewhere else. And certainly it was high time for the crooks and cops to get off our ship.

Gurin turned to Lyden. "If that is the item you claim was stolen, I will place it in your custody until the magistrate's determination."

Jamila stiffened.

Lyden said, "No."

Everyone stared at Lyden.

"No?" Gurin ran a long-fingered hand over his graying pelt. "Mzee Lyden, what *do* you want?"

The priestess drew herself up. "Captain Gurin, the College of Religion is extremely grateful that you have located the precious relic and apprehended the persons who took it. However, the matter is complex. I would like to discuss a possible resolution with Professor Patil. For now, the safest course is to secure the relic on the Terran ship."

Gurin glared at Lyden and Jamila. "Very well. For now."

Accompanied by Sergeant Danto, I took the case back to the cargo hold. I was getting used to his looks, but being that close to a Patrol sergeant still made me nervous.

"What is your clan?" he asked, as I replaced the case.

I turned to him in surprise. "I was raised among Terrans, Sergeant Danto. Terrans have families, not clans."

"You are a hybrid," he snapped. "Your implant says you are Terran, but it is clear you are a half-blood. You should be among your mother's clan. What clan?"

"My mother was Sand Clan," I lied. It was a lower caste clan, barely higher than slaves, but free. "But I'm legally registered as Terran."

I held my breath, just in case Jamila had already told him I was a runaway.

"I see," he said, with distaste. "Even so, it is shameful, to live like this, among alien peoples."

I breathed again.

Danto looked with scorn around the dim hold. "Why would you choose to consort with Terrans over your own people?"

Bastard. "You obviously know little about other races. My family taught me to appreciate the good qualities in all the people we deal with. Even Gavorans."

I slammed the vault door. To avoid following him back to the upper decks, I turned aft toward the engine room. At least there was one person on the ship who had to treat me with respect.

Archer had disassembled one of the cylinders and was reaming it with a laser abrader. He'd covered the panels with tarps to contain the dust. Most of it seemed to have found its way into his hair.

"Hey, Patch. Hand me the Prestoshine, will you?"

I stepped over pieces of engine and gave him the spray bottle and a rag. He wriggled his way farther into the cylinder bore, spritzing as he went. His voice echoed from inside the bore, "Any worron wenthay lebbus go?"

"Let us go? No, no word yet. Jamila is negotiating with the Gav priestess."

Archer scooched out, wiping the dirt from his face onto his sleeve. As I helped him put the cylinder back together, I described Lyden's meeting with Jamila, and Gurin's frustration.

"We can't get rid of them fast enough," he grumbled. "What did you think of that half-blood sergeant? He looked at me like I was something that crawled out of the bilge. He said my appearance was a disgrace."

"That was rude." Archer's appearance *was* a disgrace, but *Sparrow*'s crew was a matter for me and Kojo to deal with, not some pushy Patrol officer.

"I told *him* to try to stay clean lubing the couplings. I may get a little grimy, but my engines are spotless." He put his tools away in their case, each one into the precise slot made for it.

"You're right." I handed him a tiny spline wrench. "He's from a very upper-class clan. I guess it goes to his head."

"And he's one to talk," Archer went on. "He looks like the cat's breakfast. Cutting his hair short, the bastard, as if no one would notice he's not really a Gav, with that big nose and elephant ears."

I felt like I'd been slapped. I sat in silence, the wrench in my hand forgotten. "Some of us can't help looking funny, Archer," I said quietly. "Or being bastards."

His eyes widened. "Oh, no! I don't mean *you*. You look all right. I didn't mean…" He rocked from foot to foot.

"I'm sorry you feel that way." I stood.

"No, Patch. Wait! You know I like you!"

"Do I?"

I walked away, blinking back tears.

I went to my cabin and looked in the mirror. *Like the cat's breakfast.* Who was I to think anybody else looked strange? My features were just as misshapen.

I'd thought that Archer and I had developed an easy friendship, after he'd gotten over his shyness. I thought of him as a brother. An odd and socially inept brother. I'd been pleased as he became more friendly and confident. Confident enough to say what he really thought.

I changed to a clean jacket, washed the stray lube from my face, and ran a wide-toothed comb through my hair. I considered tying it back, or even cutting it short as I had as a child. *No. Why should I try to look like somebody I wasn't?*

To hell with Archer, and Danto, too. I crammed a beret on my head to contain the mass of curls and went looking for better company.

In the wheelhouse, Kojo and Hiram stared resentfully at *Betanda* resting to starboard, the gateway's gantry above her. As I watched, a massive Selkid cargo ship approached and paused, doing obeisance to the checkpoint. Before lumbering into the ether, she flashed her Cartel transponder to us—

whether in sympathy or mockery, I couldn't tell. If the Cartel hadn't heard already that *Sparrow* was in custody, it would know soon.

"What I want to know," Kojo said, "is why they don't just take the burzing dingus and our burzing passengers, and sort it all out among themselves? Then we could go on our way." He exchanged a glance with Hiram. "We have that client waiting for his delivery, we can't be tied up too long. Patch, can you tell us anything about the old lady?"

"Lyden? As a priestess and a matriarch, she gets a lot of deference. I'll bet she's calling the shots, even with the Corridor Patrol."

I stooped to stroke the cat. Tinker arched against my hand, but gave my thumb a soft bite to warn me against taking her for granted.

Hiram harrumphed. "I'm a little more concerned with getting this stone whatchamacallit off our ship before it makes one of us crazy. Does it give off some kind of radiation or poison or something?"

"He spoke to me," I said.

Kojo pivoted. "Who did? The tablet?"

I looked down, embarrassed. I hadn't intended to say it out loud. "Sergeant Danto. He said it was shameful to consort with aliens."

Kojo snorted. "The hell he did! He's trouble, Patch. Stay away from him."

"Don't worry," I said. "I have no interest in him at all."

For some reason, Hiram seemed to find that funny.

We waited for nearly a full day, with no word from the Patrol. I tried to concentrate on the accounts, on trade updates, on *anything* but eventually gave up and brooded in my cabin.

Finally, Sergeant Danto summoned Kojo and me to the salon.

Lyden sat at the central seat on the table's port side, flanked by Balan and her shadow Mya. Jamila sat opposite her.

Smiling, Jamila pulled Kojo into the chair next to hers. She laid a hand on his arm and turned her charm on him, full blast. "Kojo, I have wonderful news! Lyden and I have found a way forward, and we are *so* hoping you and Patch can help us."

"Oh?" Even Kojo would be wary with an opening like that.

I took a seat at the foot of the table, close to the door in case of trouble. To my annoyance, Danto didn't leave, but posted himself out of the way, staring out at *Betanda* with a dissatisfied air. No doubt he wished he were aboard her instead of tending a bunch of troublesome Terrans.

"You and Patch have been *so* helpful and accommodating in bringing us this far," Jamila gushed, "and we, that is, Lyden and I, would like to continue to charter your ship. It could be very lucrative for you."

I asked, "Where do you want to go?" There was no way I would let *Sparrow* go into Gav sectors.

Lyden answered. "We want to follow Balan's vision. We want you to take us to Nakana."

CHAPTER 12

Time to negotiate

"You want to charter *Sparrowhawk* for a voyage to Nakana?" Kojo ran a hand through his hair, leaving his curls standing on end. "You must be joking. You only have Balan's visions to think that it even exists."

"It exists," Balan said, "and I will lead us there."

"That is the purpose of the relic," Mya said, her eyes shining. Suddenly shy, she glanced quickly at Lyden before adding, "It must be. It shows the chosen one the way to Nakana."

Looking at Mya more closely, I realized she was not as young as I'd first guessed—her extreme deference to Lyden had misled me. She was a pretty thing, with large gray eyes and a softly rounded forehead fringed with a chestnut pelt sloping back from a delicate brow ridge.

I asked, "Where, exactly, would you want us to take you?"

Balan smiled smugly. "There is a planet in the outer sectors known as Kriti. The expedition will leave from there and proceed as I direct—Nakana is within sublight distance from there."

Kojo and I exchanged a glance. *Kriti*—the place we were supposed to meet Ordalo to turn over the microbial synthreactor. But I didn't think arriving with a ship full of Gavorans on pilgrimage was what Ordalo had in mind.

Kojo rubbed his jaw. "I know Kriti. Out at the edge of the Gloom, isn't it?" He pulled up the charts and located the planet in sector 377.

The charts showed Kriti as an oasis of settlement in an otherwise depressingly empty star system. The system's tenuous link to civilized sectors was a distant jump gate that connected to only a single star corridor. And on the far side of Kriti, the chart flashed a veritable wall of warnings, fencing off a vast void labeled only *Gloom*.

I stared at the chart, looking for habitable worlds. "You think Kriti is Nakana? Or maybe one of these moons?"

Jamila bit her lip. "Not exactly. Kriti got its name because the ruins there reminded Terrans of the Minoan structures on Crete. The Kriti ruins were a small outpost, roughly contemporaneous with the Cazar site we were studying. We believe that five thousand years ago, that outpost helped to guard a major cultural center in a nearby system."

Kojo sucked in a breath and leaned back. "What system? You mean inside the Gloom?"

"Correct," Lyden said. "Our scholars have long puzzled over the placement of the jump gate in that sector. The Kriti system by itself is not sufficiently important, in terms of resources, to justify a gateway, nor is the gateway as close to the only significant habitable world as one would expect. There must be some other system within sublight range of the gateway—one now hidden by the advancement of the dense ether we call the Gloom. Our expedition will search for that system."

Kojo shook his head. "You have no idea what you're saying. I've *been* to Kriti. I've *seen* the Gloom. As far as I'm concerned, life stops at Kriti."

Danto stirred. "I also have been to Kriti. It was my first posting. The sector is populated by brigands and scoundrels who spread tales about the impenetrability of the Gloom to discourage legitimate settlers. There are known pathways into the Gloom, used by outlaws to escape pursuit. With a properly equipped ship, it would be possible to investigate a specified area."

It figured that the Corridor Patrol would send a cross-blood recruit to its most remote outpost. Danto was right, of course. In their privateering days, Papa and Hiram had haunted the fringe of the Gloom whenever they needed to disappear for a while.

I swept a hand to indicate the salon's threadbare couches and worn carpet. "Properly equipped, maybe. But to investigate the Gloom you need special scanners, gravimetric monitors. Not an old space hauler." As much as I wanted to get out of our current situation, I didn't want to get mixed up with Gav Sage worshippers, headed to space beyond anybody's charts.

"They will be provided," Danto said. "Your ship is a converted military cutter. With sufficient supplies, it is well able to make a journey of several weeks' duration. You need only do what you *say* you are in the business of doing—transporting cargo and passengers."

"I have no doubt," Lyden said, "the Sages foresaw that the Gloom would overtake Nakana and left the relic to guide us. I feel certain we will discover more artifacts, perhaps even texts and prophecies. Nakana will be the key to a spiritual reawakening. For our people, it may be the beginning of a new golden era."

"Not to mention," Jamila added, "the very real possibility of discovering Sage technology. We've already been in touch with the Settlement Authority. They have authorized Evergreen University and the College of Religion to survey from orbit any planet that might have advanced technology. The Settlement Authority will lend us the equipment, as well as a scientist who will conduct the survey and, um, ensure the Authority's regulations are respected. Once we gather basic information from orbit, we'll report to the Settlement Authority to determine what further research should be done." Her dry tone made it all sound almost reasonable.

I caught Mya staring at me. I stared back until she looked away. "All this is speculation," I said. "We could spend a lifetime sailing around the Gloom and find nothing."

"The charter will be for sixty days maximum," Jamila replied. "The only question for you to consider is, how much would you charge us for such an expedition?"

Sixty days. Kojo's eyes brightened. I knew what he was thinking: The voyage would be convenient cover for our rendezvous with Ordalo. Convenient, except for one thing—our delivery was due in *fifty-three* days, and how in Zub's name could we manage it with a load full of unpredictable, religion-obsessed Gavorans?

Kojo opened his mouth, but I spoke first.

"It's too dangerous." I smiled to show my regret. "It's fun to think about going into the Gloom and finding a lost planet, but really, it's not feasible. We could be lost and never get back. Or be attacked by those brigands the sergeant mentioned. No amount of money would be worth that."

Kojo shot me a glare and touched his ear to signal he wanted to take the job.

Jamila smiled engagingly at Kojo. "A sixty-day charter, although it may take far less time than that. We are prepared to be generous with the charter price."

I tapped the table to keep eyes on me, not Kojo. "Why us? The Corridor Patrol could do this itself. Or the Settlement Authority could organize a real survey mission. Why use *Sparrowhawk*?"

Lyden wound together her long fingers. "The Settlement Authority regards the evidence as too speculative to commit to a full mission."

Kojo muttered, "No surprise there."

Jamila glanced at Danto. "We can't use a Corridor Patrol ship or any other ship with a Gavoran crew. The relic does seem to have a *disturbing* influence on Gavorans."

Danto nodded. "Even in the few days our ships have been linked, some of the guards have reported strange longings and even auditory hallucinations. Captain Gurin has limited the guards' shifts aboard your ship. However, I seem to be immune."

Thank your Terran blood, I thought.

Lyden smiled like a friendly shark. "Like you, Patch, Sergeant Danto is a hybrid; nevertheless, he is a highly valued member of Captain Gurin's crew. The Sages seem to have ordained your presence, and his, on this mission. No doubt your intermediate status will be useful."

Intermediate status. I responded with an unladylike grunt.

Mya surreptitiously glanced at Danto. Danto's jutting nose and chin and ears were flags signaling his Terran blood. Even the scant hair on his wrists and the back of his hands, so different from a proper Gavoran's sleek fur, smacked of a Terran father.

Danto returned her scrutiny with a glower and pulled his sleeves down.

I shook my head. "We're traders. Going beyond the settlements would take us out of circulation too long, with no trade opportunities. Our steady customers would find other haulers." *If* we had any steady customers left.

Kojo scratched his ear again.

I touched the back of my hand. I wasn't just negotiating—taking the job would be too damned risky.

Kojo rubbed his jaw, as if assessing the pros and cons. "The area around Kriti has a reputation for hiding pirates' lairs. Our guns could never stand up to a serious assault."

"You would be allowed to carry midrange artillery for the duration of the mission." Danto began to pace, hands clasped behind his back. "Indeed, in view of the threat from pirates and the need for secrecy, the Corridor Patrol has detailed me to lead the mission." He looked less than pleased at the honor.

I touched the back of my hand again. Now I was *really* against it. Traveling with a Settlement Authority busybody *and* a Corridor Patrol officer? And trying to deliver the synthreactor to Ordalo under Danto's prominent nose?

Danto stopped pacing and bored his gaze into Kojo's eyes. "It will be a condition that you, and everyone on your ship, maintain absolute silence about the mission and the location of Nakana. You and your crew must remain aboard ship and maintain communications silence until the mission is complete."

That made me squawk. "You mean we'd be prisoners!"

Jamila smiled. "Collaborators in a highly confidential endeavor."

I shook my head. "Maybe you can find another Terran ship."

"Unacceptable," Lyden said. "We cannot risk information spreading further."

Jamila purred, "If it's just a matter of money, I'm sure we can come to some reasonable resolution."

"Sure," Kojo said, before I could stop him. "A hundred thousand credits, in advance."

Lyden gasped, but Jamila's eyes lit up.

Danto glared. "Nonsense. We could buy the ship for that."

"But not a crew willing to go into the Gloom." Kojo looked smug.

I held up a hand. "We're not going, and that's final. Kojo is captain, but I'm the business manager. We won't take the job."

Danto's green eyes became hard. "In that case, the Patrol will inform the magistrate that your ship was apprehended carrying fugitives and extremely valuable stolen property. Your ship could be confiscated. Your licenses could be canceled."

"I saw that coming," Kojo muttered.

"We had no knowledge of that," I said. "Any magistrate would rule in our favor." I hoped.

"Doubtful," Danto said. "In any case, it would take weeks to adjudicate the case, during which time you and your crew would be held in seclusion to ensure the security of the mission. *Without* compensation."

Ancestors. Weeks in seclusion? Even if we managed to keep our ship and licenses, every moment we spent in custody would delay our delivery to Ordalo—and increase the chance the Patrol would find the synthreactor.

Damn. No help for it. "All right," I said. "I'm willing to consider it. Subject to agreement on terms."

Jamila smiled and folded her hands in front of her. "Good. Now, let's discuss price. Thirty thousand credits seems fair to me."

We settled on sixty-five thousand credits, a third up front, a third when we got to Kriti, and the last third after finishing the job.

The price was on the low side for so much time, but we were getting a lot of extra benefits. Since we faced unknown conditions, perhaps even an emergency landing without the benefits of a port's lifters, the Patrol would install some refurbished stabilizer rockets and high-efficiency units for the engines *and* would help with Archer's propulsion overhaul. I asked for a new grav generator, too, but Danto overruled it. All the provisions for the mission would come from the Patrol garrison's supplies.

On the whole, we'd end up with a better ship and enough funds to pay down some of our debts—if we survived to enjoy it.

I stared at *Betanda* while counting berths. "Jamila, Mzee Lyden, and Mya?" Mya nodded. "Sergeant Danto, Balan, and the scientist. In addition to the crew."

"And Grimbold," Danto added.

"Bad idea," Kojo said. "He's trouble."

"Another trained combatant may prove useful, and I would rather have him where I am sure he will have no opportunity to contact his friends at Rampart Militech." Danto curled a lip. "I will ensure that he causes no trouble."

I sighed. "We can do it, once we sell the cargo we're carrying and reconfigure a couple of holds into cabins. Passengers will have to share. Mzee Lyden, I'm afraid the accommodations are not very suitable for a scholar of your eminence." And age—she looked far too frail to be heading off on an exploration.

"I am quite happy to share quarters with Mya. A little discomfort is of no consequence."

Mya nodded and mumbled, "Yes, of course."

"What about our cargo? Right now, our holds are full. I need a chance to sell it."

"You will be compensated for your cargo," Danto replied. "You, your crew, and your passengers are now sequestered. There will be no outside communication except as authorized by me."

I hated losing the chance to sell the brandy almost as much as I hated the idea of carrying a bunch of Gavs around for sixty days.

I recorded all the special terms into a charter contract on my datacon. Charter party: *Corridor Patrol.* Duration: *Sixty standard days.* Destination: *To be agreed.*

"Just to be clear, Sergeant," Kojo said. "You may lead the mission, but as captain of a chartered vessel, I will retain full authority over the ship and crew. That includes the right to withdraw from the voyage if I deem it too risky to continue. Full captain's prerogatives."

Danto nodded. "Normal charter terms will be respected."

Good. Kojo could manufacture a reason to terminate the voyage when the time came to deliver the synthreactor.

I put my imprint on the contract and Danto added his. It was done.

"I'll tell the crew," Kojo said. "Jamila, I'll leave it to you and the sergeant to explain matters to Grimbold."

The cat squirmed out of Hiram's arms. "Damnit, Kojo. I haven't seen the inside of a bar or a brothel since we left Santerro. And you're talking about staying aboard and sober for two more months?"

Kojo smiled. "Sorry, Hiram. At least you can have some drinking time while we're parked at the checkpoint. I can't do much about the other. We don't have a choice here—either we take the charter or cool our heels in a Corridor Patrol isolation facility."

Hiram shuddered. "I'd rather sail, I guess. The Patrol ain't got no sense of humor."

"I don't remember much about Kriti," Kojo said. "Just how depressing it was, sailing through the Gloom."

Hiram pulled up the chart for sector 377 and stabbed a finger at the sector's sole jump gate. "The corridor from Saipan dead-ends at the Kriti system, right at the edge of the Gloom. From the gate, its ten days' hard sailing to Kriti. The planet's got a fair-sized port, serves the Terran settlements sprinkled around. A pity we're not hauling cargo: A load of used ag equipment or plague-resistant chickens would do well there."

"Instead, we'll have a hold full of power modules and survey equipment, all to chase a myth on the word of a fanatic."

I peered at the chart. Depressing was right—the listed settlements were tiny and sparse, the whole system riddled with warnings about radiation, dangerous currents, and ether too dense to navigate.

Hiram raised a bushy eyebrow. "I wouldn't mind spending a little time in Kriti. Lots of opportunities there." He cocked his head in an unspoken question.

Kojo rubbed his chin. "Maybe we can persuade Danto that we need a few days' shore leave there before we head into the Gloom."

I nodded. A sudden illness, a broken part—somehow we'd find a way to contact Ordalo to arrange delivery.

Hiram exchanged a look with Kojo. "Don't you worry, lad and missy. I'll stick with you through this job. But after that—it's time for me to stop all this flitting about and get something steadier. No surprises. I'm not getting any younger, you know."

I blinked back tears. "Oh, Hiram, you know how much we'll miss you. But I can't blame you—you've been wonderful, staying on *Sparrow* so long."

Kojo slapped Hiram's shoulder. "Thanks, old man. Just see us through this job, help us settle what we've promised. We can't ask for more than that."

Archer jittered, flapping his arms and grinning. "Explore a new planet! Fantabulous! And, Patch," he said shyly, "I'm sorry I said something stupid yesterday. I don't know how to say things sometimes. You know, I'd do anything to help you."

I laughed in surprise. "Thanks, but I can take care of myself."

"Yeah, sure."

I hugged him to show we were still friends, but I wondered if I would ever again feel quite as comfortable with Archer.

Gurin informed me the next day that the survey equipment was on its way and the midrange guns would be installed within two days. I handed him my supply list: fresh food, ration packs, medical supplies, recharged power modules, jump cells, cleaning and sanitation supplies, air and water filters, spare parts, cat food, and at Grim's request, fresh entertainment programs. I even put in new clothes for the crew. When Kojo had looked over the list, he had added cargo drones and grenades. "May as well get what we can out of this," he said.

"So, six passengers, plus Sergeant Danto and the crew, to house and feed, and keep from fighting among themselves, going mad from boredom or killing themselves over the relic."

"That's about the size of it."

I bit my lip, thinking of the complications. "It breaks my heart, but we need to move the brandy out and start converting the holds to sleeping quarters."

"Keep the premium crates, the ones in the vault," Kojo said. "And slip a crate into the wardroom." He winked. "For emergencies."

I made an invoice for the brandy, showing Danto the current price on Palermo. He paid it without complaint—what would a Gav military man know about the difference between wholesale and retail prices?

I split the down payment among the people we owed money to most urgently: the crew, our suppliers, our creditors. Archer danced from foot to foot and grinned from ear to ear, thrilled to get his back wages and a bonus. Our suppliers in Palermo would probably throw a party.

I was so happy to pay off some of what we owed, I pulled Kojo into the wardroom to show him the accounts.

"I know you don't like looking at the books, but see, I was able to give something to all the suppliers who've been dunning us and pay down nearly a quarter of the debt to that bloodsucker Branson. With this job, we've turned a corner. Once we collect the rest of the installments for this voyage and make the delivery to Ordalo, we might get free of that loan shark."

"Good."

What was the matter with Kojo? He should have been delighted, full of *I-told-you-so*. Instead, he absently stroked Tinker curled on the foot of the bunk, earning a cat-glare of annoyance.

"Kojo? In two months, we could be out of debt completely."

He didn't meet my eyes. "That's great. It's just that, well, there's something you should know."

My stomach sank. "About what?"

"About the delivery to Ordalo." He took a deep breath. "We're not going to get paid for it."

CHAPTER 13

Family reckoning

I STARED AT KOJO like he'd gone mad. "Not get paid? What are you talking about?"

Tinker, wide-eyed and ears alert at the tension in the wardroom, oozed off the bedding to slink under the bunk.

"Look," Kojo whispered, "it wasn't my idea to take Ordalo's job. It's not the kind of thing I ever wanted us to get involved in. They had me over a barrel."

For a moment, I thought I'd misheard. "Had *you* over a barrel? But Papa...You mean it was *you* who made that deal?"

He sighed wearily. "Grow up, Patch."

As if *I* was the one to blame for believing him. *Ancestors, give me strength.*

I leaned into his face. "You were gambling."

"I swear, it was a sure thing. It would have paid off—it *should* have paid off, big time! I don't know..."

I slapped my hand on the table. "I don't want to hear about it. Who?"

"A Delfin nobody, but he was just a shill. He turned my marker over to the Cartel. Delivering the goods to Kriti is the price the Cartel wants. Once we deliver to Ordalo, the Cartel will discharge the debt. But there won't be any payment."

I closed my eyes, crushed. All the risk of carrying the synthreactor, for nothing. "And if something goes wrong with the delivery?"

"It won't."

I got that sinking feeling in my stomach. "Kojo? Answer me."

His shoulders slumped. "They've got a mortgage on *Sparrowhawk*."

"You forged my imprint?" He must have. Just like he'd forged it on the charter on Santerro. *"Damn you!"*

My teeth ground. He'd let the Cartel force us to transport something their own ships didn't dare carry, under threat of taking away our home, our livelihood.

"...And I'll be indentured to Ordalo for three years." He stared miserably at the deck.

Indentured? Slavery by another name, even if it was only for a set time.

I sat down on Hiram's bunk, hard. I felt like we'd dropped into a black hole, nowhere to go but down. "How could you?"

It came out a whisper.

Kojo scrubbed a hand over his mouth. "I was suckered. You know how they work."

"So do you!"

He dropped his head into his hands. "I made a mistake. I'm sorry. It was after Dad died, and we had to buy those coils and take that loan from Branson. I thought...Patch, I really believed I could win enough to get us free. Everything would have been so simple then." He furrowed his brow, as if he was still unable to understand how things had gone wrong.

"Damn you, Kojo! *Damn you!*" I backhanded my fist into Kojo's chest hard enough to make him fall back against the locker.

I felt like my head would burst. My brother indentured? Lose *Sparrow*? Spend the rest of my life planet-bound, watching all the other ships sail away?

He rubbed his chest. "Don't blame me! This is Dad's fault."

"Papa?" I was shouting now. "How can you blame *him*?"

Resentment filled his eyes. "*I'm* the one who's wasted my life on this old bucket, rattling from one godforsaken port to another. Ever since I was *nine years old. Twenty years!* When you came aboard, just a scared little kid, I was already running *Sparrow*'s engines. I expected Dad to leave the ship to *me*. He was *married* to my mother. He *should* have left the ship to me. You—you're just an accident from a loose week on Gavora."

I felt the blood drain from my face.

My brother. Who had teased me, taught me, protected me from portside bullies, ragged me about my curls, bragged to others about my trading skills.

"Oh, hell, Patch," Kojo said more quietly. "I didn't mean that last part. It's just—look, I've always taken care of you, haven't I? When Dad died, I just assumed that he'd left the ship to me. I mean, you're still so young..."

He sighed and rubbed his hand over his face. "When I made that bet, I was trying to help, to get us out of debt. I figured, if worse came to worse, I could cover the bet by selling *Sparrow*. I could have squared everything and we'd be free to take off on our own. Stop being tied down by this old hulk."

"Old hulk." He might have been speaking some unknown language. *Sparrow* was home and family, and Papa's pride.

"But then," Kojo said, "he only left me half the business, and you wouldn't sell, and the interest on the money I owed added up."

His fury gone, he gave me that open-and-honest look, the look I had long ago learned to distrust. *Let me borrow a few sovereigns, Patch. Just this once, Patch. I'll pay you back tomorrow, Patch.* So earnest, so plausible, so charming.

"But it'll be all right. Once we make the delivery to Ordalo, they'll consider the debt paid and everything will be fine. And this charter—it's a chance for us to make enough money to get back on course."

His eyes had that hopeful expression, the one that said *this* roll of the dice is sure to be a winner.

"Papa loved me," I said.

He looked away. "I know he did. I didn't mean what I said."

"He came back for me, when I was old enough."

"Yeah, I get it. He loved you. We're a family. I just thought he would trust me to take care of you."

"He wasn't that big a fool!"

I took Kojo by the shoulders and made him face me. "You can't keep gambling like this, Kojo. Promise me. Promise you'll stop."

"I swear, Patch! Honest, I promise. Never again."

But his eyes slid away. I knew he wouldn't keep that promise.

Kojo. Good captain, lousy business partner.

I balled up a fist and pounded it against the bulkhead.

"How could you?" I whispered. "Risk the ship? And your freedom?"

All his talk about wanting to join the Cartel—just a smoke screen for when he'd be forced to work for some smuggler out on the fringe, for nothing more than a bunk and two meals a day.

Kojo didn't answer, didn't look at me.

That wasn't like him. No argument? No endless train of excuses?

I eyed him, my mind filled with suspicion. "There's something else, isn't there? Spit it out."

Then I knew, and I was overwhelmed with shame and despair.

I grabbed his jacket, forcing him to look at me. "Me, too. Is that it, Kojo? Did you indenture me to them, too?"

He avoided my eyes. "That part's probably not legally binding."

I slammed my fist against the locker. "It will be in Selkid space! Selkids indenture their sisters and daughters all the time!"

I saw myself working for some fat Selkid, run off my feet to do the lowest kind of work, mouth shut, eyes down.

A slave. Again.

I felt sick.

Kojo's eyes widened as he caught the panic in my face.

"It'll be all right, Patch. I promise. It's simple. We have fifty-two days left to make the delivery. Once that's done, everything will be fine."

"*Liar.*" I shoved him back into the bunk. "Cheating, thieving, burzing *liar.*"

I balled up my fist and punched it into the bulkhead hard enough to make the lockers rattle.

It hurt. I did it again.

Hiram opened the door, just enough to sidle in. "That guard wants to know why you're shifting bulkheads."

Tinker saw her chance and streaked out from under the bunk, through the door in an orange-and-white flash.

"Practicing featherball," Kojo said. He jerked his head sideways in a *scram* motion. Hiram looked from him to me.

Through gritted teeth, I said, "It's fine."

Hiram nodded once and ducked out again.

"Does Hiram know?" I asked.

Kojo looked away. *Of course* Hiram knew. Kojo would have needed his help to stow the synthreactor. Hiram would never have believed that Papa had agreed to carry it and not told him.

All that crap about getting old and taking a Cartel berth—I should have known there was more to it.

"Patch—"

"Shut up."

I leaned on the bulkhead, facing the blank wall, not wanting to see Kojo, not wanting to hear him. *The damn fool.*

The stupid, reckless damn fool. *Of course*, Papa hadn't left the ship to him alone—Papa knew Kojo's weaknesses as well as anyone.

Through gritted teeth, I said, "This is what you're going to do. You're going to sit down, right now, and sign a confession about the forgeries, saying I didn't know anything about the synthreactor."

"Patch..."

"And you'll execute a deed of transfer. Your share of the ship and the business and all its assets—as of today they belong to me."

His mouth dropped open. "That's my inheritance! Besides, it won't help. The Cartel's already filed the mortgage."

"It'll help after we make the delivery and the debt is discharged. I need to be sure you can never get us into this situation again." I leaned into his face. "Do it, Kojo."

He put on his stubborn face. "Not a chance! Dad left half the ship to me."

"And you squandered it on a bet." I scarcely recognized my own voice, it came out so scathingly cold. "Do you know what I can do to you for forging my imprint? For executing an indenture contract over me? Any Terran court would jail you for ten years!"

"You wouldn't!"

"Why not? *You made me a slave.*"

"Patch, I didn't..." His face grayed as he saw the full determination in my face.

Quietly, he said, "It won't come to that. I wouldn't have signed the indentures if I wasn't sure. Hiram knows Kriti, he and Dad used to sail in that sector. I even went with them once, when I was a kid. We'll make the delivery and everything will be fine."

"We'll make the delivery," I agreed. "In *my* ship. You can be captain and share the profits, but as a hired hand. I'll own the ship and the business."

"That's not fair!"

I loomed over him, staring him in the eyes. "You've never been a slave. You don't know. I would do anything, *anything* to keep from being put in that position again. Including turning you in and letting you pay the price for what you've done. From now on, *you'll* have to trust *me*."

After Kojo imprinted the contracts, I went to my cabin to get myself under control.

Kojo. He'd pushed hard after Papa's passing, to sell *Sparrow*. And it was only after I'd refused that he'd showed me the synthreactor and told me of *Papa's* promise to Ordalo.

Kojo. Of course he was willing to take on a lucrative, risky job to head into the Gloom to hunt for a mythical planet—he had nothing left to lose.

Kojo. It wasn't just me he'd betrayed. Hiram and even Archer shared the risk of carrying the synthreactor, for no payoff. And if we failed and lost *Sparrow*, what would happen to them?

Kojo. He was my brother—half-brother anyway—raised by the same father. Even setting aside this mess, how could he see things so differently? To be so ready to sell our ship? Give up being ship's captain and settle for being just another pilot?

Kojo. "You're just an accident." As if a three-year marriage contract made any difference to a man's children. As if family didn't exist without it.

And thinking of family, I needed to have a little talk with Hiram.

I cornered Hiram in the galley. "You knew."

He sighed, leaning against the freezer, holding his cup of hot tea in both hands. "Ah, missy, I told him to go to you and fess up. Told him you'd find out, soon or late, and it would be better soon."

"*You* could have told me."

"The two of you need to work it out yourselves."

One of the Gavs from the checkpoint came into the galley looking for a ration pack. I handed him one and scowled until he left.

Hiram laid a gnarled hand on my arm. "Don't be too hard on Kojo, missy. They targeted him special, 'cause o' me."

Hiram dropped his voice. "The Cartel tried over the years to get your pa and me to work for 'em. They've been trying to expand into the sectors around Kriti, and they knew we'd sailed there and learned all the backways in and around the Gloom. Your pa always turned 'em down. Now, with your pa gone, they made a play on Kojo's weak spot, to get to me."

Zub's pitchfork. No wonder Hiram was ready to jump ship.

"Kojo come to me, full of woe, and I give him my advice, to take or not, as he sees fit. Now you come to me, and I do the same."

"So, what advice do you have for me?" I asked.

"Do what you must to protect your ship, your crew, and yourself."

"I already made him sign his half of the business over to me. But how can I deal with Kojo after this? How can I trust him?"

Hiram laid a gnarled hand on my shoulder. "Kojo ain't your pa. He's a crackerjack pilot who's been put in a position he never asked for and doesn't much want. Trust him to be what he is and stop expecting him to be something he's not."

What Kojo was *not* included trustworthy with money or skilled at business. But maybe he didn't have to be, if I stepped up more.

I rubbed my eyes tiredly. "That means me taking on more responsibility. All the trades, all the cargo, all the passengers."

Hiram nodded. "That'd be best. You ain't exactly blameless in this, you know."

My head jerked up. "Me? What did I do? He lied to me, again and again. About his debts, about Ordalo—even about Papa."

That was the worst of all. He'd made me doubt Papa's trust in me, Papa's love for me.

Hiram snorted. "And you believed him. You ask why I didn't tell you? I shouldn'ta had to. Can't you see through Kojo's tales by now? Didn't you know your pa wouldn't leave you in such a bind?"

I felt like I'd been dashed with cold water. Hiram was right. I should have been suspicious of the whole business with Ordalo, but I'd fallen for Kojo's story like a frontier rube hitting the chinko table for the first time. I knew how Kojo got through life on charm, bluff, and deception, but I'd never expected him to use those talents on *me*.

I should have trusted Papa better. I'd prayed for guidance and Papa had come to me warning of lies. I'd failed to understand. Instead, I'd resented Papa and blamed him for saddling us with the risky cargo and I'd trusted my lying brother.

Forgive me, Papa. Beloved ancestors, help me find wisdom. Wisdom so I never make that mistake again.

Danto wrinkled his nose in annoyance when I asked him to transmit the contracts to the registrar. "I'd do it myself," I said, "but since you're making all communications go through you..."

He read the documents suspiciously. "Transfer ownership of *Sparrowhawk*? You make your brother a mere employee? What is the purpose of this?"

"A private matter, Sergeant," I replied frostily. "Resolving an issue of inheritance after the death of our beloved father. Do you really want to know the details?"

"I have no interest in your personal matters." He looked again at the title transfer. "But this is wrong. You list yourself as Terran."

"Under Terran law I can elect either of my ancestral races. My implant says I'm Terran and so does the existing registration. You're not questioning the registrar, are you?"

He shook his head. "But surely this matter can wait until this mission is completed."

"No, Sergeant, it can't wait. You must know that the law requires the ship's ownership to be properly recorded."

He grumpily transmitted the documents.

For the next four days, *Sparrowhawk* remained linked to *Betanda*, at rest near the checkpoint.

Jamila stayed in her stateroom when she wasn't on *Betanda* conferring with Lyden. Grimbold played hours of solitaire games in the salon, complaining to anyone who would listen. Balan moved back to his small cabin on *Sparrow*. He had started some sort of project, dictating his experiences with the bloodstone. It would probably be a best seller among the religious set on Gavora.

I shifted provisions into storerooms, cleaned emptied holds, set up cabins, and tried not to snarl and snap at everyone who crossed my path.

Kojo stayed out of my way.

Workers came aboard to install the guns and to help Archer with the upgrades on the propulsion and stabilizers. They were a silent bunch—I guessed Danto had ordered them not to mingle—and each was limited to a two-hour shift. Hiram, released from duty at the helm, "helped" by sipping from a brandy bottle, telling bawdy tales, and generally getting in the way.

Meanwhile, *Betanda*'s crew members off-loaded the brandy, leaving only the fine bottles in the vault and a crate in the wardroom. That left the main cargo hold empty, ready for the installation of the survey equipment.

That made me nervous.

In a cache hidden behind one of the bulkheads lurked the synthreactor's core, its largest component. There was nowhere else to move it to, even if we could be assured of privacy long enough to pull it out. Instead, while Gav workers came and went, I sent up battens and fussed with Prestoclean to make sure the decking showed no traces where the bulkhead wall slid open. Over each screw head I dotted a bit of dirty lube, smeared with my thumbprint, to hide the shine where the screws had recently been replaced. That was the best I could do.

Sparrowhawk was a small vessel: I couldn't avoid Kojo forever. Somehow, he and I needed to work together. I knew from experience that Kojo would soon consider the harsh words between us to be a thing of the past. In his everlasting optimism, he would resume his usual friendly demeanor, sure everything would somehow work out.

Kojo wouldn't change. Maybe he couldn't change. Hiram was right: I needed to defend myself.

Terran law would prohibit him from indenturing me without my consent, but indenturing a sister was accepted practice on Selkid worlds. I needed a way to be sure that Kojo's stupidity wouldn't land me in servitude to a bloated Selkid merchant.

Forty-nine days left to deliver the synthreactor.

We'd be ready to leave soon, I couldn't put it off any longer.

Archer was the happiest person aboard *Sparrow*, a bouncing, toe-tapping mess. His hair looked like a rat's nest and his new jacket was already a wreck.

"I have to admit," he said, jiggling from head to toe amid the engine room's clutter, "the Gavs know what they're doing.

All the maintenance on the engines is done, and the upgrades, too. It would have taken me a lot longer without their help." He turned back to polishing the controls.

I took a deep breath.

"Archer? Will you marry me?"

CHAPTER 14

Spliced

"Marry you?" For a moment, Archer was utterly still. Then, with a rush of movement, he turned back to polishing the propulsion console. "Not funny, Patch."

I placed in front of him a five-thousand-sovereign rhollium ingot. "Consider this a dowry."

That got his attention. I could tell because he calmed to a small vibration.

I pushed a heavy wrench and a detached flange off the chair. "It's Vell, the Cartel agent. He's been, well, persistent."

I'd thought a lot about how to approach Archer. Revealing the truth was out: He didn't know about the synthreactor and I had no intention of telling him. Archer was too honest to be trusted with knowledge that we were smuggling something much more illegal than the occasional hydroverter or runaway slave, and too decent to work for a captain who had tried to sell me into slavery.

But a damsel in distress would appeal to his romantic side.

"Vell's the sort who thinks any unmarried female is available for the asking. I can't avoid him—he's the agent for the whole sector. But if I were married, he'd leave me alone."

And under Selkid law, I couldn't be indentured without my husband's consent.

"But Kojo..."

"Kojo's not always with me when I deal with the Cartel. I just need an extra layer of protection." I tried to look helpless—difficult when I was as tall as Archer and a good bit heavier. "Don't worry, it will be a marriage for show only. I don't expect you to do anything."

He frowned.

"Only a three-year contract," I said, "and look, we'll exchange divorce consents. Any time you want out, all you need to do is file the divorce."

"I don't know, Patch. I mean, you know I like you!" He looked down, his hand wiggling. "But I would only want to marry someone who, you know, really loves me." He looked back at me shyly.

I made myself look desperate. "Please, Archer. I know it's a lot to ask. But if you don't feel you can do it..." I glanced reluctantly toward the upper decks. "I suppose I can ask Hiram."

"*Hiram?* No, no. I mean, it seems kind of extreme, but if you really think you need to be"—he gulped—"married, then I guess I can."

He threw back his shoulders. "I mean, of course I'll help you out. But we're stuck here on the ship. How can we get to a marriage official?"

"Kojo can do it. It's an ancient captain's prerogative. As long as the ship is in transit, the captain can officiate a marriage and hold the contract to be filed when the ship reaches port. It's a very old rule, but still perfectly valid. In the meantime, I would be legally and verifiably married and no one needs to know unless I need to, um, assert myself."

He frowned. "Well, if you're sure that's what you want."

I kissed his cheek.

In the wardroom, Kojo looked at me in horror. "Zub's beard! That is the screwiest idea you've ever had! It's bad enough you extorted my inheritance away from me—"

"Extorted?"

"—but now you're conning Archer into a sham marriage. And for what? As soon as we deliver the goods, we'll be off the hook."

"And when that happens, I'll file the divorce. But until then, I'm going to use every trick I can think of to stay out of the jam *you* landed me in."

Kojo crossed his arms. "Is this what it's going to be like from now on? You blaming me every chance you get? Never trusting me? Is that the family life you're fighting so hard to preserve? Because frankly, I'd rather do three years on a Selkid man o' war."

"Do you think I'm going to stop hating what you did just because you're sorry? Do you think I'm going to stop being afraid?"

"You don't trust me, that's the problem."

"Of course I don't! Can you blame me?"

He eyed me warily. The locker still had a dent where I'd thumped it particularly hard.

"Look, sis, we have to finish this delivery. Until then, we have to work together. I screwed up, I was wrong, I'm sorry. Just...just stop throwing it in my face, will you? Once this is done, maybe we go our separate ways. But for now, let it lie."

A crackerjack pilot, put in a position he never asked for and didn't want.

I sighed. "I trust you—I trust you to be a great pilot and captain. I *don't* trust you with money or business—leave those decisions to me."

"Fine. I can't stand dealing with the accounting anyway."

"When we've made the delivery we can decide whether or not we stick together. But for now, perform the marriage—another layer of protection will make me feel better."

"It's not exactly fair to Archer," he said.

"Why? I don't expect him to actually bed me." I laughed at the thought.

"Maybe that's the problem," Kojo muttered, but I wasn't about to rise to his jokes.

That evening, after the passengers had retired to sleep, *Sparrowhawk*'s crew gathered in the wheelhouse. For once, Archer's face was clean and his hair brushed and tied back.

"Are you sure you want to do this?" Kojo asked Archer.

"Why not? I mean, yes, I'm sure." He wiggled and jittered.

Hiram slapped Archer on the back. "Attaboy." He pulled in a confused Patrol officer as the second witness.

Kojo mumbled the words, reading from his datacon, "Under authority as captain of this vessel, duly registered...consenting adults...period of three years...Pachita Babatunji and Virgil Archer...hereby declare you married."

I whispered, "*Virgil?* Your first name is *Virgil?*"

"Shut up, Pachita."

Archer and I imprinted the marriage contract and immediately exchanged divorce consents. Archer twitched and shuffled. I kissed him on the cheek. "Thanks, Archer. You're a good friend."

"Is that it?" he asked. "But, Patch, couldn't we..."

Kojo leered at him. "Were you expecting something else?"

I punched Kojo's arm. "Stop teasing, Kojo. That's all, Archer. Like I promised, no trouble at all."

"But..."

Hiram shoved a glass of brandy into his hand. "Here you go, lad," he said kindly. "You look like you could use a drink."

"Thanks, everyone," I said, turning down the shot that Kojo offered me. "See you all tomorrow."

As I headed to my cabin, a bleary and slightly drunk Hiram called, "Best wishes to the happy couple!"

With the crates of brandy gone, the holds began filling up with power modules and provisions. There were so many jump cells I had to convert another small hold to cold storage. I checked and double-checked the lashings and balance of the load—the military jump cells were far heavier than we were used to. We would be eating them up during the first half of the journey on the ten days of long jumps Danto had laid out. Later, we would need plenty of power mods to ride the currents into the Gloom. I tried to talk to Archer about it, but he was surly and out of sorts, answering only in monosyllables. Maybe he was still hung over.

In the main hold, silent Gavoran Patrol officers installed the survey equipment: crates of specialized observation drones, consoles for monitoring atmospheric elements and imagers that could see through clouds, vegetation, and even surface soil. Soon we'd depart for Kriti.

Home.

The tablet's plaintive cry emanated from the vault every time I came near. The Patrol officers said nothing, but they worked in pairs, eyeing one another nervously, and never tarried in the hold.

I, on the other hand, wanted very much to open the vault and see the tablet again. Its strange markings and swirling colors haunted my dreams. In some sense, I told myself, the relic was also a passenger and entitled to know what was going on.

When the installation team was gone, I told the guard I needed to inspect the lashings. The guard lingered at the hatch, shifting uncomfortably as I knelt near the vault door and fiddled with the turnbuckles.

I stopped thinking and relaxed as Mother had taught me, opening myself to communion with the ancestral spirits. I imagined the emptiness of dark space beyond the galaxies. The quiet between heartbeats.

Peace.

Beautiful swirls seemed to fill the hold.

Peace and joy.

It wasn't words, just feelings entering my mind.

Home. Bring me home. Peace and joy await.

Yes, I thought. *You've won. We're taking you home.*

An image formed in my mind of a lovely pastoral world, with beasts peacefully grazing on a grassy plain. A feeling of satisfaction swept over me.

Show me the way, I asked.

Blood.

I wanted to open the case and place my hand on the relic. I felt an almost sexual urge to touch it, to pierce my skin until the blood welled out. To rub my blood into the bloodstone's incised surface.

I reached for the pad to key in the vault combination.

"Ah!" The guard cried out and raised his weapon.

In an orange-and-white streak, Tinker dashed away from his ankles.

"It's just a cat." My hands shaking, I backed away from the vault.

The guard scowled. "If you are finished, you should leave the hold."

"I'm finished."

I left the hold all right, practically running up the aft steps for the solace of my cabin. When I slammed the door behind me, I hugged myself, still shaking. The urge to touch the relic had been so strong—what *was* the relic?

Worse, I still yearned to return to the vault and touch the beautiful, lovely stone.

Peace and joy.

Spirits were comfortable friends for me, but this driving desire was something alien. Could there really be a creature imprisoned in the relic? Could it really be communicating its desperate need for sustenance and its craving to return to its place in the universe? Eternally longing, eternally hungry?

How horrible, to be left alone in the dark for endless centuries. Unable to escape, unable even to die.

If I had ever revered the Sages, that would have cured me. Maybe it made more sense to Balan, as a religious scholar. But if the Sages had really left this creature to guide us to Nakana, they must have been very cruel indeed.

Kojo straightened his dress jacket, preparing to greet our passengers. "Are all the equipment and supplies secured?"

I tucked a stray lock of hair under my beret. "All secure, cabins freshened."

Kojo quirked a smile. "You look a little stressed. What's wrong—married life doesn't agree with you?"

"Shut up." I followed him toward the passenger hatch.

I'd considered telling Kojo about the relic, but I wasn't yet feeling friendly enough toward him. My mistake had been to treat the relic like the friendly spirits of my ancestors, inviting a communication. I wouldn't make that mistake again.

Since then, I'd been in and out of the cargo hold, lashing equipment to the battens, shifting stores into the smaller holds. The relic's voice still murmured in my mind, but I'd kept my mental defenses high, remaining firmly in control. Let the damn stone whine, it was safely locked away.

Once again, Kojo and I welcomed Sergeant Danto, Lyden, and Mya aboard *Sparrowhawk*. Lyden looked the ship over with a sharp eye, as if it were up for sale. By the look on her face, she was not buying at any price.

Behind them, the Settlement Authority scientist stepped aboard.

"How very nice to meet you," she chirped. "Call me Rachel."

I had expected the Authority to send a humorless Gav, ready to spout rules and regulations to quash any attempt to open a new world to settlement. Instead, Dr. Rachel Fiori was a plump, pink little Terran, her iron-dark curls sprinkled with silver.

I carted luggage and showed everyone their cabins. Lyden declared the stateroom adequate for her and Mya, saying she was inured to hardship. Jamila and Rachel would share the adjacent cabin. In a third cabin, Danto placed his kit on the lower bunk and wordlessly tossed Grim's pack to the top. I'd let Balan keep his little cabin—I doubted anyone would want to share space with him.

Balan emerged from his cabin to follow Lyden as she settled into the salon, his eyes bright and fingers twitching, exclaiming in florid Gavoran over their great mission.

I felt a little sick watching him. Whether it was the effect of the relic or his religious fervor, he looked more like a candidate for a medical intervention than a guide to spiritual bliss.

Danto came onto the com. "Prepare to get underway in a quarter of an hour. All Corridor Patrol personnel must leave *Sparrowhawk* at this time."

The Gav guards marched stone-faced toward *Betanda*. They looked as relieved to be leaving *Sparrow* as I was to have them gone.

I did a hurried check of all the holds, engine room, and cabins. I wanted no more stowaways on this voyage.

Finally, Kojo withdrew the gangway and secured the hatches himself. He hit the com. "All hands, secure for departure."

Archer answered, "Engines ready, Captain. Jump cells ready."

Hiram followed with "Fire 'em up, lad. Rolling out."

Hiram maneuvered *Sparrow* into the gateway's arch. Blue lights turned to red as we reached jump position.

The checkpoint disappeared in a blur as we began our journey to Nakana.

CHAPTER 15

The biological effects of interspecies interactions

PAPA ALWAYS SAID to begin and end a journey with a fine meal, to give the passengers a good first impression and leave them with a fond memory. For our welcoming dinner, I used the fresh stores to make a lush pasta primavera.

The passengers dug into the food all right, but it wasn't exactly a friendly crowd. By age and rank, Lyden should have sat in the place of honor at the captain's right, but Kojo put Jamila there and Rachel on his left. Lyden appeared not to notice the slight and took the seat at the foot of the table, flanked by Mya and Balan. As the rest of us filled in the gaps, the table looked less like a welcoming dinner than a temporary truce between warring parties: four Terrans at one end, three Gavorans at the other, and me and Danto facing each other in the middle.

The viewscreens provided no diversion. The ether in this corridor was a uniform gold haze, no spots of brightness or swirls of color to break the monotony.

Awkward pleasantries soon turned to awkward silences, until Grim asked Rachel, "Why does a Terran work for the Settlement Authority, anyway? It's nothing but a tool for the Neanderthals to keep Terrans from spreading out."

"Grimbold." Danto's voice was cold. "Do you recall the terms under which you agreed to accompany this mission rather than remain in less comfortable surroundings for the next three years?"

Grim grumbled, "Follow orders and keep my mouth shut."

"Correct," Danto said. "Do so."

Rachel smiled indulgently. "The Authority is not as one-sided as you may think. There are lots of Terrans who want to see planets settled in a responsible way. No one wants a repeat of the Albo fiasco or the tragedy in the Chichester system."

Grim shrugged, as if a couple of ecological disasters wouldn't faze him. "Still, it's the Gavs who run it, right?"

Rachel wore the expression that Tinker had when she cornered a mouse. "Actually," she said, "I hold the rank of commander in the Authority."

Kojo whistled and bared his wolf grin at Danto. "Commander? I guess you're outranked, Sergeant."

I exchanged a desperate look with Kojo. Rachel wasn't the low-tier Settlement Authority flunky I'd taken her for. A Terran who made it to the rank of commander in the Gav-dominated Settlement Authority was either very savvy or a complete tool of the Gavs. Either one was trouble: The synthreactor's core was stashed inside a bulkhead barely three strides from Rachel's survey console.

"Excellent," Jamila said. "I'm so glad we have the Authority's support at such a high level. Have you experience in planetary surveys?"

Rachel let slide this reinterpretation of her role from *supervision* to *support*. "Some, but my specialty is the biological effects of interspecies interactions. I'm a physician and exobiologist."

Kojo looked up doubtfully. "That doesn't sound like the kind of science we need for this voyage."

"No?" Rachel chuckled. "An interracial mission to an unknown world, populated by an unknown species, guided by a psychoactive artifact of unknown origin? I rather thought it was right up my alley. An object that has a differential effect on Terrans and Gavorans is quite interesting. How many of you are receiving some sort of communication from the artifact?"

It was a question neither I nor Kojo had dared to ask. Jamila froze, her eyes darting around.

Balan instantly said, "I am." He glared around the table, daring anyone to dispute it.

"I am, of course," said Lyden. "The relic's desire to return home to Nakana is palpable." Mya nodded.

I stayed mum. Danto scowled.

"Excellent," Rachel said cheerfully. "There seems to be a clear demarcation between hominin subspecies. I'll need to examine each of you, and all the crew members as well, as soon as possible."

"Examine us?" I asked.

"Yes. Genetic tests, blood chemistry, that sort of thing." She waved a fork. "Nothing painful. But quite necessary in order to track any changes caused by exposure to the item. I will also ask each of you to wear medical sensors so I can keep abreast of any physical changes. I'll begin with you, Balan, first thing in the morning."

I thought an examination for Balan was a good idea. He pushed his food around on his plate, but ate almost nothing, his lips moving in some silent whisper.

"I would like to renew my link to the bloodstone," he said. "It is unconscionable to lock it away from me."

Rachel looked up, her eyes flinty. "Not yet. I need to study the artifact before anyone touches it again."

"You're going to examine the artifact?" Jamila asked. "Finally, someone's doing something sensible."

Balan appealed to Lyden in Gavoran. "This is nonsense. I am here, ready to commune with the relic. Why should a Terran, blind to its message and its beauty, be allowed access to it when we are not?"

"Because I'm less likely to die in the process," Rachel said in Terran, proving she was fluent in both languages. "Let me be clear. The Settlement Authority has authorized this mission to investigate whether there is a planet that contains technology that should be controlled. What happens to the artifact and any other technology we may find is a matter for the Settlement Authority to determine. Given the artifact's psychoactive properties, no one will touch it again until I examine it under controlled conditions."

"It must not be harmed," Lyden said.

Grim belched. "It was buried under ruins for a few thousand years. I don't think looking at it through a microscope is going to hurt it."

Balan muttered something about intolerable delay. As he pushed his food around with his fork, his long fingers twitched.

That evening, I joined Kojo in the wheelhouse. I still was angry, still didn't trust him not to go behind my back again, but we needed to work together to finish the job for Ordalo.

So I settled into the watch station to catch up, the way we used to. Not that there was much to watch—the ship's internal systems were humming along nicely, and there were no demands on the pilot during the jump.

"Any problems?" I asked.

"Huh. Nothing but problems. Look at Balan. He's always been a fanatic, but he's getting worse, and he's supposed to be our guide. Then there's Danto. What's your read on him?"

I twisted a lock of hair. "A competent police officer. He'd have to be, to make sergeant—he must have been fighting prejudice at every step. He's got a major chip on his shoulder and resents Terrans. Probably blames his Terran blood for all the trouble he's had to put up with in life."

Kojo arched a brow at me. "Do you ever feel that way?"

"Hell, no. I blame you."

He chuckled. "I almost feel sorry for the bastard. I'll bet he's been offered this mission as his first solo command—

something that's supposed to be good for his career if it succeeds, but it'll most likely be a monumental waste of time."

"What about Jamila? Why did she go along with this?"

Kojo made a sour face. "She only agreed to this crazy plan because Lyden backed her into a corner—let her off on the charges of theft and implant tampering if she helped with the archeology. Jamila's been ragging on me, trying to find a way to contact Galactic. As if *I've* got some way to wriggle out of the mess she dropped us into."

"Any chance of bypassing the com block?"

"None. Believe me, I tried. We'll need Danto's codes for anything other than a pure distress call."

Tinker entered and glared at me for occupying her seat. She jumped effortlessly to my lap and began to knead my leg, not always remembering to sheathe her claws.

"Then there's that priestess Lyden," Kojo said. "According to Jamila, she's an armed grenade, ready to detonate on contact. Utterly convinced we'll find the home of the 'blessed Sages' and that they're going to show up as soon as we hit atmo."

"Hmm. Our contract's with the Patrol and Danto says he's in command of the mission, but as a clan matriarch, Lyden outranks him. And Rachel—she's just supposed to make sure the Settlement Authority rules are followed, but she's a commander, after all." I carefully detached Tinker's talons from my leg. "Rachel reminds me of Tinker—sharp claws under soft paws."

Kojo's face lit up. "But if we play our cards right, we can use it. We have forty-seven days left to deliver the goods to Ordalo. Sooner or later, this group is bound to squabble. If things get dicey and the charter parties start to fight over where to go, I'll exercise my captain's right to terminate the mission and return to port." He stroked his chin and winked. "Maybe in Kriti, right?"

I nodded. "Not bad."

Kojo said, "I'm going to try to get friendly with Grimbold. If push comes to shove, I want him on our side."

"You can't trust him."

"I don't have to trust him, I just need to keep one step ahead of him. He may be a snake, but he's a predictable snake."

I stretched. "Whatever happens, we're facing weeks cooped up with a ship full of crooks and fanatics. You don't think there's really anything to find in the Gloom, do you?"

"The lost home of the Sages, filled with technology? More likely dust and ruins. We'll let this group of misfits play it out, at their expense."

"And somewhere along the way, we'll take care of our other business."

"Sure," he said easily. Then, with a devilish grin, he asked, "So, how's married life? Is this the honeymoon you always wanted?"

He was still laughing when I slammed the wheelhouse door behind me.

As *Sparrowhawk* settled into the days of easy travel through the star corridors, I scuttled about the ship, spelling Hiram at the helm and Archer in the engine room, producing meals and supplies when needed, and trying to ease tensions among the passengers.

Rachel fussed with her equipment behind locked doors in the cargo hold. It made me nervous, with the synthreactor's core cached in the bulkhead, but there was nothing we could do about it.

Jamila commandeered a console in the salon to study the recent images from the archeological site. Grim sat at another, watching erotic performances and making lewd comments or playing chinko against the computer. Lyden wandered between her stateroom and the salon, Mya at her elbow and always ready to bring a cup of root tea or take notes.

Balan worked on his book in his cabin or prayed in front of the cargo hold door.

The general longing for home continued to emanate from the tablet.

There was little work for the crew to do during the long jumps between outlying gates. The first three jumps each lasted more than a day and the final one was nearly three days. I would never have attempted any of them with the jump cells available to us, but Archer assured me the military cells were able to handle the load.

Archer. *I* was acting normal, shifting jump cells, taking my turn in the engine room during his breaks, checking in with him from time to time. *He* was acting odd, surly one minute, making puppy eyes at me the next.

When I pushed the handcart with a fresh jump cell into the engine room, the waiting exhausted cell was topped with a handful of pink Prestowipes, wired together into a tiny mop.

I held the mop out to Archer. "Cleaning the bore?"

He shifted from foot to foot, making no move to take it. "It's for you. It's a rose. I figured, we didn't have time to get flowers when we were married. I thought you might like something to..."

He looked at me and stopped, his pale face flushing pinker than the wipes. "Stupid idea. Forget it."

Damn. I shoved the new cell into its freezer niche. "A rose. It's a sweet thought, Archer, but the marriage—it doesn't change anything, you know."

"It must mean *something* to you."

I wondered what to say that wouldn't hurt his feelings. Hurt them any worse.

I sat on the exhausted cell, the wipes-and-wire rose in my hand. "It means I trust you. You're my best friend."

"That's all." His voice was flat. "I see."

"I don't want that to change," I said desperately. "If things got awkward between us that would be terrible."

Archer nodded slowly. "Yeah, that would be terrible."

"Thanks for understanding." I kissed him on the cheek and hauled out the used jump cell.

Later, I realized the "rose" was still in my hand. I put it away in my locker.

Rachel took the Gavorans for their medical exams first, conducting her exams on a table in the cargo hold. Soon, Balan, Lyden and Mya were wearing medical sensors on their wrists and some sort of device behind their left ears.

When my turn came on the third day of travel, I crept gingerly into the hold. The cavernous space, crammed with crates of supplies, was as familiar to me as my own cabin, but the addition of an examination table and a console with an impressive display of monitors made it seem threatening.

Home, whispered the voice from the vault.

Hell, I wanted to go home, too.

"Do I have to undress?" I asked. I didn't want her to see the graft scar on my arm.

Rachel laughed. "Not at all. Just sit here and let me do a quick physical. I would tell you there's nothing to worry about, but for some reason that tends to make people more nervous."

She took samples of blood and tissue and inserted them into her machines to work on while passing various instruments over my anatomy. I bit my lip, unable to quell my nerves. The bulkhead that hid the synthreactor core was close enough for her to touch.

She smiled, like a genial shark. "Have you ever talked to a doctor about being a hybrid?"

"No," I admitted. "Not since I was young, anyway."

After looking at her instrument readings, Rachel put down her tools and sat facing me, eyes at level.

"My instruments tell me a lot about you," she said. "You are a healthy twenty-year-old hybrid, offspring of a Terran male and Gavoran female. Do you know nearly all hybrids have a Terran father and Gavoran mother, and not the other way around?" I shook my head. "That has to do with mate selection instincts for the two races. I also know your mother was from a slave clan, and you've tried to obscure that fact by removing the brand from your arm."

I must have looked alarmed, because she patted my hand. "Don't be concerned if you're keeping that a secret," she said. "As a doctor, I'm under oath not to talk about my patients."

I nodded. *As if people never broke their oaths.*

"I know that in your early years you mostly ate Gavoran rations, the sort lower castes eat. I expect you suffered a lot of digestive problems because of it." It was true, I'd had terrible stomachaches during the time I lived with my mother. "That's a common problem with hybrids, and it's one reason many hybrid children don't thrive. You must have been six or seven years old when you came to live with Terrans, and finally had a diet you could digest properly."

I nodded, fascinated.

Rachel lightly touched the top of my head. "I envy your height. That's a lovely example of hybrid vigor, but you might have been even taller, had you received a more appropriate diet when you were young. Many hybrids also have auditory problems, but your hearing is fine."

She paused for a moment, her face serious. "However, I'm afraid you suffer from another common effect of hybridization: You're infertile. You cannot have children in the normal way. I'm sorry."

CHAPTER 16

Secrets and dreams

NO CHILDREN? *Ever?* I felt like I'd been slapped. Rachel tactfully looked away and busied herself with her instruments.

Tears filled my eyes. I had dreamed, as most girls do, of having a baby to care for, even though I wasn't ready to have one yet. To suddenly learn it would never happen...

"Of course, you can always adopt a child."

"Of course," I murmured.

"Here," she said briskly, "let me look at that graft. My, that looks nasty. The skin seal should have been changed days ago." She peeled off the transparent seal, none too gently. Underneath, it *was* nasty-looking, the skin red and oozing, the puckered edges of the graft beginning to part from the skin around it.

"I've been stuck on the ship," I mumbled. "I couldn't exactly ask the Corridor Patrol to fix it, could I?"

"I also know something else," she said, fiddling with swabs and ointment on the wound. "I know you've been hearing the voice from the relic."

I snatched my arm away. "No. Your instruments can't tell you that."

"They can. Telepathic interaction stimulates a very specific area of the amygdala. Your brain shows that activity—not nearly as much as is evident in Balan, but still, it's there."

I said nothing. I felt like she was reading my mind.

She sighed. "Everyone has secrets, Patch. I don't want to intrude, but it's part of my job to understand the effect the relic may have on members of this expedition. There." She smoothed a new skin seal over the wound. "That will heal better now. You'll still need a permanent regraft."

"Thanks." The wound under the transparent seal still looked red and raw. I pulled my sleeve down to hide it.

"Patch, for the safety of all of us, I need to know what the voice has been telling you."

I could think of no reason to keep it from her. "Home," I said. "It wants—commands—us to take it home. It says that peace and joy are there."

"And do you know where its home is? Feel drawn toward the Gloom?"

"No. When I asked it to show me, it asked for blood."

She fiddled with her instruments. "The voice you hear, what do you think it is?"

I shrugged. "A spirit, I suppose."

"Have you ever heard other spirits?"

I hesitated. "Are you going to make fun of me if I say yes?"

She smiled. "Not at all. I'm well aware that Gavorans have a long cultural history of spiritual communications."

"Then yes. But the voice of the relic is different."

Rachel asked me a lot of questions. How was the voice different? Where was I when I heard it? Had I ever touched the relic? Did I feel any need to feed it?

I answered everything I could—she seemed to know so much already, I couldn't think of any reason not to.

Finally, Rachel sat back. "Who else knows you've been hearing the voice?"

"Only Kojo."

She nodded. "You're wise to keep it to yourself. And don't trust what it tells you is true."

Could a spirit lie? I glanced nervously at the vault lurking in a dark corner of the hold. "Will I end up like Balan? He's so obsessed he barely eats anymore."

"I don't think you're in danger. Balan's physical contact with the artifact may have induced a particular vulnerability. None of the other full-blood Gavorans are experiencing his level of obsession, nor has anyone else claimed to know where Nakana is."

I nodded, only slightly comforted.

She slipped medical sensors into place on my wrist and behind my ear. "You should wear these at all times. I promise, if I see any indication you're being dangerously affected, I'll let you know."

She stared into the distance for a moment, tapping her fingers on the chair arm. "Patch, I'd like you to help me. Terrans don't seem to hear the voice. Certainly, I don't. You hear its communications, but you seem to have more resistance than the pure Gavorans. That could be valuable to me."

"What do you want me to do?"

"Assist me when I examine the artifact, to let me know if anything I do is somehow harming it. I don't want to have Balan or any of the other Gavorans so close to it. Would you be willing to help?"

I hesitated, thinking of Balan's unquestioning belief. "I don't know. I don't trust it."

"Good. That's one reason you'd be the right person to assist."

"Let me think about it," I said.

When I left the hold, Kojo drew me aside. "You were in there a long time. What took you so long?"

"She's interested in hybrids. And"—I looked down as if embarrassed—"I don't get much chance to talk to a doctor about, well, women's things."

"Oh. I guess not. Sorry, I should have thought. You're all right, then?"

I dredged up a smile. "Sure. I'm fine."

As soon as he was gone, I practically ran to my cabin. I had barely closed and locked the door before my body shook with sobs I could no longer hold back.

No little baby of my own to hold, not ever. No orange-haired child to sit on my lap.

No children to teach about my ancestors. No descendants to light a candle in my name. No succeeding generations to call upon my spirit.

It would be as if I had never lived at all.

The weight of that knowledge crashed down on me, crushing my soul.

I pulled out the scrap of my mother's scarf and held it, weeping as quietly as I could. *Beloved ancestors, help me find the wisdom to choose what is best, the strength to do what I must, and the courage to face what may come. Mother, comfort me. Grandmother, send me a sign.*

Perhaps we were too far from Gavoran sectors for Mother or Grandmother to come to me, but this ship had been Papa's home and I was sure his spirit lingered near. *Papa, please speak to me. Send me a word of comfort.*

But no comforting family spirit came.

I'd never felt so alone. I'd lost my mother, lost my father. My own brother had betrayed me. Now I'd lost my children before ever conceiving them.

I couldn't stop weeping, so I stopped trying. I just let go, sobbing into my pillow in the darkness of my cabin.

Home.

The relic's voice intruded. Insistent, unfeeling for my grief.

Quiet, I told it, angrily. *You're no help. You offer no comfort or sympathy, no advice or strength.*

Peace and joy await.

Rachel had said the voice was not to be trusted. I sent a thought to the relic: *I don't believe you. I think you're lying.*

Home. Peace.

If the bloodstone really came from the Sages, I had even more reason to distrust it. Hadn't the Sages decreed that my clan's destiny was to serve the upper castes? Slavery, passed from mother to child for generation after generation. Meek submission, promoted by aristo priests in the name of religion and long-dead aliens.

I felt the burn of righteous anger, and with it, defiance.

I'd prayed in vain for comfort. Now rage gave me what prayer had not. Papa used to laugh in times of trouble, defying the universe. Well, if my mother's spirituality couldn't help me, maybe my father's rogue nature could.

I took a deep breath and smiled. It wasn't a nice smile.

All right, bloodstone. You promise peace and joy, but you take blood. Let's see what you really are.

I went to tell Rachel I would help her.

The next morning, I joined Rachel in the hold again. At her direction, I uncrated and installed another piece of equipment, an isolation chamber. It had a large, transparent box, with its own air supply and robotic arms to manipulate whatever was inside.

She looked over the empty box. "Lovely. We're ready to begin. I'm going to remove the artifact from the vault and place it in the chamber."

"Outside its case?" I said uneasily. "Jamila said the metal of the case acts like an insulator."

"Yes, but it must be done. Perhaps only for a short time." Frowning, she glanced at the sensors on my wrist and head and checked the instruments.

"Is something wrong?"

"No." She fiddled with the console. "I'm just having some trouble calibrating for the background fields. The engines must be interfering."

I tried to keep my gaze from wandering toward the bulkhead that hid the core of the synthreactor.

Finally, she seemed ready to begin. "Are you hearing the voice now?"

"Not a voice, but I know it's there."

She went to the com node. "Balan? I'm going to examine the relic now. Let me know immediately of any stress on the relic's inhabitant." She checked her instruments. "The readings from your sensors are coming through well. All set? Lovely."

I stood up to open the vault. "No, no, my dear. I have the combinations. You sit quietly and let me know if there's any reaction from the artifact."

Rachel dictated her actions into the record as she proceeded. "Opening vault now." She checked her instruments. "Opening case."

Home. The voice ramped louder. The numbers on her various monitors flickered higher, but they meant nothing to me.

"Blood," I said.

"What do you mean?"

"It senses your blood. It kind of reached toward you."

She stayed in front of the open case for a full minute, observing the artifact without touching it.

"Stay seated, Patch," she said.

I hadn't realized I was standing. I sat again.

"It knows you are there," came Balan's voice.

"Is it stressed?" Rachel asked.

"No." Balan sounded amused. "It is not interested in you."

"Thank you." She waited another few seconds, and then laid her gloved hand briefly on the stone, then withdrew it.

"Nothing," I said.

She nodded. With a swift movement, she lifted the relic from the case and placed it into the isolation chamber. She sealed the chamber and scanned the readouts.

"No change," I said.

"I see Nakana," Balan said. "I can see its location, in a double-star system within a cloud. I must be closer, to learn its exact location."

Rachel looked at me. I shook my head. I saw nothing, heard nothing except the same whining to go home, peace and joy. Some insecure part of my mind wondered if I wasn't good enough, if my mixed race or low caste made me unworthy for an important revelation.

I shook myself. Let the Sage worshippers follow the damn thing; why should I care if I wasn't called?

Rachel ran a handheld scanner over the metal panels lining the empty case. She nodded as if satisfied, then sat where she could watch the isolation unit and its readings.

Minutes passed. I grew drowsy and allowed my eyes to close.

It was a pleasant dream, of a world of humid warmth under a greenish sky. Vegetation abounded. Beasts grazed peacefully. They were huge and hairy, warm, wandering lumps whose backs scarcely showed above the tall grasses that fed them.

Home.

There were clicks and snaps. I opened my eyes in time to see Rachel close the case's lid over the relic. She returned the case to the vault and locked the door.

"Balan? Is all well?" she asked.

"The voice has faded. You have locked it away again."

"That's right. I've finished the scans for today." She turned to me. "And you, Patch? All well?"

"Yes," I said. "I'm sorry I fell asleep."

"You received a telepathic communication," she said. "Tell me about it, please."

"It was just a dream." She clearly expected more. "Of a world with a green sky, with lots of plants and grazing animals. Very peaceful."

"I see."

"Home," I said, remembering. "I felt that this place was home. Do you think the world I saw is Nakana?"

Rachel pressed me for everything I remembered about the dream. Big animals, moving about, eating plants. Green plants, tall like grass or grain. No water visible, but a feeling of humidity and warmth. The animals had thick fur or hair, or some covering like that. But it was warm there, definitely warm.

"And a feeling of satisfaction and well-being," I said. "I can see why the relic—or spirit or creature, whatever it is—wants to go back there. A paradise, really."

"And where is this paradise?"

I had no idea.

CHAPTER 17

Spirits and angels

BALAN CAME TO THE SALON for dinner, his eyes shining, his fingers twitching. "Dr. Fiori, now that you've examined the bloodstone, I insist on being allowed access. I must speak to Suriel."

We were mid-way through the series of long jumps, and everyone should have been well rested. His fevered agitation made me lose my appetite.

Lyden's eyes widened. "Suriel?"

"I asked what I should call the soul within the relic. The name Suriel came to my mind."

Grim paused, fork halfway to his mouth. "There's somebody inside it? He must be damn small. Maybe he's like the genie in the lamp."

To Mya's questioning look, Kojo said, "That's an ancient Terran tale about a spirit trapped in a small container. When someone rubbed the lamp, the genie would come out in a puff of smoke and grant wishes."

"So Terrans *do* venerate spirits?" Mya asked shyly. "I thought Terrans had no religion."

"That's not true at all," Grim replied. "We have hundreds of religions."

"That is the same as no religion." Balan's fork clattered to his plate and he pushed away his uneaten dinner. "Even Terrans have myths of angels that serve the deity. Why can you not accept that Suriel is such a servant?"

"An angel," Kojo said in a flat tone. Grim snorted.

With exaggerated politeness, Jamila said, "Evergreen University is neutral on the angel question."

Balan turned to Lyden and complained in Gavoran, "The Terrans mock the Sages."

Rachel spoke soothingly. "We don't want to denigrate your belief, we're simply trying to understand something that we don't experience."

Lyden looked around imperiously. "I pity you, all of you, who are blind to truth. Nakana encompasses something much more important than technological advances. There we shall find the means to restore all our peoples to the harmony and peace the blessed Sages intended for us!"

The three Gav religious scholars looked rapturous, and even Danto's face was grave rather than his usual sneer. He said, "I will do everything necessary to ensure the success of this mission."

Mya gazed at him in admiration.

"I'm sure we all want the same thing," Jamila said, despite all evidence to the contrary.

"I just sail the ship," Kojo said cheerfully. "You pay me to take you to Nakana, then I'll take you to Nakana."

Feeling unsettled, I went to the engine room to talk to the one person I could usually count on to make me feel better.

"Busy?" I asked.

Archer was dangling a string for Tinker. "Hardly. These long jumps are boring."

He held his sensor-ringed wrist next to mine. "Look, matching bracelets. You know, where I come from, we'd have matching rings, too. Since we're married." He looked at me sidelong.

I laughed. "Rings are impractical. But I'm glad Rachel is monitoring us—especially Balan."

"Hmm." Archer concentrated on enticing Tinker into another pounce. "I liked Rachel. She seemed to know all about me and didn't act like there's something wrong with me."

"She was like that with me, too. She even told me things about myself I didn't know." I blinked as sadness washed over me.

He looked up. "What's wrong, Patch?"

"Oh, nothing. Nothing to worry about." But I couldn't stop my lip from quivering and my eyes from filling with tears. I turned my head away.

Archer awkwardly put an arm around me. "Tell me about it. After all, we're married now."

I blotted my eyes on my sleeve. "It's nothing, really. It's just that Rachel told me...I can't have babies."

Archer stopped jittering for a moment. "Babies? You want to have a baby?"

"Well, not right now, idiot. It's just that I always assumed I would have children someday. I was disappointed to learn that I...I can't." Misery washed over me so strongly I could barely get the last words out.

He peered at me anxiously. "You can adopt. There must be lots of babies who need parents."

I scooped up Tinker. She allowed me to cuddle her for two seconds before she twisted out of my arms and stalked off. "Maybe it's better this way. Maybe I don't need to be bogged down by a family. I can just concentrate on business, and not worry about other things, right?"

Archer's face bore a combination of sadness and disappointment. "Sure. Business." Shoulders slumped, he turned to check a pinging readout.

"Don't you want to hear about the passengers?" I began to chatter, telling him about Balan's book, Lyden's religious fervor, and Mya's devotion to Lyden. "They're all obsessed with the relic—all the Gavs say they hear it talking to them." I watched Archer's face to see if he would scorn their belief, but he just looked thoughtful.

"What do they think it is?" he asked.

"Balan says there's an angel named Suriel who lives inside it. Kojo says it's like an ancient Earth spirit that granted wishes."

He brushed that aside. "Not a spirit. Not if it feeds. But it somehow survived five thousand years without food or water." Both feet tapped to a rhythm only Archer could hear. "Spores can do that. Fungi. Some animals like frogs and fish can survive months, even years in a dormant state when their habitat freezes or dries up."

"You think the voice comes from a fungus or a fish? Balan would be very disappointed."

"Actually, if it weren't for the blood part, I would think it came from a machine." His hand jiggled pensively.

"A machine?"

He shrugged. "If I were going to leave a map in a place where someone would find it hundreds or thousands of years later, I wouldn't rely on a living creature. I'd build a machine."

Sometimes I forgot how smart Archer was. "That's clever. But why would anybody do that?"

"There was a war at the time, right? Maybe it's military secrets."

I rubbed my arms, feeling suddenly cold. "I hope not. When war and religion get mixed up, things get very bad."

Three nights later, we were coasting in the last, long jump before powering up for the sublight leg to Kriti.

In the small hours, I wakened from a dream. I'd fallen into a bottomless well amid swirling darkness. Papa had stood far above me—I'd stretched my hand to him, but he was out of reach.

Feeling uneasy, I got up to make a routine round of the ship.

All was quiet in the wheelhouse. Hiram dozed at the helm, the monitors set to ping if anything needed attention. Through the canopy, the ether's golden haze had given way to a dusky brown, like sailing through broth. The wardroom door was closed and silent.

I crept down the aft steps to the engine room. Archer snoozed peacefully in his nook, relying on the monitors to alert him if adjustments were needed. Even in his sleep, he twitched like Tinker dreaming of the hunt.

The cargo holds were all locked and silent, except for the tablet's whining to go home. I made a quick check of the panel that hid the synthreactor core: The dirt and lube I'd rubbed onto the screwheads seemed undisturbed.

On the passenger deck, the cabins were shut and quiet, except for the faint drone of Balan's voice—something about Suriel, probably dictating his book to the console. In the salon, nothing stirred except the warning blips on the scanner.

I was getting ready to turn in when shouts came from the wardroom.

"You moved the chit!"

"You're a liar!"

I ran up the companionway to the command deck. Hiram hovered bleary-eyed at the wheelhouse door. "Best settle 'em, missy." He disappeared back to the helm.

I threw open the wardroom door in time to see Grimbold take a swing at Kojo. Dice and rhollium coins skidded across the deck.

Tinker streaked out, skidding around a corner to disappear down the companionway.

Kojo ducked as Grim's right fist swept past his ear. Grim's left didn't miss—he buried it into Kojo's midriff.

That left Grim completely open as I slammed my joined fists into his side. He toppled against the bunk as Kojo doubled over onto the deck.

I grabbed Grim's shoulder and shoved him out of the wardroom and into the passage.

"He was cheating!" Grim gasped, rubbing his side.

"Liar," Kojo panted, his arms crossed over his middle.

Danto pounded up the companionway, wearing a form-fitting undershirt and shorts that showed off his sinewy, lightly furred limbs. He carried a stunner in his hand.

"I will not tolerate fighting," he said. "Lock Grimbold in the hold."

As if Danto had the right to give orders. As if we had a spare hold to use as a brig.

Grim yelped, "Me? *He* started it."

"I'll deal with this, Sergeant," I snapped. "Kojo, give him back his money."

"Patch, it was a fair—"

"Doesn't matter," I said. "Give it back."

Kojo pulled coins from his pocket and thrust them into Grim's hands.

"New rule," I said, as Grim counted his money. "No gambling, except against the entertainment console."

"I thought *he* was captain," Grim sneered.

"He is." I stepped in, to stand nose to nose and eye to eye with Grimbold. "But I'm the one letting you walk away under your own power with your money in your pocket. Keep it there."

Grim sidestepped Danto and stalked off, grumbling. With a groan, Kojo collapsed onto the bunk.

"Good night, Sergeant," I said. "There will be no more disturbance."

Danto took a step closer, close enough for a blow—or a kiss.

Still keyed up from the tussle, I braced myself, ready to fight back in either case. I was very much aware of those long, furred, unclad limbs.

For a moment we stood face-to-face. Now that I was used to him, he didn't seem ugly. His beaky nose would have been distinguished in a Terran. And the small scar was not unattractive. His physique, though thin for a Gavoran, was more than acceptable by Terran standards. It was just that his features were such an odd mixture. Like mine.

Danto holstered his stunner. "You handled the situation well," he said.

A compliment? I shrugged. "A few words over dice, not much of a situation."

For another moment he stood close enough for me to feel the warmth from his body, as if he were waiting for something.

I stepped back. "Kojo? Are you all right?"

Kojo responded with a grunt.

Reverting to his familiar irritated scowl, Danto turned and followed Grimbold.

Ancestors, but he was changeable.

Too late, I remembered: A Gav man expected the woman to make the first move. An opportunity lost? Maybe, but a dalliance with Danto would complicate an already fraught voyage. With a sigh, I stooped to collect scattered dice and coins.

"I wasn't cheating," Kojo said.

"Don't we have enough problems? You promised not to gamble. And I thought you were trying to be friendly with Grim."

Kojo leaned close. "I am," he whispered. "That was just a little show for Danto. Let him think we're at each other's throats, but when the chips are down, Grimbold's with us."

Kojo rubbed his stomach and winced. "I just wish he wasn't so convincing."

CHAPTER 18

Myth and destiny

A LONG SLIDE and a bone-jarring thump signaled our exit from the star corridor into the Kriti system. The jump gate lights glowed starkly against the murk of the Gloom.

We paused only long enough for Danto to relay his report to the Corridor Patrol. Then *Sparrow*'s engines, quiet during the long days of jumps, roared back to life in all their thumping, wheezing glory. The smooth calm of the star corridors gave way to the trembling and hitches of sailing through swirling ether.

I passed out headache meds and nausea patches. "We have ten days of rough sailing before we get to Kriti. Strap in whenever you're sitting or sleeping and keep everything stowed."

Mya rubbed her arms and shivered, peering at the salon's viewscreen. "That dark shadow—it looks like a storm."

"That is the Gloom," Danto told her. "The ether there is so dense it blocks the light of stars beyond. It is...unsettling."

Mya gazed at him. "Horrible."

Rachel sipped tea with a feline smile. "You were posted on Kriti, Sergeant. Are you looking forward to seeing the place again?"

I hoped so. Maybe he and Rachel would relax enough on Kriti that Kojo and I could take care of our other business.

Twice more in the last few days I'd sat next to Rachel while she swabbed samples of dust and stains from the relic's surface. Each time, I'd found a moment when her back was turned to assure myself that the panel hiding the bulkhead cache showed no sign of disturbance. But how could we find a way to off-load the synthreactor with Rachel constantly in and out of the cargo hold and monitoring our every move?

Thirty-eight days left to deliver the synthreactor.

Danto rose, scowling even more fiercely than usual. "Looking forward to seeing Kriti? I had hoped never to see that cesspool again."

After three days and nights of rough sublight travel, only Rachel, Kojo and Grim seemed to have an appetite for breakfast. Jamila and Mya stared morosely at their plates. I hadn't eaten much myself, but that was just because the damn relic had whined all night, disturbing my sleep.

Balan lurched into the salon, holding onto the bulkhead as if in need of support. His face was damp with sweat, his pelt dull, and his eyes reddened.

He glared at Rachel. "Dr. Fiori! You must let me into the cargo hold. I must be closer to the relic."

Rachel rose and laid a hand on his shoulder. "I'm sorry Balan, but it's doing you harm."

He jerked his arm away, jittering like Archer on a bad day.

"He looks strung out to me," Grim said, munching a biscuit. "Maybe you better check his cabin for dope."

Lyden spoke gently. "Balan, you do look ill. Let Dr. Fiori help you back to your cabin."

"No!" Balan turned to the old woman, a manic hatred in his eyes. "I know what you want. Only *I* have given blood to the relic. Only *I* have the right to commune with Suriel."

Rachel spoke sharply. "That's enough, Balan. Return to your quarters. Danto, see that he goes. I'll get my med kit."

Danto grabbed Balan's arm and marched him down the passage. Balan's protests faded until the door to his cabin cut them off entirely.

"Zub's horns and pitchfork," Kojo said softly. He looked at me, eyes filled with concern.

I scrunched my nose at him to prove that I was fine, but inside I was shaken. Was I going to become like Balan?

Jamila rounded on Lyden. "Now do you see? Now do you understand? That's how he was at the dig site. That thing is a danger! Do you want to expose yourself to that? To expose Mya?"

Lyden responded calmly. "Sacrifice is always necessary for great advances."

Grim harrumphed. "Easy to say when it's somebody else making the sacrifice."

I cleared the table, trying to calm my nerves. It was only a rock. How could it make Balan so ill? Even if there was a spirit within the bloodstone, I'd never heard of a spirit affecting anyone that way.

When Rachel and Danto returned, she addressed the group. "I've given Balan a sedative. He'll sleep now."

Kojo's dark face was more serious than usual. "Rachel, I'm responsible for the safety of my passengers and crew. Is there any chance someone else will end up like Balan?" His glance slid toward me.

"I doubt it," Rachel replied. "Balan has a much stronger connection to the relic than anyone else. His neural activity spikes whenever the relic is taken from the shielding in the case. No one else has that extreme a reaction. Grim is correct that Balan is reacting like an addict. It's not just that the relic wants blood—Balan has a physical craving to keep renewing that tie."

Kojo grimaced. "Hell. It sounds like a vampire!"

At Mya's questioning look, Grim leered. "Vampires look like us but feed on blood—people's blood. And live forever."

Mya's face wrinkled in disgust. "Horrible."

"It's just a folk tale," Kojo said. "Part of the story is that if a victim survives the first attack, the victim becomes the vampire's willing slave. He or she gets some sort of satisfaction from giving blood to the vampire." Kojo kept an eye on me as he spoke, as if I was about to rustle up a blood breakfast.

"I assure you, the relic does not house a vampire," Rachel snapped. She paused, considering. "However, its proximity does appear to affect Balan. From now on, I'll leave the relic in its protective case in the vault—I have all the samples I need. That should help."

I couldn't be so calm about it. "Balan's the only one who knows how to get to Nakana. You can't keep him sedated for the rest of the trip."

"We need not rely on Balan until we reach Kriti," Danto said. "In the meantime, Dr. Fiori will care for Balan and inform me if his condition worsens."

"And if it does, what then?" Kojo looked around at the group. "It's still nine days to Kriti. Suppose that burzing thing starts to affect Lyden like that, or Mya, or you? We could turn around now. A day back to the jump gate, then a couple of jumps to a decent med center. Every hour we continue, we're in more danger."

"Every hour we continue, we are closer to Kriti and the med center there," Danto said. "I have no doubt Dr. Fiori can manage until then. We go on."

"That makes sense to me," I said, touching my ear to signal Kojo. I appreciated that he wanted to off-load the passengers as soon as we could, but why go backward just when we were getting close? We still had more than thirty days to make delivery. If Balan got worse, it would make a good excuse to scrap the mission—and leave us in an excellent position to complete our other business.

Kojo rubbed his chin a moment, then nodded. "All right. For now."

Later, I knocked on door to Lyden and Mya's stateroom, wanting only to leave clean towels.

Lyden opened the door and immediately drew me into the cabin. "Dear Patch, come in. Perhaps you will join us in prayers for the success and safety of our mission."

Damn. A religious ambush. "Thank you, Mzee. But I wasn't raised in your religion. I say my prayers as I was taught by my family."

"But you do pray? Excellent." Lyden enthroned herself on the stateroom's only chair. "I'm glad that Terran atheism has not entirely destroyed your innate spirituality."

Mya perched on one of the bunks. "Every Gavoran child is born knowing in her soul that the spirits guide our lives. With teaching, you could better fulfill your destiny."

"Destiny?" I squirmed uncomfortably, my arms loaded with towels. "I'm just here to keep the ship running and the passengers comfortable."

Lyden smiled knowingly. "Each of us has a purpose to fulfill in the Sages' plan. Surely you feel the desire, the need, to serve a purpose? To be more than someone who lives and dies without knowing why?"

"Everyone wants to think their life means something." I recalled my barrenness with a pang.

Lyden nodded regally. "We pure Gavorans are dangerously sensitive to the relic, but because you exist between worlds and between peoples, you can carry us safely. I believe the Sages have chosen you and your brother to bear us on this journey— you are not of our faith, not affected by the relic's power, but necessary to carry it and us to Nakana. Perhaps this is to be your destiny, your legacy of service to our people."

If I had a destiny, I hoped was something more than being Lyden's luggage carrier. "You don't really think the Sages will be waiting on Nakana, do you? Assuming we find it. I mean, no one has seen them for five thousand years."

Mya leaned forward, eyes shining. "The Sages may not have manifested themselves corporally in the present age, but they continue to guide us, not only through the sacred texts but through their continuing spiritual presence. Perhaps the time has come for them to return to us in a more direct form."

A celestial check-in? Not something I was eager for. "Yes, well, if that's all…" I edged toward the door.

Lyden said, "My dear, forgive me for inquiring, but I am puzzled. Have you taken a vow of chastity?"

That stopped me, out of sheer surprise. "Chastity? Why would I?"

"I only wondered why you have not called Sergeant Danto to you. He seems a competent young male, and a hybrid like yourself."

I felt myself blushing. "Mzee Lyden, an accomplished Star Clan man might not welcome advances from me. I'm sure he usually has offers from much more attractive females." I glanced toward Mya. She sat stone-faced, not meeting my eyes.

"My dear Patch," Lyden said with an amused smile, "it is not the place of a male to object when a female chooses him—if they are not compatible, they need not remain together. In the absence of a matriarch from your own clan—Sand Clan, I believe?—let me advise you. You are of an age to provide your clan with offspring. Given your limited options, Danto would be a suitable choice for your first child."

I struggled to hold my temper. "I have plenty of *options* among Terrans, thank you. Besides, I thought maybe Mya had an interest in Danto."

Lyden sniffed. "Absolutely not. Mya has an excellent future. She should not be sullied by taking a mixed-race companion, however accomplished he may be."

Mya wore the tense smile of someone clenching her teeth. Lyden didn't appear to notice.

"Thanks for the advice. I'll keep it in mind."

I escaped to my cabin. *Nosy old bag.* Danto wasn't good enough for Mya, but perfectly fine for me?

In my cabin's tiny mirror, I examined my face, cataloging the ways it differed from the Gavoran ideal. Nose too big, ears too prominent, lips too full, all surrounded by that mane of orange curls. Danto might be a half-blood like me, but he'd been raised to appreciate Gav standards of beauty. Mya would be much more to his liking.

In irritation, I crammed my beret back on, tucking stray hair underneath. "Limited options"? Maybe I was odd-looking, but that didn't prevent the occasional portside tumble with a friendly Terran. Why would I swap the variety of my travels on *Sparrow* for a life tied to a single city or a single man? I'd never aspired to a protracted Terran-style relationship—the arrangement with Archer was just for show. And now that I knew babies would not be a part of my life—all the more reason to spend my life unfettered by a man.

Feeling the need for an antidote to Gavoran religion, I went to the salon and sat near Jamila, diligently working at her console.

"Do you mind?" I asked. "Lyden's been telling me about the Sages."

Jamila smirked. "Feeling enlightened?"

"More like mugged." I rubbed my fingers where Lyden had clutched them. "Mythology aside, what do we really know about the Sages?"

Jamila tapped a finger to her lips. "Unfortunately, everything we know is distorted by Gavoran religion. No direct writings or artifacts, just the 'prophecies' that some ancient Gavoran claimed were dictated by the Sages. That's one reason—a big one—to be skeptical about the relic."

"But the Sages were real?"

"Oh, yes. All our faster-than-light travel through the star corridors relies on science far beyond what Gavs or Terrans or Selkids could manage. The Gavs may have built the beacons and gateways, but they clearly learned the design from some more advanced culture—a culture that vanished thousands of years ago."

"How important is Lyden?" I asked. "Is she really influential in the College of Religion?"

Jamila wagged a hand. "Right now, she's just the leader of a splinter group that thinks Gavs have been too affected by alien influences—meaning Terrans, of course. Young Gavs see Terrans choosing their own careers, forming their own colonies, and governing themselves, and have started to agitate for fewer clan restrictions. A few matriarchs like Lyden think the best response is to clamp down on dissent." She grinned. "As an anthropologist, I could tell them the likely outcome of *that*."

I nodded. Xenophobia would explain Lyden's eagerness to keep Mya away from a cross-blood.

"Lyden's just a fringe player now," Jamila said, "but if she can claim some new revelation from the Sages, who knows? She might actually spark a Gav religious revival."

"Mya certainly seems to be under her thumb."

Jamila dropped her voice. "Don't be taken in by Mya's shy schoolgirl act—she's as ambitious as they come. She's chosen to be a rising star in Lyden's tiny movement instead of one among many in the mainstream, even if that means fetching and carrying for a demanding old lady. Of course," she added, "Mya may also believe the Sages are about to reappear and begin a new age. People believe all sorts of unlikely things."

I stood to go. "What about you? Do *you* think we'll find the Sage homeworld?"

Jamila turned back to her console. "I'm an archeologist. If there's an unknown archeological site out there, I want to be on the spot when they find it."

That night I dreamed of male embraces. I couldn't quite see my lover's face, but his arms were long and strong and lightly furred. A deep joy filled me as my skin touched his, as his heart beat next to mine. His long fingers touched my face, my lips, my breasts...

Suddenly, my dream was filled with anxious struggles and shrill alarms. I heard Papa warning me about something. Maybe about faithless men.

I awakened with the sheet twisted around me. The alarm sounded again, a shrill buzz. Were we under attack? In a moment, I was up and running barefoot to the wheelhouse.

Hiram was at the helm, flustered. Beside him, Danto hissed furiously. "What have you done?"

The scanner was blizzed with static noise. "Is it an attack?" I asked. No ship was visible through the canopy.

"Radiation field," Hiram said, gesturing toward the scanner. "Tell your boyfriend to quit yelling."

I caught a whiff of brandy.

"What's going on?" Kojo crowded into the wheelhouse. A bit late, I thought. He must have been with Jamila.

"You pilot has drifted off course," Danto said, tightly. "The man is incompetent." The alarm ceased its buzz, and the scanner's blizz began to clear.

Hiram turned sheepishly to Kojo. "Sorry, Captain. I must have been a little sleepy. Look, we're out of the field already. I just drifted off for a few minutes."

Kojo clenched his fists. "Hiram, where is it?"

"Where's what?" Hiram said innocently.

"The bottle. I can smell the brandy from here."

"Ah, lad, it was just a little pick-me-up."

Kojo reached under the pilot's seat and came up with a bottle, half-empty.

"Out!"

"Kojo, honest…"

"Out," Kojo took over the helm. "Go sleep it off. I'll deal with you later."

Hiram slunk away.

"Such behavior is completely unacceptable," Danto said. "He must be disciplined."

I shoved myself between them. "That's enough!"

Danto and Kojo both turned to me in surprise.

My balled fists were on my hips like an angry matron. "Sergeant Danto, this is a civilian ship and a civilian crew.

Hiram is quite reliable within his limits. Our crew is entitled to reasonable rest periods and shore leave. They've had neither because of you, and that damned bloodstone."

I stabbed a finger at his chest. "You lead the mission, but you don't command this ship. It's not your place to criticize Hiram or any other member of this crew."

"It is my place to complete this mission. If another pilot were available, I would ban that man from the helm."

"We'll deal with it, Sergeant," Kojo said.

"Do so." Danto gazed at me for a moment, then left.

"Well," Kojo said with a sly grin, "you sure told him."

"Humph. Gav men are used to taking orders from females."

"And that flimsy nightshirt might have helped as well." Kojo laughed as I realized I was wearing very little indeed.

CHAPTER 19

Distress call

THE NEXT DAY, I felt better than I had in a while, having slept surprisingly well after the night's excitement. The good mood seemed to be catching—despite the growing darkness, the ship's course was calmer and the passengers were less fractious. Jamila and Lyden conversed quietly at Jamila's console, translating the inscriptions from the walls of the ruined Cazar temple, while Grim played chinko and made an occasional sarcastic contribution. Rachel cheerfully reported that Balan had slept well and she was keeping him tranqed.

Even Hiram was in a good mood, although I expected him to be hung over. "Never better!" he claimed. "Just what I needed, a little drink and a good sleep."

In the afternoon, after Lyden had retired to her cabin for a rest, Danto sat near the viewscreens, gazing at the darkening vista where the dense ether clouds blocked out the stars. Mya soon joined him, listening raptly as he described the perils of radiation sources and ether maelstroms. As she let her hand linger on his arm, he bent his head toward hers.

The interest is definitely mutual, I thought, clearing the table of lunch leavings. No wonder Lyden had tried to push me in Danto's direction.

A pang of envy washed over me as I remembered my dream of embraces from strong, furred arms. But that was foolish—why should I dream of Danto, of all people? Maybe it was just the novelty of imagining an affair with a hybrid, someone who understood what it was like to be in-between.

I shook my head to clear it. This whole day had been a little strange, too bright somehow, too full of emotional highs and lows.

Danto's voice sounded through the com. "Captain to the helm. We've received a distress call."

I ran up to the wheelhouse, arriving just behind Kojo.

Sparrow seemed to be sailing in ink. Aside from a hazy glow to starboard, the ship sailed in darkness as deep as an ocean.

Without visual cues, we were dependent on the scanners. They lit with warnings of a large debris field filled with radiation.

"What's up?" Kojo asked.

Danto nodded toward the scanner. "Distress signal, intermittent, from that debris field." His fingers were already keying in his codes to open the hailer. "This is *Sparrowhawk*, answering..."

Kojo slapped his hand down, cutting off the hail. "Are you crazy? That's an old pirate trick!"

Danto looked daggers at Kojo. "I cannot ignore a distress call. I am changing course to investigate."

Kojo glared back. "You're not in a Patrol cruiser, Sergeant. This is a civilian ship and your duty is to protect *us*. Look at the scanner. You see the distress call, but do you see a ship?"

"The radiation may have..."

Kojo hit the com. "Archer, we may have trouble. Prepare escape thrusters, just in case. Hiram, to helm. Passengers, secure for turbulence."

I pointed to the scanner. "Something's coming."

A blip had appeared from behind and below us, approaching fast.

Danto glanced at the blip. "Terran ship, predator class."

Our transponder pinged. I stared at it, unbelieving. A Terran ship with a Selkid Trading Cartel transponder? And what would a Cartel ship be doing here, so far from Selkid sectors?

"What the Zub?" Hiram slipped into the wheelhouse. "A Cartel flash? Out here?"

The ship came into view, a smudge in the murk. Its hail sounded throughout *Sparrow*. "Rampart corvette *Kamok* hailing the Cartel-sanctioned cutter *Sparrowhawk*. Cooperate with us and we will escort you to your destination, protecting you from the illegitimate coercion of the Corridor Patrol."

"Illegitimate?" Danto cried.

"We are here to recover a stone artifact belonging to Rampart Militech. In accordance with the articles of the Selkid Trading Cartel, fair compensation will be paid for assisting the recovery. Resist and we will take the item by force."

Rampart had joined the Cartel—and they wanted the relic.

Damn! That meant the Cartel knew we had the "sacred relic" they'd been looking for ever since we left Santerro. We'd carried a valuable item out of Selkid space without giving the Cartel their cut and disobeyed a Cartel order to turn it over to them. Either of those infractions would see us blacklisted in Selkid sectors—and that would be the least of our worries. If we were in default of our Cartel obligations, then even if we delivered the synthreactor as promised, the Cartel might refuse to release the mortgage on *Sparrowhawk* or Kojo's indenture...or mine.

How had they found us?

Danto returned the hail. "*Kamok*, this is Sergeant Danto of the Corridor Patrol. *Sparrowhawk* is under the protection and in the custody of the Corridor Patrol. Any interference will be treated as an act of piracy."

Kamok answered, "*Sparrowhawk* is a private vessel, operating under Cartel articles. The Corridor Patrol has commandeered *Sparrowhawk* in order to prevent a Cartel member from taking delivery of an important item of cargo. That is an abuse of authority whose legitimacy is challenged by Rampart and the Cartel. We demand the Patrol release *Sparrowhawk* and allow her to proceed with her free trade."

I felt a glimmer of hope. If Rampart and the Cartel thought the Patrol had coerced us, maybe we had a chance. Maybe if we gave *Kamok* the artifact now, we could convince them that we hadn't known it was the thing the Cartel had been looking for.

"Kojo," I said, "we have to give them the damned thing. The Patrol can track them down later. Let the College of

Religion, Rampart, and the Cartel fight over the relic in court—somewhere we're not caught in the middle."

"Are you cowards?" Danto snapped. "I will not allow my first command to be tainted by surrender."

"This is a space hauler, not a battle cruiser."

Kojo nudged me. "Danto's right. Surrendering to raiders is never a good idea. Trust me, it would be better to fight them off if we have to."

My stomach sank. What was Kojo up to?

Danto hit the hailer. "Stand down, *Kamok*. *Sparrowhawk* and her crew and cargo will remain in Corridor Patrol custody. Any interference will be met with…"

Kamok fired a concussive blast.

CHAPTER 20

Battle stations

KAMOK SPED TOWARD *Sparrowhawk*, extending booms tipped with grapplers.

Danto ran for the gun turret.

Kojo shouted, "Patch—drones! I'll help with engines." He hit the com. "Archer, ready thrusters. Half bore, two seconds. All hands, strap in."

As I flew down the companionway, Kojo close behind me, a second blast rocked *Sparrowhawk*, tumbling Kojo into me hard enough to knock my breath away. Kojo cursed and stepped over me, heading for the aft steps.

I took a moment to check that the passengers in the salon were secured. Lyden seemed to be praying, Grim looked sick, and Rachel simply looked interested. Through the viewscreen, we saw our guns fire three concussive blasts in quick succession, followed by a burst of armed projectiles. Several hit *Kamok* but failed to penetrate her hull.

"Engaging thrusters," Kojo warned on the com. "Now!"

I grabbed for a chair as the thrusters slammed us into a new course. Screams and vomit filled the salon.

As soon as I was back on my feet, I ordered, "Grim! Help me with the drones!" He was a military man, he must know how to fight.

"Me?" But he stumbled down the steps behind me to the lower decks.

With Grim grumbling and cursing, we muscled a heavy cargo drone out of its locker and shoved it onto the launch bay.

Something was wrong.

There were only eight drones in the locker. We'd restocked at the checkpoint—there should have been a full load of nine drones. Where was the ninth?

And why was the relic silent? It should have been pleading to go home.

Then I knew—it was gone. *Kojo!*

While Grim locked on the mooring lines, I ran to the magazine for grenades.

Damn! Kojo had once again gone behind my back. No wonder he was ready to fight—if we couldn't produce the tablet, then surrendering to the Cartel ship wouldn't solve our problems.

I armed the grenades and banged them into the drone's payload. We shoved the drone into the airlock. From the drone console, I opened the airlock to space and launched the drone. "Drone away. Grenades armed for remote detonation."

Danto responded on the com. "Prepare another. I'll control them from the turret."

Absurdly, tears filled my eyes. I didn't want the relic to be gone. I wanted to talk to it, to learn about its past, to understand its nature. I *missed* it! How could Kojo make such a decision without me—again!

I sniffed. "Come on, Grim. Another drone."

Grim paused in front of the open magazine, then took out his high-class stunner and stuck it in his belt. "Now's our chance. I don't want to die for this. Just dump the burzing relic out the airlock and get out of their way. Let Rampart and the Cartel and the burzing gorillas fight over it."

The idea would have had some appeal, except we didn't have the relic to surrender. "Shut up. You want to explain that to Danto?"

After another moment of hesitation, he reached for the drone. "All right, but you make sure you tell that jumped-up sergeant how helpful I am."

A concussion blast nearly knocked both of us off our feet.

"Where is that drone?" Danto demanded over the com.

Struggling against the reeling of the ship and the slow-to-adjust grav generator, Grim and I managed to get the drone to the launch bay. Hiram was sidewinding, trying to stay away from *Kamok*'s grapplers. Rachel's heavy analyzers strained against their lashings.

Just when I'd begun to lock the drone in, the bucking ship took a lurch that slammed me to the bulkhead and sent Grim flying across the hold. The drone collapsed toward me, held back by only a single mooring line.

"Pincer!" Danto shouted. The viewscreen showed a small vessel approaching at high speed from above and behind us, grapplers deployed.

I leaned against the bulkhead and pushed my feet against the drone, using my legs to tip it back into position. Once it was upright, Grim, moaning and rubbing his side, wrangled a second mooring line onto the drone, then shoved it into position for launch.

Sparrow shimmied as Hiram dodged blasts from the looming *Kamok* while trying to evade the grapplers of the smaller attacker at our flank.

"Helm's sluggish," Hiram said. "They must have hit something."

Flashes. Danto fired *Sparrow*'s guns at the smaller ship, a Selkid harrier-class vessel, designed for short range.

I ran to the grenade case and set three grenades to detonate on signal.

Another jolt made the ship shudder.

Kojo called on the com, "Propulsion's hit! Patch? Where's that burzing drone?" It sounded like all hell was breaking loose among the engines.

"Almost ready!" I loaded the grenades and slammed down the payload hatch. Grim pushed the drone into the airlock. I hit the launch lever. "Drone away!"

From the com node came unintelligible shouts.

With a flash, the drone exploded near the harrier. A moment later, the shock wave hit *Sparrowhawk*. As the ship lurched, Grim and I dragged another drone into the launch bay.

"Son of Satan," Grim swore. "Grapplers."

The harrier filled the viewscreen, its grapplers reaching out like claws. I ran to the magazine.

With my arms full of grenades, there was a crunch. *Sparrow* tilted sickeningly.

I fell against cases of supplies, dropping grenades to the deck. Grim scrambled on his knees to retrieve them.

"Patch, we need another drone!" Hiram called.

The ship swayed and bumped, Hiram doing some fancy tacking. Gray-faced, Grim thrust the grenades at me to set and load into the drone.

Damnit, I didn't want the relic to be gone. I told myself not to be foolish. The relic had brought us nothing but trouble. It had killed Deprata and made Balan half-crazy. It was like one of Kojo's vampires. All day, I'd felt better than I had in a long time—because it was gone. Even Balan, dosed with tranqs, had seemed stronger and healthier.

How could I want it back? I told myself to be grateful the voice was silenced.

I shut the drone's payload hatch.

Balan leaped into the hold. "Where is it!" He grabbed Grim and threw him to the deck.

"What have you done with it?" Balan pulled frantically at the vault door. "Open it! Open it!"

Damn—his meds must have worn off.

"Balan, the drone!" I shouted back. "Help me with the drone!" I pulled myself up and ran to the launch bay. "Help me, Balan! Grim, get up." I shoved the drone in the airlock. Grim rose to one knee, his stun pistol in his hand, aiming at Balan frantically trying to open the vault.

Danto's shout came over the com, "Grapplers! Brace!"

There was a booming crash as the hull crunched into something solid. There was no recoil—the magnetic grapplers had *Sparrow*.

Kojo called on the com, "Patch! Get out of there!"

I ran to the magazine and grabbed two stun pistols. "Balan!" I threw one to him.

A blast tore through the cargo hatch.

Ancestors! We were being boarded!

There was little cover in the tidy cargo hold. I had nothing between me and the boarding party but a stun pistol. *Strength and courage*, I prayed. *This is my ship and I will defend it.*

Balan stood before the vault, pistol at the ready. The cargo hatch yawned open.

A flash came from beyond the hatch. I fired at whoever was beyond.

Zing! Grim fired his stun pistol—and Balan went down.

"Put down the weapon, Patch," Grim ordered. "Time to be reasonable."

So much for Grim being on our side when the chips were down.

From somewhere beyond the blasted hatch, a Selkid translator plug screeched, "Drop your weapons!"

I hesitated too long. A stun blast from the hatch threw me against the cases of supplies.

My vision grayed. Roaring filled my ears. I tried to lift the stunner, but my limbs wouldn't move.

As my vision began to clear, the room spun sickeningly. Balan was on the deck, propped against the vault door. Unmoving.

Grim had his hands in the air, his stunner at his feet. "Don't shoot! I'm on your side."

Four members of the harrier's crew poured through the blasted hatch—armored Terrans and two Selkids. One picked up the dropped weapons as others moved out to the rest of the ship. I couldn't move yet, but I heard stun blasts.

A stranger's voice echoed through the com. "No one needs to get hurt. All we want is the artifact. Hand it over and you can go on your way."

I wasn't fool enough to believe that, but apparently Grim was.

Hands still raised, Grimbold said, "It's in the vault. Patch here can open it for us. No one here's going to fight you."

Kojo's voice came over the com. "This is the captain. I've taken control back from the Corridor Patrol. We have no quarrel with Rampart or the Cartel. You can have the tablet, just leave us in peace. Patch, open the vault and let them take the case. That's an order."

He said *the case*, not *the tablet*. *Razzle-dazzle.* Kojo must have cooked something up with Danto.

Grim nodded. "C'mon, Patch. Open the vault. It's the smart thing to do."

"Give me a moment. My head's still spinning." I closed my eyes and took deep breaths, putting my hands to the sides of my head to try to make the room stop turning. *Play for time.* I had to give Kojo and Danto a chance to make their play. Tentatively I sat up.

"Come on," an intruder said. He pointed his stunner at me. "Open it or we'll blast the door."

"Wait!" Grimbold cried. "Let her open the vault! Don't take a chance on damaging the artifact."

A mercenary grabbed Balan by the leg and dragged him to one side.

"I'm going." I crawled to the vault door, not trusting myself to get to my feet. Once there, I leaned against it and closed my eyes again, as if still too dizzy to stand. It wasn't far from the truth.

"Stop stalling," a Selkid squawked, flippering my shoulder.

I pulled myself up. I tried the combination, but I must have made a mistake. I shook my head and tried again.

"Come on, Patch," Grim said. "Hand it over."

Finally, the vault door opened. I stepped aside, leaning against the bulkhead for support.

"There! There's the case!" Grim reached in and hefted it out.

"Open it," the Selkid's translator screeched.

"I can't," Grim said. "I don't have the combination."

"Then what good are you?" The Selkid fired his stunner, point-blank, straight into Grim's unprotected torso.

Grim slammed back into the bulkhead. My nerves winced reflexively.

"I saw that coming," I muttered, not moving.

"Any rhollium in there?" The shooter examined the crates in the vault. "Santerro brandy? Not bad! Take these cases to my cabin," his translator barked. Two mercenaries holstered their weapons, loosed the lashings, and picked up a couple of the heavy crates.

"You two"—he pointed—"lock down the helm and guns. Put the crew in one of the holds." From a sheath at his back, he took out a knife the size of my forearm and began to pry open the case's clasp.

There was a flurry at the door.

"*No!*" Balan lurched into the nearest intruder, slamming him against the bulkhead. The Selkid crumpled like a broken toy, his dorsal spine kinked at its most vulnerable junction. Balan snatched up the dead man's pistol.

Zing! Balan's stun shot hit the man holding the tablet's case. The impact shoved the mercenary's body back against the crates of supplies and sent the case flying.

As I dived for the fallen stunner, the two intruders carrying brandy dropped the crates and reached for their pistols.

They weren't fast enough. One fell back heavily, reeling from the blast from Balan's stunner. The other shot off a stun blast as he dived for cover, but missed his target.

I had to use both hands and a knee to aim the heavy Selkid weapon, but I didn't miss. With a *zing*, my shot sent the intruder out of the cargo hold, back into his own ship.

Sounds of more fighting came from the main part of the ship.

Balan picked up the tablet's case and held it triumphantly. He shouted in Gavoran, "For the Sages!"

A blast from a stun rifle slammed Balan to the deck. His head hit the bulkhead with a sickening crunch. The artifact's case careened across the hold.

I hurried to Balan. His eyes were fixed, but I still heard rasping breaths. Blood seeped from the back of his head.

Another form came through the blasted hatch from the harrier. Still kneeling over Balan, I lifted the awkward Selkid weapon, hoping it had had time to recharge.

Before I had a chance to fire, a shot came from behind me, dropping the intruder.

"Patch, are you injured?" It was Danto, a pistol in each hand.

"Not much," I said, "but Balan's in a bad way. They blasted the cargo hatch—we'll need to seal off the hold." Grim began to stir and moan.

"Where is the relic?" Danto asked.

I had almost forgotten about it. I pointed to the case. "Take Balan. There's an armed drone ready to launch, caught between the ships."

"Release the drone and bring the relic." Danto let loose another shot at the hatch, and then dragged Balan into the passage.

I hit the launch lever to release the drone. There was nowhere for it to go, it was trapped between the harrier and *Sparrowhawk*. If the drone detonated in that position, it would rip the cargo hold apart.

I grabbed the relic's case and sent another shot zinging toward the hatch, in case more of the harrier's crew were thinking of boarding. Danto returned, dragging a mercenary's inert form, and threw it onto the deck. Danto took Grimbold by the collar and pulled him out of the cargo hold. I was right behind.

As soon as we were clear of the door, I sealed off the hold. *Damn*. All the good brandy, locked in a hold with a blasted hatch. Even if the Rampart crew didn't take it, if the hold was opened to space, it wouldn't survive exposure to the cold.

And the biggest piece of the synthreactor—it might be a long time before we could dig it out of a frozen bulkhead.

"What about Balan?" I asked, kneeling beside his body.

"He is gone," Danto said. "Secure the ship. I must return to the guns."

Danto was right. The young Gavoran was no longer breathing. My eyes teared up. Balan had died bravely, for no purpose whatsoever.

"All right there, Patch?" Hiram asked through the com.

"Fine, thanks." I looked around. My abs were still cramping, but I could live with that. The bloodied body of another mercenary lay in the passageway.

I picked up all the loose stunners and went to the engine room. "Kojo? Archer? Are you hurt?"

Archer was doing something complicated to the propulsion unit. He looked up, his face white. "Are you all right, Patch?"

"We can handle this," Kojo said. "Make sure no intruders are aboard."

I went to the salon. "Rachel? Mzee Lyden? Mya? Jamila?"

"We are here," Lyden said weakly. "We are uninjured." They were still secured in their seats. Jamila looked ill, Lyden austere, like a tortured saint.

Mya's eyes were wide with excitement. "Is it over? Are they gone?"

The viewscreens showed *Kamok*, far off, spewing debris from a hull breach.

"Not yet."

Flashes lit the ether and staccato shocks shook *Sparrow*. Danto was firing on the harrier, trying to get it to break its hold.

"Can I help?" Rachel asked.

"Can you handle a stunner?"

She smiled. "Certainly."

I handed Rachel a stun pistol. "Jamila, Mya," I said, "help Rachel. If there are any mercenaries still alive on the ship, put them somewhere and keep them there. Shoot them if you have to."

"Me?" Mya cried.

I climbed to the wheelhouse.

"Good to see you," Hiram muttered as I slipped into the watch station.

"There's an armed drone caught between *Sparrow* and the harrier. Can we break away from the harrier?"

"No. I'm trying to stay behind it. Let the burzing slugs stay between us and that Rampart predator."

Kamok, still firing, was slowly falling behind. The harrier gripping *Sparrow* was trying to rotate, trying to drag *Sparrow* into a position where *Kamok*'s guns could reach her, while Hiram was using our damaged propulsion to stay behind the harrier.

I took the drone controls. "How bad is our propulsion hit?" I asked.

"Bad enough." Hiram concentrated on maneuvering the ship.

"Try rocking the ship, if you can, so I can free up the drone."

"Could damage the hull."

"The cargo hold hatch is already breached," I said.

Hiram grunted and put the ship into a shimmy. I worked the drone controls this way and that. "Got it!"

The drone drifted free. I kept it in the shadow of *Sparrow*, out of sight of the harrier.

"Work it over toward its underbelly," Hiram said in a tight voice.

"Not its grapplers?"

"Not with our hatch breached. Blow its exhaust ports and smoke the filthy vermin out."

I smiled. Trust Hiram to know the best way to capture a ship.

I let the drone crawl toward the harrier's lower hull until its imager showed me the exhaust ports. Danto continued firing sporadically, keeping the harrier's attention.

"Brace!" I hit the detonation signal.

The drone blew with a silent shimmer of light on the underside of the harrier. The harrier bucked, pulling *Sparrowhawk* with it.

At first, it seemed like the maneuver didn't help. *Sparrow* was still held fast by the harrier's grapplers, Danto firing at the harrier.

Kamok, in the distance, had drifted out of range.

The seconds stretched out, as I tried to think of something else to do.

"*Sparrowhawk*, this is the harrier *Mock One*. We surrender. Our ship is in distress. Get us out of here!"

CHAPTER 21

Damages

ONE GOOD THING about having a Corridor Patrol officer aboard: Danto knew how to take prisoners. Two members of the harrier's crew had been on their vessel when smoke had driven them to surrender. Danto quickly put them in improvised restraints and shoved them into his cabin with their two injured crewmates, with Jamila guarding the door.

Kamok had been severely damaged—Hiram said he didn't expect she would make it to a port. Even so, he stayed on alert in the wheelhouse.

I kissed the bald spot on the top of his head. "That's for the fancy sailing."

"Humph. Reminded me of the old days. I'm too old now for this sort of excitement."

I had nothing worse than some deep bruising and a sore skull. Kojo and Archer both had bandaged arms, burned when they had manually shut down the damaged propulsion cylinders. Kojo was haggard, face pinched with pain and worry. Archer was too tired to twitch.

I made a silent prayer of thanks that they weren't hurt worse. "What about the others?" I asked Rachel.

She leaned against the bulkhead with a weary sigh. "Jamila and Mya are shaken but unhurt. Grimbold will recover from the stun blast if he takes it easy for a day or two. It's Lyden who concerns me—the stress was rough on her. She's resting now. I don't think she's in immediate danger, but she's not as strong as she pretends."

As for *Sparrow*, she was still coupled to the harrier. There had been some leakage in the link between the ships, but Archer had jumped in with a can of Prestoseal—no enviro suit, no helmet—and patched the leaks before Kojo had a chance to tell him not to. His quick action kept the hold from exposure to space, saving Rachel's equipment as well as the good brandy.

In the cargo hold, I re-secured the equipment that had jostled loose and put the cases of brandy and the tablet's case back in the vault. I didn't need to open the case to know the relic wasn't in it. *I didn't get to say goodbye*, I thought, and then laughed at my own foolishness.

Most important, the bulkhead cache seemed to be intact. In my prayer of gratitude to the ancestors, I made sure to include thanks that the synthreactor hadn't been blown to bits.

Over the next day, we rested in shifts between doing the most necessary tasks. While Danto interrogated the prisoners, Kojo and Archer went between the two ships, reviewing the damage, sealing rips in the hull, and scavenging the harrier to make the most urgent repairs.

"They hit a propulsion port," Kojo said. "The pressure built up and damaged our engines. Thank Zub the harrier's a Selkid vessel—we can switch one of her couplings for ours."

The harrier's engine room was coated with oily dust. I resolved to be more tolerant of Archer's fastidious habits. Archer himself was on the deck, on his back, struggling one-handed with a wrench as big as a boot.

"Here, let me," I said. "You'll hurt your arm worse and then where will we be?"

"Dead in the ether with a bunch of religious fanatics for company," Archer grumbled. "Not too much different than where we are now." He scooched over and let me wrangle the giant wrench onto the lug. Together, we freed the coupling.

Crammed together with Archer under the coupling housing, a wave of tiredness and relief swept over me. I laid my head on his shoulder. "I'm glad you weren't hurt worse."

"We make a good team," he said softly.

Kojo's face peered under the housing. "Did you two fall asleep in there? Get moving."

Back in *Sparrow*, Archer wriggled into the engine's battered innards while Kojo and I provided the brawn to pull out the bent flanges of our damaged coupling.

When we were done, Kojo straightened, his face drawn with pain and exhaustion. "Time to head to port. No sense trying to go on, with Balan gone. We can tow the harrier, sell it for scrap."

"What about Rampart and the Cartel? What will they think of us blasting one of their ships out of the ether?"

Kojo slumped. "We'll blame the Patrol, tell everyone Danto forced us to fight. It's the best we can hope for."

One task that couldn't wait was disposing of the bodies of Balan and the two mercenaries. As soon as Rachel certified the deaths, I wheeled a corpse-filled handcart to the waste recycler. I flushed the mercenaries first— it would take days for *Sparrow* to digest so much organic material.

Danto walked in as I straightened Balan's head to a more natural position.

"I'm sorry about Balan," I said. I hadn't liked him, but he'd deserved a better end than mad obsession and a blast from a brigand's weapon. "He died bravely."

"As befits a son of Wind Clan." Danto knelt to adjust the sheet I'd used for a shroud. "You also showed great courage in facing the pirates."

Scarcely realizing what I was doing, I threw my arms around his neck and hugged him. "And you," I said, my voice muffled in his shoulder. I loosened my grip and said more clearly, "You saved us all, killing the intruders. Thank you."

You're a fool, I told myself. *Dirty and sweaty and just a mess. He must think you're ridiculous.*

Danto pulled my arms away with his familiar irritation. "I am a sergeant of the Patrol. That is what I am trained to do."

"Of course." I looked down in embarrassment. "But I'm grateful all the same."

"Oh, there you are, Danto." Kojo leaned against the door, Archer close behind him. "When you're able to break away, I'd like to talk about returning to port."

How long had he and Archer been standing there?

"In the salon, then," Danto said.

As we followed Kojo and Danto, Archer hissed at me, "Patch, for a smart person, sometimes you can be really thick."

Lyden and Mya sat at the salon table with Rachel and Jamila. Kojo, looking battered, sat on a couch with Archer and Hiram. I stood at the door, where I could keep an eye on Danto's cabin, which housed the prisoners—two Rampart Terrans crammed in with two big Selkids from the Cartel. I hoped they were very cramped.

Grimbold reclined on an easy chair, still sore from the stunblast he'd caught.

I wasn't sympathetic. "You had your fancy stunner. Why the Zub didn't you use it against the people trying to hijack our ship?"

"Why didn't you just give them the damned artifact?" he snapped back. "I understand Danto getting all combative—his career would never survive a surrender. But I expected you and Kojo would put saving all our lives ahead of saving the burzing piece of rock."

The starless ether seemed to press on us, stifling in its featureless murk.

"Ship's status?" Danto asked.

Kojo rubbed his chin. "We can cannibalize the harrier to make *Sparrowhawk* operational, at least long enough to get to Kriti. We need to leave the harrier intact and with enough supplies to put the prisoners back in her—we just can't manage four hostiles on top of our current passengers and crew." Kojo glanced over at Archer. "And our engineer is injured."

"Weapons," Archer said, jiggling a foot.

"Right. We've used a lot of the ammunition for the guns and we've used a third of the drones and grenades. If we have to defend ourselves again, we'll be in a bad way." Kojo turned to the old pilot. "Hiram?"

"The aft scanner's down."

"Right. Patch?"

"The water recycler was damaged."

"Medical supplies are depleted," Rachel added.

Danto paced. "I have already relayed a message to the Patrol requesting assistance and prisoner transport; however, it will take at least two days for my messages to reach a beacon and be relayed to the Patrol, and at least five more days for a Patrol cruiser to come to our assistance."

The prospect of hanging around for a week was not appealing. "How did they know where to find us?" I asked.

"According to the prisoners," Danto replied, "the Rampart mercenaries first tried to obtain the artifact on the route to Oakdale, acting on Grimbold's information. The Selkid Trading Cartel learned of this attack in some way." He looked questioningly at Kojo.

Kojo stirred, trying to find a comfortable position. "Automatic distress signal sent by the transponder to the nearest beacon, with the specs of the attacker. That's the whole purpose—to discourage attacks on Cartel-sanctioned ships."

"Indeed," Danto said. "In any case, the Cartel learned of the attack on *Sparrowhawk* and traced the brigands to Rampart. They were extremely displeased that Rampart had dared to target a Cartel member in a Selkid sector."

Kojo nodded. "I'll bet they were. Makes them look bad."

Danto resumed his pacing. "Apparently, as a defense, Rampart Militech told the Cartel the artifact has tremendous commercial value and offered to share the profits in exchange for the Cartel's help in obtaining it. Cartel members reported *Sparrowhawk* had been seen in Corridor Patrol custody at the sector 102 checkpoint." He stared at Grimbold. "Somehow, the Cartel also learned we were bound for Kriti."

"Not from me!" Grim shot a resentful look at Danto. "I never heard of Kriti until after you dragooned me and cut off all communication. You tore my whole kit apart, looking for a transmitter. As if I would even know what our position is, in this endless corner of nowhere."

Danto loomed menacingly. "It must have been you. No one else could have revealed our destination to the Cartel."

With a twinkle in her eye, Rachel said, "I'm afraid that's not true, Sergeant. The Settlement Authority was buzzing with rumors of an expedition into the Gloom near Kriti—I heard about it from three different people before I volunteered for the assignment. I have no doubt the Selkid delegates would have let the Cartel know."

All heads swiveled to Lyden. Perfectly calm, she said, "Everyone I spoke to in the Authority promised to keep the matter confidential."

Great—*we'd* been sequestered and threatened with detention to keep us quiet, while *she'd* been lobbying every department in the Settlement Authority to launch the expedition.

Kojo closed his eyes and shook his head. "Amateurs."

Danto must have been thinking the same—he looked like he'd swallowed a lemon. "I see. In any case, Rampart and the

Cartel sent a joint mission to find *Sparrowhawk* and bring back the artifact."

A price on our heads. I felt sick.

Kojo put his head in his hands and moaned. "Well, the mission's over now. Without Balan, there's no point in looking for Nakana. And Kriti's out of the question—Rampart's ships might be there, gunning for *Sparrow*. We need to repair *Sparrow* and hide out until the Patrol can get here and protect us."

And salvage what we could. I was recalculating. Kojo was right: We couldn't risk Kriti, but if we dropped the synthreactor pieces somewhere near the jump gate, that might be close enough to satisfy Ordalo. Then, if we could convince the Cartel and Rampart Militech that *Sparrow* had resisted *Kamok* only because we'd been commandeered by the Patrol, we had a slim chance of explaining our way out of trouble. But first, we had to get the passengers out of the way long enough to resurrect the synthreactor bits from their hiding places and get them into drones, and somehow launch the drones without being detected.

Jamila turned to Lyden. "I know this is a tragic setback, but we must make the best of it. Perhaps another expedition, better equipped, after we've had time to study the artifact."

"We must go on," Lyden said. "I shall be our guide. I will form the blood link with the relic, and Suriel will speak to me."

Rachel's brow knitted. "That wouldn't be wise. We know the effects of linking with the relic are both debilitating and addictive. If anyone else attempts it, it should be someone with the strength to withstand the stress."

"Please, Mzee," Mya said. "Your health is too important to risk. I will do it."

Kojo tensed. "That's a bad idea," he said. "*Sparrow* is damaged and there may be more Rampart hunters out there. We should sail back to the gate and jump to somewhere safe." Maybe he'd expected to get to Kriti before anyone opened the relic's case and realized it was gone, but he hadn't counted on Balan being killed.

"We shall go on," Lyden pronounced. "If it is too dangerous to travel to Kriti, the danger can be avoided by proceeding directly to Nakana."

Danto looked thoughtful. "We can spend the next seven days until the Patrol arrives in hiding, dodging brigands as the captain suggests, or spend it usefully, searching for Nakana."

"No!" Jamila looked around wildly for support. "This is madness. We need to go back for supplies. For repairs."

Danto shook his head. "We have taken enough equipment and supplies from the harrier to last several weeks. If we are within range of Nakana, then Mzee Lyden is right. Going there directly is the best course." He looked at Mya and Lyden. "If the College of Religion can provide the location of Nakana, the Corridor Patrol will complete our mission."

Kojo stood to face Danto. "Sorry, Sergeant. For the safety of the ship, crew, and passengers, the mission ends now. I'm invoking the captain's prerogative, as provided in the charter terms, to terminate the voyage because of adverse conditions. You've done your job and called for help. Now we'll head back to the jump gate to meet the Patrol."

Danto bridled. "This mission is under *my* command."

"But *I* command the ship and crew," Kojo insisted.

Gavoran and Terran confronted one another, their faces so dissimilar but wearing identically stubborn expressions. I tensed, ready to jump in to protect Kojo.

Lyden spoke up. "Sergeant Danto, bring the relic here."

"Why?" Kojo asked, a little too quickly.

"Yes," Jamila added, "why? You know it's dangerous. Shouldn't you leave it where it is?"

Lyden narrowed her eyes. "Bring it."

Damn! Lyden must have realized the relic had gone silent.

Danto considered for a moment, then went.

Ancestors. Nothing to do but see how it played out.

Jamila darted a glance to Kojo, who gazed fixedly at the darkness beyond the viewscreen. Lyden watched the two of them speculatively. Rachel frowned, deep in thought.

Danto returned with the heavy case and laid it on the table. He opened it.

Nestled inside were three bottles of excellent Santerro brandy.

CHAPTER 22

Captain's prerogative

MYA MOANED. Lyden moved her lips as if in prayer.

Danto turned to me and snarled, "Where is the relic?"

My mouth dropped open. "How should *I* know?"

Archer sat up, eyes startled wide.

Danto switched his gaze to Kojo. "Captain, the artifact was in your custody. Where is it?"

Kojo snorted. "Crap. The dingus was in *your* custody, Sergeant. The burzing thing is of no concern to me or my crew."

"It was of concern to Balan," Grim said. "Maybe he took it."

"Probably Grimbold," Hiram offered. "Ask him a few more questions, why don't you?"

Danto looked ready to interrogate Grim again, but Lyden snapped, "Don't be a fool, Sergeant. She took it. Professor Patil. No doubt with the assistance of Captain Babatunji. And"—she closed her eyes again—"I believe it is no longer on this ship."

"Captain." Danto loomed over Kojo.

"Sergeant, allow me." Lyden gazed at Jamila the way a snake looks at a mouse. "Professor Patil, you and I have not always agreed on research methods, particularly where the relic is concerned. Nevertheless, I have always respected your learning and your skill. I quite understand that the relic has an allure that is difficult to resist. Although you do not believe in its sacred nature, its effect on Deprata and Balan must surely convince you that persons exposed to it, including yourself, may be vulnerable to impulses they cannot fully control."

Jamila looked down, twisting her fingers in her lap.

Damn. Ten to one she was going to blame Kojo.

Lyden leaned forward. "It was you who took the relic from the dig and it is obvious you have taken it again. I ask you now to think of your reputation, your fine career, your future! Tell us about it now and I promise, no more will be said. I will attribute this lapse to the influence of the relic. But if you persist in lying, then..."

Jamila looked up, with actual tears in her eyes. "It was Kojo who took it from the case. He sent it off the ship in a drone. We were planning to go back later and find it. To save it for posterity! For science!" She began to weep, decorously. "I just couldn't bear the thought of it disappearing into some temple on Gavora without having the opportunity to study it fully!"

Grim gaped at Jamila. "You lying...*you* were double-crossing *me*?"

Danto's eyes hadn't left Kojo. "The radiation field," he said.

"Yeah," Kojo admitted. "I ordered Hiram to make a little diversion, and the radiation masked the trail of the drone leaving."

Kojo looked around the room solemnly. "Listen. I don't know about angels or demons or any of that religious stuff, but Lyden's right about one thing. That tablet has a bad influence on the people around it. I saw what it was doing to Balan, and it scared the hell out of me. I could even see my sister acting a little—different." He didn't look at me. "Captain's prerogative. As captain, I judged that *thing* to be a danger to my ship and my crew and I got it off the ship. Any decent captain would do the same. And, by the way," Kojo added, "Patch knew nothing about it."

Danto looked at us both coldly. "I do not believe that. She is the owner of this vessel."

"Oh, you should believe him." I fixed a steely eye on my brother. "Going behind my back is becoming a habit with Kojo."

"You fools!" Mya cried. "Suriel will freeze in the cold of space! You have killed him!"

"Relax," Kojo said. "The drones are designed to transport delicate cargo. It's shielded from radiation and its internal environment will be stable for at least a year."

"We must return and find it," Mya said.

Kojo shrugged. "Why? This ship's in no shape for exploring. Leave the drone where it is for now. You can recover it when you're ready. Launch a real expedition. Let the rest of us get on with our lives."

"Suppose the Cartel backtracks and finds it?" Grim asked. "It's worth a fortune and we won't see a dracham!"

"Or perhaps you will sell its location for a price," Danto said coldly. "None of you can be trusted. Up to now, I have been patient, but I cannot tolerate interference with the mission. Captain Babatunji, you will return to the radiation field and recover the relic, and if it is possible to do so, we will use it to locate Nakana."

Kojo turned his good hand palm up. "Let's be reasonable, Sergeant. I promise, I'll take you back to the radiation field and help to recover the burzing tablet, even though I personally would prefer to blast it into the nearest star. I'll swear under oath to help you recover it and not interfere with what you want to do with it—*after* the Patrol escorts *Sparrowhawk* to someplace safe for rest and repairs. We'll leave the extra passengers behind. There's no need for secrecy anymore—the Cartel and Rampart already know as much as we do about the location of Nakana. And without passengers, Patch doesn't need to be here, either."

"Kojo!" I cried.

Kojo ignored me. "I'm asking this both as a captain, to protect my ship and crew, and as a man, to protect my sister."

Archer nodded vigorously.

"*My* ship and crew," I said. "Kojo, I'm going with you."

Danto looked ready to explode. "That is enough!" He thumped his chest. "All of you will do as I order. Do you think I know nothing about you? All of you?"

He pointed an accusing finger at Grim. "Grimbold, do you think I know nothing about your criminal history?"

Grim moved his hand as if brushing away a fly. "Youthful indiscretion."

"Jamila Patil, do you think I know nothing about rumors of antiquities being pilfered from your sites and sold to private collectors?"

Jamila smiled nervously.

"And Kojo Babatunji."

Kojo widened his eyes as if interested to know what Danto would say.

"This ship has been apprehended four times carrying illegal cargo, and its captain has escaped with only minor penalties due to the illicit influence of the Selkid Cartel."

Hiram nudged Archer with a grin.

"None of which happened since I've been captain," Kojo said.

Danto glared at Kojo. "Nevertheless, if proven, this ship and everything in it could be impounded. You, Captain, are dangerously prone to gambling—your debts are a matter of record. And your crew? A drunken pilot and a mentally deficient engineer!"

I jumped up. "Danto! Stop this!"

He switched his glare to me. "And Patch," he snarled. "Did you think I was fooled by your claim to be a member of Sand Clan?"

Archer had flinched at Danto's insult. Now he stopped twitching entirely.

"Watch your mouth, Danto," Kojo warned.

Lyden's eyes narrowed.

Danto thundered on. "I saw the scar on your arm the night we were in the radiation field. You are a runaway slave—a heretic and a renegade. A traitor to your masters, to your clan, and to the Sages. Once we return to Gavoran sectors, it will take only a moment to find your true background and your clan will deal with you as you deserve." Loathing filled his voice. "The lying mongrel spawn of a heretic slave and a Terran outlaw."

Archer stood up, his fist clenched. Hiram grabbed his arm, with a quiet, "Steady on."

I stepped up to Danto, eye to eye. "Yes, my mother was a slave. She was kind and honest, a woman of great courage, who suffered and died because she smuggled me to freedom. Palermo granted me asylum and has registered me as a free Terran. I have every right to live as I choose. And if I'm a mongrel, Sergeant, then so are you."

"Quite right," Rachel chirped. "Well said."

Danto looked around the tattered salon, a commander left with extremely unpromising troops. "None of you can be trusted," he said, "and yet we are trapped in this situation. I will do as I must to complete this mission and there will be no further complaints or objections until it is done."

"We have rights," Grim began.

"No longer. Captain Babatunji, you have claimed captain's prerogative under the charter terms. But the terms of your contract must yield to the law. Under the emergency powers of the Corridor Patrol, I hereby commandeer this vessel and assume the captaincy. You and your crew are now under my command."

"Can he do that?" Jamila hissed.

His face taut with anger, Kojo nodded.

"Jamila Patil and Grimbold…"

"We're civilians," Grim said.

"You are under suspicion of theft. You can cooperate with my orders or you will be transferred to the harrier with the prisoners and taken into custody by the Corridor Patrol. Choose now."

"Great choice," Grim muttered, "since they already shot me." He shrugged. "I'm in."

Jamila made a twisted smile. "Happy to cooperate, *Captain* Danto."

"Good." Danto looked around again. "Any trouble will be dealt with swiftly and severely. Dr. Fiori." He turned to Rachel, who had been watching with interest.

"All of this is moot if we don't repair the ship," Rachel said. "May I suggest that repairs should be the first order of business? Until then, our survival is at risk."

Danto took a deep breath. "You are correct, Dr. Fiori. Kojo, you and the crew will use whatever you can from the harrier to make repairs and resupply this ship."

"Maybe I'm too mentally deficient," Archer muttered.

Danto ignored him. "Disable the harrier's engines, but leave the hull sufficiently intact to house the prisoners for a period of twelve days. That will allow ample time for the Patrol to find them."

"And what happens if we meet another Rampart ship?" Kojo asked warily. "*Kamok* will have relayed a message to any other Cartel escort ships in the sector. They'll be looking for us."

"All the more reason to proceed directly to Nakana," Danto said. "The company is dismissed. Proceed with repairs. Tomorrow we return to the radiation field."

As the group began to drift away, Archer took a step toward Danto, his face set and hand balled into a fist. "You have no right to talk to Patch that way."

I hurried to step between them. "I've been called worse." Danto could probably break Archer's slender body with one hand.

Danto took a breath. "I...I apologize for the harshness of my words. I should not have yielded to the stress of the situation."

I spun to face him. "For your words, Sergeant? Not for your judgment of my character?"

Danto lowered his impressive brow. "All Gavorans, even slaves, revere honor and loyalty. When a slave abandons her duty, she rejects the very basis of our society."

"There's no honor in slavery," I said. "None of us can change the circumstances of our birth, but it's the choices we make afterward that count. And as for Archer, he's smarter, braver, and more loyal than any of your damn Corridor Patrol."

I stomped out, leaving both Danto and Archer gaping in surprise.

That evening, I found a few minutes to speak to Kojo in the wheelhouse. The view through the canopy was bleak—black punctuated by dark gray. The scanner showed the blip of the distant jump gate and flashed warnings about the beginning of the Gloom.

After making sure all the com nodes were off, I said, "I'm worried."

"You're worried? I'm goddamn petrified."

"What were you thinking? You knew Balan would insist on seeing the tablet."

Kojo waved a hand tiredly. "I thought Rachel would keep him tranqed until we got to Kriti. Once we got near enough, I was going to engineer a fire in the hold and pretend to dump the case along with some of the cargo. The mission would be over, we'd go to Kriti, get rid of all these burzing passengers, and finally take care of our other business."

"And go back later to pick up the relic for Jamila?"

He flashed his *you-caught-me* grin. "Well, maybe. If the price was good."

"Looks like Ordalo will have to wait."

"It can't wait long. We've only got thirty-one days left to deliver." Kojo ran a hand through his hair. "Zub's beard! I don't know whether to hope we find Nakana quick, or that we don't find it at all. Either way, we need to get moving and end this burzing mission. At this point, I'd shake hands with Zub himself if it would get us back to our old life."

That night, I had trouble falling asleep. Maybe the relic had been a whining annoyance, but now it was gone, I missed it.

Lying mongrel spawn of a heretic slave and a Terran outlaw. I'd been an idiot for letting myself dream of Danto. My mother was braver than any Star Clan warrior, and Papa was cannier.

Once, when I was small, the landlord's daughter had called me a big, ugly half-breed. Papa had taken me on his lap and soothed my anger and told me I had a strength and beauty different from any other. He'd promised we would go together to faraway worlds to meet all the different peoples of the universe—a promise he'd kept.

I got up and took out my mother's old scarf. *Thank you, Mother, for my life and my freedom. Thank you, Papa, for raising me to be strong and proud.*

CHAPTER 23

Hunger and obsession

WE DID WELL out of the harrier. We left enough power mods in the crippled ship to run her environmental system until the Patrol could take custody of the four prisoners; otherwise, we scavenged everything we could detach. We took a very nice military-grade scanner to replace our damaged one, and Archer used the harrier's spare parts to bring the water recycler back into operation. Her stores replenished our power modules and ammunition, and the food from her pantry even lent some variety to our meals—although with Balan's seat glaringly vacant, no one had much appetite. Medical supplies were still low—there had been a lot of injuries to the survivors of both ships, and we had to leave a med kit with the harrier's crew.

I hoped the Patrol wouldn't delay in picking them up.

Rachel wasted no time in moving her things into Balan's cabin. When I let Kojo know, he brightened at the thought that Jamila had a private cabin again.

Finally, after a brief memorial service for Balan and some much-needed rest, *Sparrow*'s engines roared back to life and the harrier's hulk faded into the ether.

A day later, we were back in the dim, swirling ether of the radiation field.

Kojo peered at the scanner. "Zub's pitchfork. It should be here."

The atmosphere in the wheelhouse was tense with Kojo, Danto, and me crowded into it. I'd been trying to avoid Danto, but as we neared the radiation field, I'd begun to hear the voice of the relic.

This time, the bloodstone's call was more urgent, more insistent.

Hunger.

I stood behind Kojo and rested my hands on his shoulders.

At the watch station, Danto tapped his fingers against the console. "If you really hoped to recover the relic," he said, "sending it into a radiation field was a poor plan."

Kojo made tiny adjustments to our heading. "I didn't care about the relic. Still don't. It's Jamila who wanted to retrieve it, I just wanted to get it off the ship."

I squeezed Kojo's left shoulder.

He shook his head at the scanner. "Not in this area. Let's move a little to port." He adjusted the position of *Sparrowhawk*. I squeezed his shoulder again, and he moved farther to port.

Ping.

"Ah," Danto said, "there's the drone's signal."

"Standard recovery, Patch," Kojo said.

"Right." I headed for the cargo hold.

Hunger. Give me your blood.

In the cargo hold, I concentrated on maneuvering the drone into the hold, matching the drone's movement to the ship's and painstakingly working it into the airlock. Rachel stayed at my side, checking my neural scans. The Gavs, even Danto, had wanted to crowd into the hold while I brought the relic back, but Rachel had locked them out, saying she needed to concentrate on monitoring the readouts.

Blood.

"You hear it, don't you?" Rachel asked softly.

I nodded. "It's hungry."

My hands shook on the drone controls. The drone was in position, but I hesitated to lock it down. "Once we got close to the radiation field, I heard it calling. I even knew where it was. Was that what Balan and Deprata felt, at the dig site?"

"Probably."

"Am I going loony, like they did? Will all of us get that way? Maybe we should just attach a couple of grenades to it and blast it to pieces."

Rachel put a hand on my shoulder. "Terrans aren't affected, and I promise, I'll watch out for you. As long as you don't touch it, I think you'll be all right. Remember, Balan and Deprata were religious scholars, already primed to believe they were receiving messages from their gods. If you'll keep your

Terran skepticism in mind, it will help you resist whatever you hear from the relic."

I nodded. Terran skepticism. *Remember, it lies.* "And what if Lyden's right? Suppose the bloodstone really is the voice of the Sages calling?"

"If it is, I'll gladly hand the relic over to the Gavoran priesthood," she said. "Otherwise, it's going to the Settlement Authority for study."

A couple of clicks and the recovery was complete, the drone locked in. I opened the airlock inner doors and dragged the drone into the launch bay.

"Don't open it yet," Rachel said. "First, sit quietly and let me monitor you. What is it telling you?"

Suriel called to me, *Give me a taste of your blood.*

"It's asking for blood. I feel an…an urge to touch the relic." I pictured a slit in my skin, the blood welling up.

Rachel opened the drone's payload hatch and used clamps to retrieve the tablet. The relic seemed to pulse in frustration, as if willing the tools to slip.

"Be careful," I said. "It wants blood."

"Mmm." Rachel carefully placed the tablet in the metal case.

I let out a breath as the case muted the relic's call.

Rachel said, "Done. Let's go join the others. By the way, I've changed the combination. As of now, I'm the only one who can open the vault."

Lyden paced the salon. "This interference by Terran atheists must not continue. The relic is a gift of the Sages. Suriel *calls* to me. You must give me access to the relic now."

Danto nodded. "Dr. Fiori, there is little point in delay. The goal of the mission is to find Nakana. We can only do so if one of us communes with the relic."

"I should like to make some further observations first," Rachel said.

"Observations?" Lyden's voice rose in pitch and decibels. "What use are your observations when your science blinds you to the deeper truths of the spirit? I pity you Terrans. You seem to have no souls at all."

"Lyden, I understand your wanting to make a connection with Suriel," Rachel said carefully, "however, I'm not convinced you are the best person. We all saw the strain the relic put on Balan. Mya is younger and stronger…"

Lyden looked pinched, as if she hadn't been eating well. Even Mya's pretty face was beginning to look hollow-eyed.

Blood.

For the first time, I felt sorry for Lyden and Mya. Everywhere I went on the ship, whatever I was doing, I heard the voice of the relic asking to be fed. It was more than an annoyance now—it was a desire, a deep longing. The full-bloods must be hearing its demands far more clearly.

Mya clasped her hands together. "Please, Mzee Lyden. Do not risk yourself. Allow me to carry this burden."

"Nonsense," Lyden replied. "I am perfectly well. As the leader of the religious delegation on this mission, it is my duty to link with Suriel."

Mya laid a hand on Lyden's thin shoulder. "Then you should prepare yourself, Mzee Lyden. Perhaps we could spend some time in prayer and meditation."

Rachel drummed her fingers on the table thoughtfully. "An excellent idea. The medical monitors are showing increased neural activity among the Gavorans, and I want to observe this for a few hours before anyone interacts with the relic. Get some rest, Lyden, and eat something. In the morning you can connect with the relic."

Lyden glared at Rachel. "Very well. But tomorrow, I must join with Suriel. Mya, come."

She swept out, nearly running down Kojo as he was coming into the salon.

Mya paused to speak to us—looking primarily to Danto. "Soon. Soon we will reach Nakana. It will be the beginning of a new age, a new dedication to the will of the Sages. And *we* will be the ones to bring it to our people." With great dignity, she followed Lyden, and Danto trailed behind.

Kojo nudged Rachel. "Mya and Lyden are both going around the bend. Maybe you should tranq them."

Rachel gazed after the Gavs. "The relic is affecting them, but they're not mad. Gavorans take it for granted that spirits exist and speak to us—their entire religion is based on it. It's we Terrans who can't perceive their reality, like being color-blind or deaf to sounds other animals hear clearly."

Kojo harrumphed and jerked his head toward the command deck. I followed him up the companionway to the wardroom.

When he shut the door behind me, he asked, "Why is Rachel dragging her feet? We need to get this mission over with. I'm tired of being pushed around in our own ship."

"Rachel's just being careful. Lyden's awfully old to be making a blood sacrifice."

"She's loopy."

"The relic is getting to her, Mya too. It's hungry."

He darted a look at me. "What about you?"

"I'm fine." Except for hearing the damn thing every waking hour and in my dreams. "Ouch."

Tinker jumped down—she'd bit my hand to let me know I'd been holding her too tight. A tiny speck of blood welled up, and I sucked it off.

That night, I tossed and turned in my bunk, kept awake by a hunger that had nothing to do with food.

"Sometimes, Patch, you can't step aside. Sometimes you need to stand up and fight."

Papa stood next to my bunk, in his old jacket, his brow furrowed.

"Papa?"

"Be strong," he said. "Be brave." Then he was gone.

I got up, too restless to sleep. *Be strong, be brave?* What help was that? Papa was gone to the afterlife, what did he know about mystical relics and yearning for something out of reach?

Blood.

I dressed and left my cabin.

All was quiet. No sound from the command deck. All the doors to the salon and passenger cabins were closed.

I crept down the aft steps. The cargo hold was empty, the flickering lights of Rachel's monitors providing a soft glow.

The bulkhead that hid the synthreactor seemed undisturbed, the lube I'd used to cover the screws was still smeared with my thumbprint.

Touch me. Give me blood.

I sat on the deck beside the vault door.

Speak to me, Suriel, I thought. *Balan is gone. Tell me, where is Nakana?*

Blood.

I relaxed and let the thoughts come in. Swirls of yellow and red filled my mind, and a deep hunger. I yearned to open the vault, unlock the case, and stroke the relic. I ached to hold it to my breast, to open my vein, and bathe the relic in my blood.

"Patch?" A hand touched my shoulder.

Rachel knelt beside me. "Why are you here?"

"I...I want to feed Suriel." Tears filled my eyes. "Can't I be the one to feed it?"

"No." She eased me up and away from the vault. "Go back to bed now. Believe me, you don't want to be the one to feed it."

As she walked me toward the passage, I said, "It's strange, isn't it? Up until Kojo sent it away, it was just an annoyance, wanting to go home. Now, the relic wants my blood. And I want to, like it's my duty. Would it be so bad if I did?"

Rachel's brows drew together. "I think it might be very bad. Get some sleep, Patch. And you mustn't come to the cargo hold again without me."

She shut the door behind me, locking herself in the hold with her equipment—and Suriel.

Sometime during the night, Lyden died.

CHAPTER 24

Blood sacrifice

THE PASSENGERS had been picking at breakfast in the salon, casting baleful looks at the somber vista from the viewscreens. Danto sat next to Mya, his glances and her fleeting touches telling a tale of their growing closeness. Kojo munched stolidly on a rusk, Jamila frowned at her tea, Grim sat at a console with an endless game of solitaire.

I pushed around some porridge, feeling slow and tetchy after a night with little sleep.

Rachel walked in with her usual briskness. "I'm afraid I have sad news. Lyden has died."

Mya gasped. Kojo's head jerked up, his eyes wide.

"I'm sorry," Rachel said. "Her medical sensor ceased registering during the night. I went just now to check on the reason and found her."

Danto rose immediately. "Show me. The rest of you, stay here."

Mya buried her face in her hands. I went to her side. "Oh, Mya. I'm so sorry."

"So am I." Jamila joined us and took Mya's hand. "I had no idea she was ill."

"Nor did I," Mya sniffed. "Of course, she is—was—quite elderly. Perhaps the strain of this voyage, of preparing to commune with Suriel..."

Grim snorted. Jamila shot him an angry look.

"What? It *is* a little fortuitous, isn't it?" Grim asked. "I mean, my condolences and all that, but maybe now we can do something sensible. Sell the artifact to Rampart Militech or Galactic Conglomerate—let them take the risks of finding Nakana, and the trouble of arguing with the Neanderthals."

"You are hateful," Mya spat out. "How can you think of your own selfish interests while our beloved Lyden lies still warm?"

"She may be your beloved Lyden," Grim muttered, "but she's certainly not mine."

"Shut up, Grim," Kojo said.

Danto strode into the salon frowning ferociously. "Dr. Fiori is attempting to determine the cause of death. In the meantime, each of you will give me a detailed statement of your movements during the night."

"That's insulting," Jamila said. "None of us wished her harm."

Kojo shrugged. "I slept until midnight, when I went on helm duty."

"I was in bed, asleep." Jamila folded her arms and leaned against the bulkhead. "Alone."

"Crap," Grim said. "You know where I was—I'm stuck sharing a cabin with you."

Danto shook his head. "I made a security check during the night. You could have left the cabin during that time."

Grim scowled. "I didn't. You can't pin anything on me."

"I stayed in the salon, to give Lyden solitude, as she requested." Mya nodded toward the couch. "It was not comfortable, and I did not sleep well."

"I spent most of the night in my cabin," I said, "but I did get up around midnight to check on things."

"What things?" Danto asked.

"I often do rounds at night. Last night, I went to the hold to be sure Rachel's equipment was secure. She was up, too, and I spoke to her."

Danto looked at us all, clearly unsatisfied.

"Look," Kojo said. "You're a Patrol officer. It's natural that you should suspect something fishy—that's your job. But most likely the lady just expired naturally. The real question is what we do now."

"There is no question," Mya replied. "We must continue. We owe this to Lyden."

"That's the third Gavoran death associated with the artifact," Jamila said. "Surely, Sergeant, you can see the danger. It should be turned over to Terran scientists who can handle it safely."

"Professor Patil, you are speaking nonsense." Danto paced the threadbare carpet. "Deprata was a suicide and Balan was a victim of pirates. Lyden had not even touched the bloodstone. Whatever caused her death, it was not the relic."

"Heart failure," Rachel said as she walked in. "Lyden suffered a head injury and experienced a heart attack."

"A head injury?" Mya exclaimed. "How?"

"She fell against the bunk. When I found her, she was on the floor, dressed in nightclothes. She may have experienced chest pain and fell when she tried to rise from bed. Or she may have fallen, and the shock or pain brought on the heart attack. Either alone could have been fatal." Rachel poured herself some tea.

I sighed in relief. "So it was a natural death, then, or accidental."

"Maybe she was pushed," Grim suggested.

Rachel shook her head. "I've checked everyone's sensor readings. She was alone in her stateroom when she suffered the attack, shortly after midnight. Mya, you visited her earlier. Did she complain of pain or dizziness?"

Mya twisted her fingers together. "She seemed as usual. I offered again to take the burden from her, but she became quite sharp with me. I thought it best to leave her alone."

"That is true," Danto said. "Mya was upset by Lyden's insistence, and we spoke in the salon."

Kojo looked to Mya with sympathy. "I'm sorry, Mya. We can hold a memorial whenever you wish."

"We should probably hold off on doing anything with the relic," Jamila said. "Out of respect."

"No!" Mya grasped Danto's arm. "Sergeant Danto, Rachel." She looked desperately from one to the other. "You agreed to allow access to the relic today. We must do it, today! Now! Suriel calls—I must go to it. I must feed it."

Rachel paused only a moment. "Yes, I can see the urge is becoming stronger. Very well, but I will require controlled conditions."

Mya sat in the chair next to the isolation unit. She looked thin and flushed but smiled as if she were meeting her lover. Danto paced nearby. I sat to the side by the drone control console.

My insides roiled, not from hunger, but from envy and fear. I wanted—needed—to touch the artifact, to sate the longing gnawing at my mind. My own desires disturbed and disgusted me.

Rachel used heavy gloves to open the case and place the relic within the isolation chamber. I had a brief glimpse of the tablet's underside—channels etched into the stone in converging spirals.

"Ahh!" Immediately, Mya reached both hands toward it, but Rachel closed the chamber over the dark stone. Rachel spent a minute looking at the readouts.

I felt seething frustration from the relic, mirrored by the yearning on Mya's face.

I wished it was me sitting in the chair. I wished it very much.

"All right," Rachel said. "You may insert your arm."

Mya put her arm into the port and let her hand caress the relic. Under her hand, the stone seemed to pulse in somber colors.

Blood! Blood!

To see her stroking the relic made me burn with envy. I should have turned away, but instead I stared in fascination. I ached to be there beside Mya, to touch the cool stone, to let my blood cover its surface.

Mya's eyes were closed. She whispered, "A knife."

"Step back, please," Rachel said. Danto and I both had strained forward.

Rachel manipulated the instrument arm within the chamber. A mechanical appendage tipped with a scalpel appeared. "Stay still," Rachel murmured.

The scalpel made a short cut on Mya's forearm. Crimson drops slid to the surface of the relic.

Mya gasped. "More," she whispered. "More."

Blood gathered in the channels, forming thin streams that disappeared into the relic like rain flowing on sand.

A sigh of satisfaction crept into my mind. The hunger and desire began to abate.

Rachel scanned the readouts. After a few more drops, Rachel withdrew the scalpel, letting the flow of blood slow.

Mya remained seated, eyes closed, caressing the relic with her bloody hand. "Show me," she whispered. "Show me Nakana."

Her eyes snapped open, gazing at something far beyond the dingy walls of the cargo hold.

"Green plants," she said. "Fields and hills covered with grass. Animals! Water and warmth."

I saw them, too, and felt the warm humidity.

Mya breathed a long, satisfied sigh. "Thank you, Suriel. I am blessed, truly blessed."

"Where?" Danto demanded. "Look, Mya, here are the star charts. This is our position, between the gateway and Kriti. Where is Nakana?"

"It's beautiful," Mya sighed. "And we are close now. I will show the way."

Rachel glanced at me.

I shook my head. I had no clue where to go.

Home. Peace and joy.

The relic's familiar whine was a welcome relief after a night of gnawing bloodlust. I hadn't realized how keyed up I'd been with the relic's demand to feed.

From the helm, I listened on the com while in the salon Hiram, Danto, and Kojo pored over the charts and their skimpy information about this area of space. Rachel was with them to keep the peace and Mya was there because she wouldn't leave Danto's side.

Hiram drawled, "Sergeant, we done everything you said. Patched up *Sparrow*, put up with your insults, come back for that bloody bit of rock. But now you're talkin' about going into the Gloom. There ain't no beacons in there, lad, and no one to come rescue us if anything happens. I was counting on starting out closer to Kriti, using one of the known trails as far as we could."

Danto's voice was testy, "But look at the location Mya has specified—it is closer to our current position than to Kriti. If we go directly from here, we could be at the target location in only four days."

Hiram grunted. "That Nakana planet ain't gonna have a big welcome sign on it, lad. How are we gonna know if we're in the right place?"

"I will know it." Mya's voice was high and clipped. Her desperation to feed the relic had changed to a high-strung giddiness. "Suriel has shown it to me. The system is a double star, hidden in a cloud."

Rachel's light voice asked, "Hiram, if we do as Danto suggests and travel into the Gloom from here, will we be able to find our way back again?"

"Huh. That Selkid scanner we scavenged is pretty damn good." He paused. "If we stick to the quiet places and leave a trail of breadcrumbs behind, the locators can guide us back out."

Kojo spoke up. "We wouldn't be able to stay long—we don't know the conditions inside the Gloom and locators can drift."

"Agreed," Danto said. "If we do not find a system such as Mya has described within two days of reaching the target location, we will proceed to Kriti. By then, the Patrol post on Kriti will have received my reports and be ready to escort *Sparrowhawk* to safety."

Kojo said thoughtfully, "Four days in, two days to explore. Survey would take how long?"

"No more than three days," Rachel said.

"Then twelve days to retrace our steps and move on to Kriti. That puts us in port within twenty-one days on the outside, sooner if there's nothing there." I could almost see Kojo rubbing his chin.

That timeline would have us in Kriti at least seven days prior to our deadline. With luck, we could deploy drones with the synthreactor before then—once the flyby was finished, both Danto and Rachel would be more relaxed and less vigilant. We could drop the synthreactor somewhere at the edge of the Gloom—before the Patrol escort could find us—

and find some way to relay its location to Ordalo. It would be tight, but it could work.

"Rachel, you've been awful quiet," Kojo said. "The survey will be under your supervision. What do you think?"

After a pause, Rachel said, "I've had a great deal to think about. If we have sufficient supplies to go to this cloud, locate Nakana, and conduct up to three days of survey before preceding to Kriti, then I agree we should go ahead. If there *is* a Sage planet out there, we need to place it under Settlement Authority control as soon as possible."

"Very well," Danto said. "We will proceed immediately."

Rachel's voice became brisk. "Danto, I want your word of honor as a Patrol officer that you will break off the mission and return to Kriti, if and when I tell you to do so. The Settlement Authority's orders include getting this mission's personnel back alive and in good health. We've already lost two members. I must have your assurance that you will comply if, in my judgment, the risk is too great."

"If you insist, Dr. Fiori. You have my word of honor."

"Thank you."

"Sorry, Hiram," Kojo said. "The drinks and the companionship will have to wait awhile longer."

CHAPTER 25

The Gloom

UNRELIEVED, IMPENETRABLE darkness. To call the view through the canopy "black" was an understatement. *Black* is a pigment with a character of its own, or simply a space empty of light. The Gloom was altogether different, a vast field of energy and subatomic particles that sucked the light out of the sky, that absorbed every stray photon and reflected nothing. Simply being there made me think of death—not the friendly, rousing afterlife I'd been raised to believe in, but a total obliteration of a soul.

I stationed myself at the drone console in the cargo hold with a raft of lightweight locator buoys ready for deployment. The locator was the type we used for in-transit deliveries to be picked up by our customers—just the sort of thing we'd use for the synthreactor.

"Buoy one launched," I reported. The locator gave a single ping, then went silent—it would only activate again in response to a coded hail. We wanted no bounty hunters following us.

"Ready, then," Kojo responded. "Archer, full engines."

With a hiccup from the grav generator and a roar from the engines, *Sparrow* turned her back on the last vestiges of light and headed into the Gloom.

It was eerie, sailing through the Gloom. No visible cues, no ping of beacons, it was hard to sense whether we were progressing at all. Our scanner marked currents and grav fluctuations, but Hiram and Kojo stayed in a quiet channel and kept track of distance traveled by pinging the buoys. We dropped buoys at intervals of two hours, never more than a third of our scanner range—I wanted to be damn sure we could find our way out if one of the locators drifted away or stopped working.

After dropping the first two buoys, I took the time to deal with Lyden's remains. Rachel had left Lyden in her nightclothes, lying peacefully on the deck. In death, her face was shrunken and bony. She looked much older than I had realized, as if she'd held onto vibrancy by force of will.

I wrapped her in a sheet and placed her next to the recycling chute and invited the subdued passengers in for a memorial. Pale and swaying, Mya rushed through the long Sage prayers. With a final *May the blessings of the Sages be with you*, she turned to Danto. He wrapped his long arms around her and she sobbed into his chest.

Out of a sense of delicacy, I waited until Mya and Danto left to flush Lyden's corpse down the recycling chute. From there, I went to the engine room. I'd had very little time to visit with Archer lately, but to be honest, he'd been so testy I'd been avoiding him.

"How are the engines?" I asked.

"Fine. Much better than before the upgrades." He squirted some Prestofreeze into the power mod coolers.

"And your arm?"

"Oh." He flexed it. "A little twinge now and then. It's fine, really."

"Good." I racked my mind for something else neutral to talk about.

He flapped his hands. "I'm sorry, Patch. About Lyden."

"Lyden? Well, it's too bad she passed away while on our ship, but"—I shrugged—"she wasn't particularly dear to me. In fact, I didn't like her much."

"I thought, with you spending so much time with her and the other Gavs—well, I thought maybe you were starting to have second thoughts." He carefully wiped the excess lube from the port and closed it.

"What do you mean? Second thoughts about what?"

"About being more Terran than Gav. I mean, it would be understandable, if you thought you would be more at home with them." He shifted from foot to foot.

I looked at him with astonishment. "Archer, are you out of your mind? More at home? With *them*? How could you even think that?"

"Well, you hardly ever come to talk to me anymore. And what with getting to know Balan and Danto...After all, it's not like we're really married."

"You're space-happy. You didn't know Papa long, but he was the best father I could have had. So, no, I don't have any 'second thoughts' and it will be a hot day in black space before I want to live with Gavorans." I took a breath. "And if you think I'm being too friendly with the passengers, well, that's not any of your business, is it? Like you said, it's not like we're really married."

After a day in the Gloom, dinner was quiet. The darkened viewscreens seemed to oppress the passengers' mood—except for Mya.

"A beautiful world awaits us," she said dreamily. "I saw it. I saw it all. An atmosphere rich in water vapor. Huge seas, extending over vast portions of the surface. Land masses covered with vegetation. Lush, grassy plains and mountains covered with green plants. And wildlife!" It was strange, hearing Mya describe the place I had seen in a dream. "Herds of herbivores, covered with fur. All imbued with a feeling of peace and satisfaction."

Peace and joy.

Mya smiled around the room, her flushed face and twitching hands at odds with her serene expression.

"Sounds nice," Kojo said.

Grim snorted. "Sounds unreal. Where are the Sages, then? Where's all the technology? There must be cities, right? Transportation? Factories and farms? People?"

Mya's smile faltered. "I saw nothing like that. Perhaps the Sages have evolved beyond the need for such things."

"If it *is* a Sage planet, Mya," Jamila said gently, "most likely the Sages left it long ago." Mya's face stiffened. Jamila added hurriedly, "But even if we find only a single ruined structure, the boon to our knowledge will be invaluable. It will be one of the greatest finds of our lifetime."

I asked Rachel if she'd learned any more about the relic.

"I did," she said. "It's been very helpful to be able to see Mya's interaction with the relic. Her blood not only triggered additional telepathic signals, she also received a high dose of endorphins. Essentially, the relic gave her an emotional reward for cooperating. Its effect is similar to an addictive intoxicant."

"It makes you high?" Grim asked.

"Essentially, yes."

"Ha! I knew Balan was strung out!"

Mya bridled. "You are belittling a profound religious experience."

"Not at all," Rachel said. "Your experience is real, as verified by my instruments. I am merely examining the mechanism."

"Suriel is a person, not technology," Mya insisted.

"If there is a life form within the relic," Rachel said, "the relic must contain some very sophisticated technology to keep it alive. I don't want to use a high-intensity imager to learn more—that might harm the relic. But there is one thing that would help—a control subject. In fact, you, Grim."

Grim started. "Me? For what?"

"To donate a little blood."

"You must be joking!"

"It's necessary. By having a Terran interact with the relic, I'll have a control sample and I can understand more about the relic's process."

"But why me?"

Rachel smiled. "Because *you* are the least essential Terran on the ship."

Later that evening, after dropping another locator, I joined Kojo in the wheelhouse. We'd had little time to talk since entering the Gloom.

"What's wrong with Tinker?" I asked. The cat was restless, meowing, twining between my ankles as if she wanted attention, but refusing to stay put when I lifted her to my lap.

"I don't know," Kojo said. "Hiram said she was getting spooked by the Gloom. How are we doing on breadcrumbs?" He was keeping *Sparrow* on a route that twisted between hazards, sticking to the calmest channels so that the locators would remain in position long enough to get us out.

"The locators? Fine, we have plenty. Why are they called *breadcrumbs*?"

"In the old story, two children who were taken into the woods left a trail of breadcrumbs to find their way home."

"Did they? Find their way home?"

Kojo rubbed his chin. "Come to think of it, no. Birds ate the breadcrumbs."

That didn't sound encouraging.

Meow, meow. Tinker clawed at the hem of my pants.

"Maybe she's hungry," I said.

"She's got food, I checked. If she keeps this up, I'm going to lock her in one of the holds."

Looking through the canopy was like looking into a mirror in a dark room—you might imagine anything and convince yourself it was real. If a stray current pushed the locators out of place, we would spend the last days of our lives looking into that void.

I rubbed my arms and shivered, even though the environmental controls were working fine. "Do you think we made the right decision, coming into the Gloom like this instead of going to Kriti?"

Kojo clucked his tongue. "You can't look back, Patch. Once you've dealt the cards, you've got to play your hand."

Rachel entered. Tinker immediately abandoned my ankles and rubbed up against Rachel's.

"Do you need something?" Kojo asked, frowning. We tried to keep the command deck off limits to passengers.

"Just a few words with you and Patch." Rachel reached down to stroke Tinker. "Oh, dear. Gone into heat already, kitty?"

Meow, meow.

Kojo laughed. "Is that all it is? She's definitely getting locked in a hold."

Rachel smiled. "You should do something permanent or eventually you'll be up to your ears in kittens. Patch, what are you hearing from Suriel?"

"No more hunger. Promises of peace and joy on Nakana. Constant urging for us to go there, just like when you first came aboard."

She nodded. "Good. However, I wanted to let you know that what I see on the monitors is a slow, steady rise in telepathic activity. In your case, a small but consistent increase from when I first came aboard."

Kojo eyed me worriedly. "What about Mya?"

"Mya's neural activity is greatly enhanced since she connected with the relic. I'm more concerned about Danto. His neural activity has also increased in the last few days, and it continues to grow more pronounced."

I felt cold. "Danto? I didn't know he was hearing the relic."

Kojo rubbed his jaw. "That's not good. Is that why you made him promise to end the mission on your decision?" I asked.

"Yes, and I expect him to honor his word. But I wanted to make you both aware, in case action is needed."

Kojo nodded. "Thanks, Rachel."

Rachel paused. "This may not be significant, but he's also moved into the stateroom with Mya."

Kojo's eyebrows jumped. "*That* was fast."

"I'm not surprised," I said. "Mya's been interested in him from the beginning, maybe just because he's different, but Lyden disapproved. Now she's free to do what she wants."

"Exactly. No more need to meet in the salon at midnight."

Rachel gave Tinker's ears a final scratch, saying, "Good kitty."

Meow, meow.

After Rachel left, Kojo lifted his eyebrows at me.

"Don't look at me," I said. "I don't know anything about cats."

"Not Tinker, idiot. Danto."

I shrugged. "I can't read Danto at all. He certainly doesn't confide in me. Mya's welcome to him, I'll stick to kitties."

"Good. And, uh…put Tinker somewhere, will you? She's driving me crazy."

Sleep was hard to come by, only in part because of Tinker yowling in the small stores hold under my cabin. My dreams were filled with the constant urging—badgering—to get to Nakana. A place of peace, joy and beauty. Warm, humid air, and hairy beasts munching the meadows. I was sick of the place and I'd never even been there.

I liked cities, I told myself. Small ports with lots of cargo for an independent hauler. Kriti would be nice. Rich ale and lots of interesting people, if you're not picky about legalities. No doubt Hiram would find a dozen old friends and I would hear a few stories about Papa. I fell asleep thinking of Papa, but woke in a damp sweat, with the smell of grass and wet fur lingering from my dreams.

Grimbold squirmed in the chair next to the isolation unit, where Mya had sat two days before. He eyed the isolation box. Within it, the bloodstone rested like a coiled cobra.

"Do I have a choice about this?" Grim asked, stroking his mustache.

Rachel smiled. "Your cooperation is much appreciated and will be duly noted in any future criminal proceedings."

"Not funny."

"Insert your arm into the isolation unit. You're not squeamish about a little blood, are you? After your distinguished military career?"

He gave her a sidelong look. "You know about that, eh?"

Grim stuck his arm into the isolation chamber port. Rachel sealed the opening tightly around his arm. Within the chamber, the relic's deep colors seemed to pulse with anticipation.

"Wow. It really is something, isn't it?" Grim gazed at the relic.

Rachel dictated her actions as the readings adjusted to Grim's presence. "Place your hand on the relic, please." More readings. Finally, Rachel used the manipulators to make an incision. Blood dripped into the relic's channels and was quickly absorbed. Rachel waited, staring at the instruments.

Grim frowned. "Is that it? Isn't it supposed to make me feel high or something?"

"Apparently not." Rachel kept her attention on the instruments. "Just stay still, please."

She made him stay for nearly an hour before releasing him with thanks.

"Those gorillas are crazy," he mumbled. "Map, my ass. It's just a burzing rock."

I slammed the door behind him.

Rachel asked, "How was this time different?"

"The relic was quiet," I said. "This time it wasn't hungry. There was a little pause when it tasted the blood, but then it went back to the usual longing for home. Like it didn't care about Grimbold's blood."

Rachel nodded. "It already has what it wants."

Over a dinner of Selkid rations—not bad if you added enough piri piri sauce—Rachel discussed her findings.

"There definitely is a living being within the relic. It breathes in oxygen and releases carbon dioxide, as we do, but in minute amounts. It seems to derive nutrition from blood—after giving it blood today, there was an increased rate of respiration, indicating a digestion process. That process must be very efficient—there was very little waste produced."

"Fine," Grim said. "It breathes and eats and craps. Big deal."

Rachel went on. "More interesting is the difference in neural activity. Mya's blood was followed by increased telepathic activity in her, and only in her. Grim's blood did not elicit any increase in neural activity in anyone."

"Suriel only reveals the truth to the worthy," Mya said.

"Thanks very much, I'm sure," Grim muttered.

"The point," Rachel said, "is that the relic generates several distinct types of expressive telepathic communications, and the relic's response seems to discriminate between individuals based on their blood."

"Maybe it just wasn't hungry," Kojo offered. "Maybe it only needs one dose."

"Perhaps," Rachel said, "but remember that it interacted with both Deprata and Balan. I suspect the relic uses the blood both for nutrition and to test blood factors. If the blood has whatever factor it's looking for, the relic directs a specific telepathic message directed only to the donor, probably through the donor's physical contact with the relic. That specific message is the direction to the planet we have been calling Nakana, coupled with an intense desire to go there, as well as the psychological reward of stimulation of pleasure centers in the brain. A very potent mix."

Jamila dabbed her napkin to her lips. "Fascinating. I knew there would be a logical explanation, once Terran science could examine the artifact."

Mya looked toward the ceiling. "Science tells us only the irrelevant mechanics. The truth is spiritual."

"One final thing." Rachel swept the group with a serious gaze. "Whether because of the passage of time or the proximity to Nakana, in the past few days there's been a measurable increase in the strength of the telepathic activity. Mya, Danto, and Patch"—she looked at each of us—"you should know that you may be at risk. The telepathic activity may become very strong. Perhaps even hard to resist."

The Terrans, even Kojo, looked at us with concern.

"I'm fine," I said.

"That is nonsense," Danto said. "I am completely in control."

Mya said stirred restlessly. "As soon as we reach Nakana, everything will be fine. We are getting close."

CHAPTER 26

Lightning and thunder

WE GATHERED in the salon, glued to the viewscreens. For the first time in days, there was something to see. Amid the inky blackness, the deep gray smudge might have been just a trick on eyes desperate for some relief from the dark. But according to the scanner, the gray smudge was a debris cloud, the remains of some cosmic explosion that drove ether, energy, and matter from the center to form a thin-skinned bubble. And within the bubble was a double-star system with at least five planets.

"I'll be burzed," Kojo said. "We found it."

"I don't believe it!" Jamila peered into the screens, her eyes alight.

It was the middle of the fourth day traveling the Gloom, just as Mya had predicted. She had spent that last day pacing nonstop, rubbing her hands and talking to herself—or maybe to the relic, it was hard to tell. Now she lounged, eyes closed and a smug smile on her face. "Nakana. We have found it."

Home!

I felt drawn to the viewscreen as well, eager to see what the debris cloud hid. Just rocks and ruins? Or a lush, grassy planet of busy cities and unimaginable technology? Somehow I felt sure that life and intelligence awaited us.

"The cloud may be the result of a nova," Danto said, "caused by an exchange of matter between the suns. Or perhaps a weapon. But once we pass through the outer layer of dust and debris, there should be little obstruction."

The viewscreen didn't change, but the scanner flashed, warning of energy discharges and turbulence. A second later, a low frequency wave shook *Sparrow*.

Rachel's gaze was fixed on the scanner, her brows drawn together. "Kojo, those energy surges…"

Kojo peered at the scanner. "Those discharges are generated by the cloud, like a wall of lightning and thunder and hail the size of mountains. The cloud is still expanding, so we'd have to fight the outward thrust. It will be like pushing through a thicket."

He looked around the gathered company. "If we try to penetrate the cloud, it will be a terrible strain on the ship and the crew. We could be risking the ship. We've found the system. Maybe that's enough for this expedition."

Kojo looked at me, one eyebrow lifted, and touched the back of his hand.

He was giving us a chance to back out of the mission and proceed to Kriti. I'd checked the scanner myself—Kojo was exaggerating the risk. It would be a rough ride, but *Sparrow* could handle the strain.

I touched my ear. "I think we can do it."

Kojo blinked. He must have expected me to take the quick way out. But we'd come so far—I was sure we could make it all the way. And maybe we *would* find a planet full of advanced tech. The ship and crew who discovered *that* would never have to scrape the bottom of the barrel for jobs nobody else wanted.

Kojo grinned. "All right, then. Everybody get some rest. It will be like trying to take a boat up a set of rapids—once we begin, we can't stop until we're on the other side."

In the cargo hold, Tinker wound around my legs as I helped Rachel secure her equipment for a rough passage into the cloud. I picked up the cat and cuddled her for a moment, glad to have her back to normal.

While Rachel was absorbed with her equipment, I strolled over to the cache bulkhead. A glance showed the screwheads still covered with smears of lube, no sign of disturbance. Relieved, I returned to Rachel's side.

Rachel checked her monitors, then drew me close. "I'm concerned about Danto," she said quietly. "His neural activity has increased. He's been monitoring all of us through the com nodes whenever he can."

I shrugged. "He's in command now. Monitoring operations is normal."

"I want you and Kojo to be armed at all times."

That seemed an overreaction, but if the Settlement Authority commander wanted to mutiny against the Patrol sergeant who'd taken command of my ship, I was happy to go along.

Rachel checked her monitors. Danto was with Mya in the salon, and Kojo was in the engine room. She pointed to the magazine and said out loud, "Thank you, Patch. Just finish that one and you can go."

I withdrew two stun pistols and placed them under my jacket with a smile. "Call if you need more help, Rachel."

In the engine room, Kojo manned the engines while Archer slept. "They're running well," Kojo said. "Straight up, the upgrades are sweet. Everything copacetic with Rachel?"

"She has some concerns about going into the cloud." I nodded toward the com node as I handed him one of the pistols.

"I see." He tucked the pistol into his belt and drew his jacket over it. "Anything specific?"

"Just general nervousness. You should probably stay close to the wheelhouse, in case Hiram needs a break."

Kojo smiled wolfishly. "That's just what I was planning to do."

A few hours later, *Sparrow* faced the energy wall like a minnow facing a tsunami. It was beautiful—and terrifying. The haze swirled in deepest reds and dark oranges, sparking with energy charges that arced across vast distances.

I had doubled the lashings on Rachel's equipment and the stores in the cargo hold and padded the food and dishes in the galley before locking everything down.

Rachel passed out anti-nausea patches, and tranqs for those who weren't operating the ship. Even Tinker got a tiny dose of tranquilizer. She mewed unhappily as I added extra padding to her snug retreat.

Rachel and Mya opted to watch from the salon. Jamila said she couldn't bear to watch and went to her cabin. Grim said he could die in bed more comfortably than in the salon.

Kojo came on the com. "Time to man your posts."

Kojo and Hiram would both be needed in the wheelhouse. Danto went to man the guns, to fire concussives if we needed to blast debris out of our path.

I went to help Archer. We'd need power mods, lots of them.

"This is going to be a rough ride," I warned him. He bounced and vibrated for a moment then, without warning, he gathered me into a big hug.

"Look," he said, "whatever happens, I'm glad we're married. I'm going to look after you." He kissed me, right on the lips.

"You're daft," I said. "And I can take care of myself." But I held onto him a little longer than strictly necessary. It had been a very nice kiss, and his arms around me were warm and comfortable, his vibration no more than a kitten's purr.

Hiram's voice came over the com. "Fire up those engines, lad. Time to earn your keep."

Sparrow started delicately, approaching the energy wall slowly. At Kojo's command, we ramped up power and began to push against the wall.

"Build up power slowly," Kojo ordered. "We don't want to shoot through and be out of control on the other side of the energy field." Archer and I brought more and more power to bear.

Kojo called, "Danto? How about a little help?"

A concussive charge shot from our bow and detonated against the wall. The disruption was enough to pierce the first layer.

Sparrow leaped forward and began to penetrate the cloud.

Over the next few hours, we pushed into the wall of energy. Like a man trying to run up an icy hill, *Sparrow* thrust forward, slipped back, and thrust forward again, as the straining engines forced the ship deeper into the cloud. With every bit of headway, we triggered plasma bursts and energy pulses that rattled and shook the ship like a terrier shaking a rat. Even with the nausea medication, Archer and the passengers emptied their stomachs in the first two minutes, and even I was sick. The pressure waves made my head ache terribly.

I was glad Lyden, frail as she was, had been spared this.

Shearing forces made *Sparrowhawk* shimmy sideways again, throwing me off my feet as I exchanged a spent power mod for a fresh one.

Kojo called back, "More power!"

Archer, face sweaty and breathing heavily, shook his head and called into the com, "Kojo, we're at max. We can't keep this up. We need the escape thrusters!"

"Do it!" Kojo called. "Quarter bore, two seconds. Punch it!"

Archer whispered, "Yes." As soon as I strapped in, he hit the thrusters.

Suddenly we were rushing through violent waves of energy, like a sailboat heading into a monsoon. Energy pulses enveloped *Sparrow* as our passage disrupted charged pockets of ions. The thrusters shoved the ship forward, deeper and deeper, as Hiram and Kojo used the maneuvering rockets to keep the ship heading into the energy waves. Any attempt to turn would be suicidal.

Each time a power mod reached the point of exhaustion, I unstrapped long enough to shove another into its place. After the fourth, Archer eyed our dwindling supply of mods, looking ill. He whispered under his breath, "This is not good."

I glanced at the viewscreen. It was darker ahead, the haze of dust thinning. Certainly, there were fewer flashes of igniting plasma. Were we nearing the end of the energy wall?

"Reverse!" Kojo yelled. "Slow! Slow! Danto, guns!"

We shunted power away from the rear propulsion toward the retro rockets. *Sparrow* slewed sickeningly.

Then the waves were gone.

We shot into a field of debris. Huge boulders loomed up, much too fast.

Danto fired blasts that arced before us, thrusting rocks out of our way. We decelerated further, trying to match the orbit of the debris.

"Good!" Kojo said. "Steady on engines! Let Hiram take it."

Sparrowhawk danced and pirouetted among stones the size of huts, rocks the size of mountains. Hiram kept us moving just a little faster than the debris around us, plying the maneuvering rockets to dodge obstructions as beautifully as a floating leaf swirls past rocks. Each time a congregation of rubble approached, Danto would fire a concussive to push it aside. It was lovely.

Gradually, the debris thinned.

We were inside the bubble. At the distant center, huge twin suns revolved around one another in tight formation, energy streaming between them. And somewhere below us, closer to the center, was Nakana.

"There's nothing here," Kojo said.

We were all at breakfast the next day, in high orbit around the fifth planet, the one Mya claimed was Nakana.

"It's exactly as Mya said it would be—habitable conditions, three moons. We've scanned everything around, but there's nothing here. No ships, no communications, no energy readings. Nothing. It gives me the creeps."

"There will be signs," Mya said, drowsily stirring her porridge. Rachel had given her a mild tranq. "The Sages will have left signs for us."

I was drowsy myself—the night had brought me little rest. My dreams had been filled with huge, shaggy beasts that grazed on lush grasses. I'd rested my hand against the flank of one and felt its slow pulse. The warmth of its body had enveloped me. I'd breathed in the scent of grass and fur and dung. I'd known it was a dream, but I'd wanted it to be real, to be there touching the warm body, so badly that I'd ached with longing.

Home. Take me home.

"The society that once lived here may have left or died out," Jamila said. "It happens. People become dissatisfied and move on, or suffer a catastrophic war or natural disaster. We'll know more when we send a probe to look under the clouds."

"Or maybe this is the wrong place and Nakana is somewhere else," Grim grumped. "Or maybe Nakana's just a myth, nowhere at all."

"There will be traces," Jamila said. "Cities, roads. We'll see them."

"Certainly, from here in orbit, Nakana looks habitable," Rachel agreed, munching some toast. "The scanners indicate that the lower atmosphere is rich in nitrogen and has enough oxygen to be breathable. The cloud cover is composed largely of water vapor. There are large seas encircling major land masses and abundant vegetation."

Mya said, "As soon as we land, we will be able to see for ourselves."

Kojo and I froze. "Land?" I said. "On an unexplored planet?"

"Yes!" Mya clapped her hands.

"No," Rachel said. "We will *not* land. That would far exceed our mission and would contravene protocol for planetary exploration. This mission is for a preliminary survey only, to be conducted from orbit. I'll deploy the first three drones this morning." She laid her hand over Mya's. "I'm sorry, Mya. There will be other expeditions to explore more extensively."

"But we must," Mya whispered. "Suriel wants us to go there."

Rachel had me install some sort of sterilization unit into the drone launch airlock. One by one, we deployed three survey drones into low orbits after they'd been treated with a lightning-bright blue light to kill any microbes on their surface. Soon, Rachel was directing me where to send the drones. Data and images began to pour in.

Mya, Danto, and Jamila gathered around Rachel's screens and monitors, fascinated by the new world. When Grim and even Archer complained that they wanted to see, too, I routed the images to all the ship's viewscreens and opened the com nodes so everyone could join the fun.

Rachel kept up a running commentary. "The air temperatures are within habitable ranges, particularly in the equatorial regions...The seas show significant temperature gradations, indicating strong circulating currents...Look, there, a mountain range. Lovely. There's ice or snow on the tops. Indecent amounts of vegetation. It's fueling the atmosphere with oxygen, and helping to sequester the carbon."

"Paradise," Mya said.

Jamila pointed. "There, you can see lines on the land on the lidar images. They could be roads, hidden under the vegetation cover."

"Perhaps," Rachel said, "perhaps. Hmm. Significant carbon dioxide. It could be volcanic activity, but it could indicate living beings that breathe in oxygen and breathe out carbon dioxide like we do."

"Or industrial activity?" Jamila asked.

"No sign of that. On Earth, insect life and herbivores are responsible for vast amounts of carbon dioxide in the atmosphere."

"It is all as Suriel revealed," Mya affirmed. "A lovely, fertile land, filled with life!"

And in fact, Rachel soon pointed out a forest of moving specks. "Animal life," she said. "Big, like elephants. They're moving across the plains. Some sort of migration."

"It's beautiful," I said. "Look at the animals, and all that water. It could be a new ag planet—you could feed billions of people from here."

We spent all day at it. As I brought a tray of samosas into the cargo hold, Jamila turned, eyes shining, and exclaimed, "A city! We found a city!"

The lidar imager showed sprawling heaps of boulders covered by shrubs. "It doesn't look much like a city," I said.

Jamila tapped the screen. "See these straight lines radiating out?" There were six of them, glowing faintly, stretching toward the sea, the mountains, and the plains. "Those are roads, converging on the ruins of a population center. I can't wait to write this up." She glowed with anticipation of professional accolades. "We've done it! We've discovered Nakana."

I leaned against the bulkhead and closed my eyes while Jamila and Rachel parsed through the images, speculated about mining processes, water production, and atmospheric modification. A wave of longing swept over me.

Home. Take me home.

"We must go home," Mya said.

Jamila laughed. "Home? We just got here."

"Nakana," Mya replied. "Nakana is our home, our true home. We must go to the surface."

Rachel said lightly, "Sorry. Not this trip."

Danto stepped close enough to loom over Rachel. "Dr. Fiori, your caution is unwarranted. Everything the relic has revealed to Balan and Mya has proved true. As a scientist, that should be enough to convince you the voice of the relic can be trusted. We are called to Nakana—we must go."

Rachel smiled sadly. "I will certainly include my observations about the trustworthiness of the relic in my report. However, like you, Danto, I have my orders. We will not land."

Danto stiffened, his face rigid.

Rachel raised her voice to address the group. "Patch and I need to get ready for the next step, a probe to gather samples from the surface. That requires isolation procedures, so all of you will have to leave. Danto, will you remain a minute, and ask Kojo to join us? I want to discuss the drone recovery process."

As Danto went to the com node, Rachel whispered to me, "Be ready."

I drifted a few steps back so I was behind Danto.

Kojo walked in with a cheery, "Hello, Rachel. What's up?"

As Danto turned to Kojo, it took only a moment for Rachel to pull out a stun pistol.

"Sergeant Danto," she said formally, "you are relieved of command."

"You? You have no right!" By that time, Kojo and I had our stunners trained on him. "Do you dare to commit mutiny?"

Rachel replied, "Commander, remember? As medical officer on this ship and under the regulations of the Settlement Authority, I am instructing Captain Babatunji to relieve you on the grounds that you are medically unfit for command. I am now taking control of the mission."

Kojo bared his wolf grin and took away Danto's stunner. "Good. This simplifies things."

"I'm sorry, Sergeant," Rachel said. "I take this action only out of an abundance of caution. It's clear from the neural sensor that you've been hearing the voice of the relic. Proximity to the planet seems to be causing a spike in telepathic activity."

Danto glowered. "You will regret this."

Rachel—half Danto's size and twice his age—didn't back down. With some kindness, she said, "I have no choice. It's clear the relic has affected some of your actions. I promise you, you'll be commended for your leadership in bringing this mission to a successful conclusion. I have no doubt your actions—*all* your actions—have been, to your best judgment, necessary for the success of the mission, and I will include that statement in my report. However, the danger of your judgment being impaired by the relic is too great. You are relieved."

Rachel put away her stunner. "Kojo, I am formally instructing you to continue with the mission to complete the preliminary survey, which will take only another day. After that, we'll return to the nearest convenient port."

"No!" Danto cried. "We must go to the surface! The mission requires it! The Sages require it!"

"Your word of honor, Sergeant," Rachel reminded him. "You gave your word of honor to leave when I said you must."

"My duty to the Sages supersedes my personal honor!"

"I know," Rachel said gently. "That's why I must relieve you of command."

CHAPTER 27

Nakana

SPARROWHAWK WAS OURS again. I felt like a long illness had passed.

Kojo gave Mya the option of moving her things into another cabin or being locked up in the stateroom with Danto. She chose Danto, as long as Rachel agreed to route the planet images to her console.

Once the lovers were locked into Mya's stateroom, Kojo turned to me with a sigh. "Finally, our luck has changed. Let's finish the survey and get the Zub out of here." He went to tell Hiram the good news.

Jamila grinned when I told her of the change of command. "Excellent! The sooner we finish the survey, the sooner I'll be able to launch an excavation."

"Good for Rachel," Grim said. "She's got more balls than Kojo. I'm glad *somebody* finally had the nerve to do something sensible."

I gave him a stun pistol so he could keep an eye on Danto and Mya when they needed to use the sanitary facilities.

"Don't worry," Grim said with a nasty smile. "I'll be sure that bastard stays in his place."

"None of that. They're not prisoners. Rachel just wants to keep them out of the way until we leave the system."

That night, I hoped for a glimpse of Papa, maybe even some advice from the spirit realm. Instead, my dreams took me back to the warm grassland and the shaggy beasts. The longing to be there with them was desperately acute. I felt sorry for Mya—if she felt Suriel's desire so much more intensely than I did, she must be in misery.

Early the next morning, I joined Rachel as she monitored the three survey drones as they sent streams of data about the planet to her computers.

Blankets and a pillow were stacked neatly next to the bulkhead.

"Did you spend the night here?" I asked, uneasy. She would have been within arm's length of the synthreactor.

"I expect to spend every night here until the survey is complete and we're in Kriti," she said, with less than her usual good cheer. "The relic's effect on the company is…unhealthy. The sooner we finish the mission, the better."

Ancestors! With Rachel camping in the cargo hold, how would we ever unload the synthreactor?

At her direction, I moved the sampling probe into the airlock. She let the sterilizing blue light bathe it with all three sample pods open, and then sterilized it again with the pods closed. As big as a cargo drone, the probe had similar rockets for hovering and fine positioning even in strong gravity.

I deployed the probe straight into the lower atmosphere.

"The winds will be strong," Rachel warned.

"I pilot a space hauler. I know how to deliver a drone full of cargo." I sent the probe toward a sea near the planet's equator, where the winds would be calmer. It was quiet enough there on the open water to take a seawater sample before sending the probe over the nearby land mass.

"I want to see that wildlife," she said.

The rocky coast of the continent opened out to one of the grassy plains that seemed to cover Nakana. And there they were, massive beasts feeding on the grasses.

There were many, many of the beasts, in different sizes and shapes. The biggest had the long, shaggy hair I'd seen in my dream. "Magnificent," Rachel murmured. "Bigger than elephants."

The tall grass obscured their legs, but the animals moved with an undulating motion that suggested more than four feet. Their heads were low, constantly eating. I could see their heavy necks straining as the animals pulled at the grass to break it off. They were always moving, not just walking, but wagging several appendages, arms or tails maybe. Their perpetual motion reminded me of Archer.

Standing apart were thinner, taller animals that followed the larger ones, eating what was left behind. I wanted to see them closer, but every time I flew the probe near, the animals moved away.

Rachel said, "The probe frightens them. See that patch of dust? It looks like a wallow. Try to take a dirt sample from there." I obliged. "Lovely. Now let the probe rest there quietly. Maybe one of the animals will approach."

Sure enough, in only a few minutes, a beast came near. Its broad flank was covered with long reddish fur, just as in my dreams. I could almost feel the heat radiating from its body, and almost feel its pulse through the probe controls. One of its tails waved like a happy puppy's.

"Excellent," Rachel said softly. "Now open the third sample pod and leave it open. We might actually capture a stray hair or two. See the temperature change? The animal is warm-blooded. Good, you can close it now. Move the probe away slowly."

I raised the probe until we could get a better view of the beast, resting in the dust wallow.

"Six legs," Rachel observed. "Long hairy covering. Wide mouth, small appendages near the mouth, possibly to assist feeding. At least six sensory organs on its head. Multiple auxiliary extremities."

I raised the probe higher and we saw several similar animals nearby. As we watched, an animal approached the one resting in the wallow and nudged it. The wallower obligingly stood up and walked away. The newcomer took its place, wriggling in the dirt.

Jamila called from the salon. "Did you see that? Indicative of social dominance."

A short way off, several stockier animals browsed. Their bodies had a delta shape, with a head at the center of a blunt side, four long legs along the other two sides, and two shorter arm-like extensions extending from the rear, grooming their short fur. I could see little of their heads, because they kept them down, grazing the cropped grass.

"They don't look up," I said.

Rachel said, "Hmm?"

"They don't look up to check for predators. They just keep eating."

"Perhaps sight is not an important sense for them, or there are few predators." As we watched, they moved on. "They're thin," mused Rachel, "although the grass is plentiful. Perhaps it has low nutrition value. Try to get closer to the grass."

We watched the fascinating scene for quite a while.

The probe's power monitor beeped. "Rachel, the power's getting low."

"All right. We've got our samples. Bring the probe back into orbit for retrieval."

I fired the probe's thrusters, scattering the animals. When the probe was far above the beasts, I ignited the main rocket to accelerate it into orbit. The winds were fierce—I had to fight to get it beyond the atmosphere, into an elliptical orbit. Once it reached apogee, I would boost it higher to bring it aboard.

I called Kojo on the com. "Good news. We've finished sampling and are beginning retrieval. How are Mya and Danto?"

"Danto's brooding," Kojo replied. "Mya's fretting. If she gets worse, I'll have to tranq her again. I won't be happy till we get out of here."

As the heavy sampling probe spiraled higher, I began to maneuver the three smaller survey drones into position for the touchy process of retrieval while both the drone and the ship were in orbit.

Amazing. For once, everything was going right. Against all odds, we'd found Nakana and finished the survey. We had twenty-two days left to deliver the synthreactor—enough time to get out of the Gloom and head for Kriti. Along the way, we'd find some way to distract Rachel long enough to dig out the synthreactor pieces and drop them into orbit around some lonely moon. Soon we'd be free of Ordalo's threat, and free of Danto, Mya, Rachel, and this crazy mission.

Jamila called on the com. "I've found another city! It's farther from the equator, in a temperate region. Can you send the drone closer so we can get a better view?" She gave us the coordinates.

"Fine," Rachel said with a sigh. "Patch, direct one of the survey drones over that site—just one pass. Go ahead and start recovering the others."

Jamila delivered some rations, for which I was grateful. "Can't we just leave the observation drones in place?" she asked, peering into the cargo hold. "I can use them when I come back for the excavation."

"Protocol requires that we leave nothing behind," Rachel said.

"But an orbiting drone couldn't possibly cause any harm."

"Until it's hit by a meteor and forms a debris field around the planet?" Rachel shook her head. "No. Nothing left behind." She shut the door decisively.

"Look sharp, missy," Hiram called from the wheelhouse. "I've matched our orbit to the first survey drone's. It's all lined up for you."

"Thanks, Hiram." I maneuvered the drone into retrieval position and let it float into the airlock. "Locking down."

Intense blue light blazed from the airlock's shielded window. "Sterilization complete."

While the second survey drone approached the retrieval point, I crated the first. The sampling probe was climbing nicely, and the third survey drone was beginning to arc toward the pole.

"Heads up, missy," Hiram called. "Second drone should be in range."

The second survey drone zipped into the airlock and went through the sterilization cycle.

The sample probe was still in low orbit, climbing slowly as it circled the planet. The rockets were using a lot of power to shift the heavy probe and its load of samples.

"Hiram," I called, "the sampling probe is low on power. Can we get closer?"

"Moving in," Hiram called. "Easy, missy. Preparing to cut acceleration. Three, two, one, cut."

I halted the probe's rockets just as *Sparrow* stopped accelerating, so the probe seemed to be drifting nearby, with only a slight swerve to starboard. A few quick bursts from the probe's maneuvering rockets brought it toward the airlock.

Closer, closer. There was a clang as the probe touched the mooring pad. *Boom!* The interlocks clamped shut. The blue sterilizing lights blazed behind the shielded airlock window.

"There." I breathed in relief. "Got it, Hiram! Thanks!"

"My pleasure, missy." With a short rocket thrust, *Sparrowhawk* accelerated upward to a safer orbit.

Rachel smiled. "Nicely done, Patch. Just the last drone to bring in."

"Won't the sterilizer kill the samples?"

"They're shielded inside the sample pods. The pods will stay sealed until we get to a proper lab."

The remaining survey drone was high over the surface, moving from the polar ice to mountainous woodland. Cloud wisps obscured the visible-light image, but the lidar images were still clear. As the drone's orbit carried it farther from the pole, the surface became hilly, green with shrubs or trees rather than grasses.

"There's the city," Jamila called.

It looked like a long, low mound of rocky blocks covered with scrub, but as the drone passed over the mound, a hint of straight lines appeared within the jumble of blocks. Streets in a ruined city? Jamila and her fellow archeologists would have their jobs guaranteed for years investigating it.

"Well spotted, Jamila," Rachel said.

Chirp.

I paused in crating the heavy sampling probe. The sound had erupted from one of Rachel's consoles.

Rachel checked her monitors with furrowed brow. *Chirp.* A second chirp sounded, then a third. The view of the city faded into the distance as the drone moved away. After a pause, there was another chirp, then silence.

I checked the scanner. I checked again, scarcely able to breathe.

A beacon.

Hiram called the from wheelhouse. "Kojo, missy, did you see that? A beacon pulse. Out here in the Gloom, a goddamned burzing *beacon*."

The sampling probe forgotten, I turned to Rachel. "A beacon—Sage technology. It's true, then. It *must* be true. We found Nakana."

The sacred texts that had guided Gavoran culture since the Sages had first brought our ancestors out of Earth were coming to life before my eyes.

Beloved friends! Peace and joy await.

Rachel laid a hand on my shoulder. "A few random energy pulses. Nothing to get excited about."

Random? Nothing to get excited about? Rachel was either lying or being deliberately obtuse. The jump gates, the beacons, terraforming tech—everything that made interstellar colonization possible, we owed to the Sages. And here, hidden in the Gloom, was the origin of it all.

Danto called from the stateroom. "Dr. Fiori, that beacon pulse was unmistakably Sage technology. You can no longer deny us—we must go to the planet to investigate."

In the background, Mya moaned, "The Sages call to us. We must respond!"

Rachel announced into the com, "Calm down, friends. You're jumping to conclusions. The energy pulses could be natural, the result of geothermal action or seismic movement. Whatever it is, further investigation will need to wait for a better-equipped expedition. Once we gather in the last drone, we'll leave. It's time to go home."

Home. Peace and joy.

I shot a look at her. Why was Rachel denying the obvious?

"But Suriel!" Mya cried. "Suriel must be taken to Nakana."

"The relic has brought us here," Rachel said. "Suriel has succeeded. You should all be very proud. We've done our job and completed the preliminary survey despite considerable adversity. Now it's time for us to leave and let the Settlement Authority take control."

The com buzzed with Danto's demands and Mya's hysteria. Kojo cut in with, "I'm going to have to tranq them both. Grim, cover me."

I turned on Rachel, angry at her attempts to hide the truth. "That wasn't just a random energy pulse or an earthquake. That was a *beacon*."

"Missy?" Hiram called from the wheelhouse. "What are you doing? The third drone is coming into range."

"Right, Hiram, I see it. Just a little excitement about that pulse."

"Well, pay attention."

I returned to the drone console, forcing myself to concentrate on steering the drone closer. "The third survey drone is coming into position. Rachel, Danto has a point. Finding a beacon out here…"

"Carry on, Patch," Rachel said. "We'll be on our way home soon."

Home!

With a rattle of the lock, the cargo hold door opened. Kojo walked in.

Blood dripped from his scalp.

"I'm sorry," he said. "Danto…"

Danto stepped into the doorway, holding Jamila in front of him, a stun pistol pointed at her neck.

CHAPTER 28

Command and control

JAMILA WHIMPERED. She stood in the doorway, Danto's stunner pointed directly at the point where her spine joined her skull.

I froze. A stunner blast from point-blank range would leave her paralyzed—or dead.

Danto said, "I will destroy Professor Patil if you do not do exactly as I say. Stand away from the consoles and keep your hands in sight."

Kojo held his hands high. "He cold-cocked me when I went in with tranqs. Grim tried to fight, but Danto almost killed him. Better do what he says."

Kojo hurt? Danto back in control? That changed everything.

Mya stepped in from behind Danto. "Do not resist. I have Kojo's pistol."

She waved it, pointing it vaguely toward me and Rachel.

Mya looked terrible. Thin, eyes red, she trembled noticeably.

"Your weapons," Danto said. "Place them on the floor and kick them to me. Carefully."

Kojo nodded to me. "Do it."

"Of course." Opening my jacket so Danto could see what I was doing, I lifted the stunner from my belt and placed it on the deck. Rachel did the same.

I booted the stunner across the deck. "You don't have to hurt anyone, Danto. I'll do whatever you want."

"That's right," Rachel said. "There's no reason for more violence."

Mya gazed at the vault with longing. "Now, give me the relic. We must take it to Nakana."

"There's no need to go to the surface," Rachel soothed. "We can put the relic in a drone and send it there. We'll do it now, if you want."

Kojo caught my eye and lowered one hand long enough to rub his nose—*be ready*. He sidestepped, closer to the vault.

My stomach dropped. Kojo was going to try some razzle-dazzle.

He inched into position—close enough to make a play for Mya's pistol when she went to the vault. In her weakened condition, he might succeed. All he needed was a few moments' diversion.

I knew exactly what to do.

"Kojo, stop," I shouted. "Get away from the vault." His eyes widened in surprise.

I turned to Mya. "Rachel's lying. She won't let the relic go. That's the protocol—nothing left behind. She'll take Suriel away from Nakana, to be lonely forever."

Rachel cried, "Patch, don't."

Hiram squawked on the com that the drone was drifting out of range and what the Zub was I doing?

I was doing what I had to do.

Home.

Mya and Danto turned toward me, but Jamila moaned and sagged, dragging Danto's arm downward.

Kojo leaped for Mya.

He wasn't close enough. With a sickening *zing*, Mya shot her stunner straight into Kojo's chest.

Kojo spun and slammed to the deck, face-first.

I cried out and took a step toward him, but Danto threw Jamila at me. We fell together in a tangle of limbs.

With an animal scream, Mya rushed at Rachel, pummeling her to the deck. "Give it to me!" she shouted. "Give me the relic."

I shoved Jamila off me and again tried to get to Kojo.

Danto's stunner blast slammed me back into the bulkhead. My head bounced into the wall.

I fell into darkness deeper than the Gloom.

Home. Peace and joy.

When my head began to clear, Rachel was curled on the deck while Mya kicked at her. Jamila tried to pull Mya away, but Mya shoved her down with a disgusted grunt.

Kojo lay motionless near the vault.

I pushed myself up to lean against the chair—too fast. My vision grayed again.

"Stop, Mya!" Jamila tried again to drag Mya away from Rachel.

Cramps doubled me over—the stun shot had hit me full-on. I clutched my belly and concentrated on slow, deep breaths.

As I tried to focus, Danto picked up the loose stun pistols and shoved them into his belt. It was a fine collection and they'd done us no good at all.

"Mya, stop that," Danto said.

Mya kicked once more. "Why? She wants to take Suriel away."

"We will need her," Danto said, "to set the captain's arm."

Kojo stirred but was too dazed to get up. Danto stood over him. "Captain Babatunji, you are relieved of command. On medical grounds."

He lifted Kojo's left arm. With a well-placed kick to the elbow, Danto shattered the bone.

Kojo's yell of pain faded quickly as he lost consciousness.

Tears ran down my face.

Danto walked over to me and looked down. "Patch, you lying bastard slave, you will do everything I say, without question, or I will hurt Kojo. I will break his bones until you comply."

"Yes," I promised. "Absolutely. I'll do everything you say. Please don't hurt him any more."

Danto smiled nastily. "Good. Now inform the crew that I am in command."

Shaking and holding my aching middle, I managed to get to my console seat and hit the com. "Hiram, Archer?"

"What's going on, missy? I'll need to make another pass at that drone."

"Forget the drone. Danto is in command."

"What do you mean, *in command*?" Archer called.

"Kojo is hurt and Danto will hurt him worse if we don't do as he says."

"Why, the mutinous son of a sea slug…"

"Patch!" Archer cried. "Are you all right?"

"Quiet," Danto ordered. "You will take the ship to the surface, near the woodland city."

Rachel struggled to sit up. Blood dripped from her nose and cuts on her forehead. "You can't go to the surface. You don't know…"

Mya cut her off. "We know what Suriel orders us to do."

"Patch?" Hiram asked.

"You heard Danto," I said. "Follow his orders. Take us down. I'll send the city's coordinates. Find a landing spot nearby."

"All right, missy."

"But, Patch," Archer began.

"Archer, just do what Danto says. It'll be all right."

I turned to Rachel. She'd managed to sit up and was holding her battered head.

"Rachel? How bad are you hurt? Can you help Kojo?"

"Superficial only. Danto, please let me tend to the injuries."

"Do so. Professor Patil will assist you."

Jamila took the med kit from the locker and helped Rachel go to Kojo. Danto left Mya to hold a stunner on us.

None of us were much of a threat.

After a minute, Danto returned, dragging a moaning, bloody-headed Grimbold.

Mya turned to me. "Now, open the vault and bring me the bloodstone."

Supporting myself on crates, I staggered to the vault. Rachel recited the combination.

Home! Peace and joy await!

Mya panted with anticipation. "Bring it to me. Bring it to me."

I laid the case on the table and worked the combination. The relic, nestled in the padding, looked brighter and shinier than before. It was beautiful.

Before I could reach for the relic, Mya snatched it up and hugged it. "A knife," she ordered. "Bring me a knife."

Jamila brought a huge scalpel from the med kit. She must have taken the largest she could find and didn't bother to sterilize it.

Mya didn't care. She laid the relic on the table and made a long cut in her arm.

Blood welled out. The smell of it made me dizzy.

Danto stood beside Mya, his hand on her shoulder. It would have been a touching scene except for the stunner in his hand.

Despair brought tears to my eyes. *My brother. My ship. The relic.* I was in danger of losing them all.

As her blood flowed into the relic's channels, Mya closed her eyes, moaning softly. She pulled Danto's hand down to the relic and cut into the flesh at the base of his thumb. As his blood mingled with hers, he gasped and stiffened, letting the stunner dip.

I moved forward, just a little.

The stunner snapped up. "Step back," Danto snarled.

"Let me go to Kojo, please."

"Go."

Bent and leaning on whatever consoles and crates were in reach, I stepped over Grim and knelt next to Kojo.

He was very pale. His eyes fluttered as Jamila cut away his shirt to expose his left arm and chest. His arm, already swelling, had a bend where no bend should be.

Rachel joined us. Her face was bruised and an eye was beginning to blacken. "We need to set the bone now, before the swelling gets worse."

Rachel injected Kojo with something from the med kit. "Patch, stand behind me. Jamila, kneel beside him and brace his body against the wall. Have the splint ready."

Rachel sat on the deck and placed the sole of her left foot against Kojo's armpit. She gently worked the splint under his arm and slipped her bent right leg underneath, so that the arm, supported by the splint, was angled toward me.

"Now pull," Rachel said.

I pulled his wrist. Kojo cried out, his face contorted in pain.

Long seconds ticked by while Rachel pushed the bits into place and strapped the splint into position.

Kojo stopped yelling. Eyes closed, face covered in sweat, his breath came in ragged gasps.

"Stop. Lay it down gently. Good, good." Rachel applied cold compresses. "That's all I can do for now. When the swelling goes down, I'll use the imagers to adjust the splint better."

I wiped dirt and tears from my cheeks. How had everything changed so quickly?

"How's Grimbold?" Jamila asked. He'd begun to stir and moan.

"Concussion. Help me move the imager over so I can see how bad it is."

I turned, only to find Danto right behind me, holding his stunner aimed at Kojo.

Danto's hand still dripped blood. "The magazine. Remove all the weapons and place them in the vault."

Our arms collection was not extensive. I carried the stun pistols and rifles into the vault and laid them on top of the fine brandy. *Ancestors!* It was a long time since we'd loaded those crates in Santerro.

When I was done, Danto kept two stunners in his belt and laid the rest inside. He ordered me to stand away while he changed the combination. "You will all remain here until I send for you," he said.

I nodded, still feeling dazed from the stun shot.

Jamila looked pleadingly at Danto. "Danto—Sergeant. You're a respected officer of the Corridor Patrol. Remember your oaths. Remember your mission. You can't really mean to abandon your duty like this."

"I follow a higher duty, a duty to the Sages," he said.

"Even if it means harming us?"

"Yes." Danto nodded toward Rachel. "Ask Dr. Fiori. She knows the lengths to which I'll go."

He went to Mya, still sitting with the relic. At his touch, she rose, cradling the relic like a child, and followed him out.

Jamila looked at Rachel. "What does he mean?"

Rachel slumped, her face bloody and eye swollen. "I believe Danto killed Lyden."

Jamila gasped. "Killed her? He couldn't have. You said Lyden was alone."

Rachel placed more cold compresses on Kojo's arm. "That's what I thought, at first. But when I took a second look, Danto's readings for that night were off—and they were identical to Mya's. Mya must have worn both sets of sensors to make it seem like they were together in the salon."

Poor Lyden. Betrayed by the one closest to her. I closed my eyes and leaned against the bulkhead, utterly drained.

Jamila covered her face with her hands. "You could have told us. Now we're trapped here with a killer."

Rachel shook her head. "I wasn't sure, though I took the precaution of arming Kojo and Patch. I still don't have any evidence. Lyden fell and her heart stopped. It would be impossible to prove he caused it."

"Patch?" Archer stood tentatively at the door. I crossed the room to him, still clutching my aching middle.

"You shouldn't be here," I whispered. He grabbed me and gave me a hug.

"Ow! Not so hard."

"Oh, sorry. I just wanted to see if you were all right." He looked with dismay at the casualties. "And Kojo, too."

"We'll be fine," I said. "As soon as we get to Nakana."

"What do you want me to do?" he whispered. "If we work together, maybe I can overpower him."

The idea of slight, jumpy Archer taking on a hulking Corridor Patrol officer was almost funny.

I shook my head. "Please, don't try anything. Go back to the engines and help with the landing. Just do as Danto says. Everything will be fine."

"All right." He looked at me worriedly. "If you're sure."

"I'm sure. Go on now," I said.

Kojo roused enough to sit up, and Jamila tended him gently.

"The splint helps," he said with a grimace. "And whatever Rachel shot me up with. What does that bastard Danto think he's doing?"

"Standard military strategy," Rachel said. "Disable your biggest threat first. He needs you alive, to help pilot the ship on the way home, but now you won't be able to fight him, and he knows Patch will obey him if he threatens you."

Kojo scowled at me. "Why the Zub didn't you do something? I could have grabbed Mya's pistol if you'd helped."

"We need to take the relic to the surface," I said.

"We should just drop the burzing thing out an airlock."

"No," I said. "We shouldn't be fighting Danto and Mya. We should be helping them. They're right. This is what we should be doing, going down to the surface."

"What?" Kojo said. "Why?"

"That's what we're supposed to do, take the relic home. They'll be waiting for us there."

"Waiting? Who?"

I shook my head. The answer was obvious. "The Sages, of course. Who do think activated that beacon?"

Kojo just stared, his face paling to dusky gray.

"You should rest," I said. "I'm sorry you're so hurt. But everything will be fine, once we land on Nakana."

Come! Come, beloved friends! Peace and joy await.

CHAPTER 29

Peace and joy

SPARROWHAWK DESCENDED slowly into the atmosphere. Soon, we'd be able to see for ourselves the lush grasslands and beautiful beasts. I could hardly wait. Nakana waited for us, a place of peace and joy, the home of welcoming friends.

"The Sages? What are you talking about?" Kojo stared at me as if I'd lost my mind. Rachel went to check the monitors.

It had become very clear to me, since receiving the first energy pulse. This was Nakana. This was home. "Can't you feel them calling us?" I asked.

Poor Kojo. Never to hear the beautiful voices.

Rachel laid a hand on my shoulder. "I understand."

Something pricked my neck.

I fell to the deck, my legs suddenly limp.

Jamila cried, "Patch? What's wrong?"

"Don't worry," Rachel said. "I gave her a temporary paralytic. It'll wear off." She began tying my hands and feet.

"What are you doing? Kojo! Tell her to stop!" I wanted to resist, but I couldn't move.

Kojo looked ready to cry. "Rachel?"

"I'm sorry, Patch," Rachel said. "Your sensors show you're being profoundly influenced telepathically."

"Of course I am. I hear them quite clearly. The answer's in the city. You don't need to tie me up. I'll help us to go there and find them."

Rachel was being very slow to understand. But then, she was just a Terran, not graced with the ability to hear the Sages' call.

Come! Come, beloved friends!

"Danto was right," Rachel said. "That energy spike from the city had all the characteristics of a beacon. Sage technology. I suspect this beacon is drawing in anyone who has Gavoran genetics."

"Patch," Kojo said. "Fight it. You're not a Gav slave, you're a free Terran."

"Don't worry, Kojo," I assured him. "I'm just fine." Poor Kojo. He might be my half-brother but he was just a Terran. How could he understand?

I was exhausted and my middle hurt, but I was happy. I didn't mind being trussed up on the dirty deck, as long as we were getting closer to Nakana. I felt more at peace than I'd been in months.

All would be well once we arrived on the planet. I'd thought *Sparrowhawk* was my home and that Kojo was my family. But now I knew that home and family were waiting for me on Nakana. Kojo didn't need me, didn't want *Sparrow*. He could go his own way and I could stay here and we'd both be happy.

Soon we'd be there, among the sweet grasslands and the beautiful long-haired beasts.

Sparrowhawk made its final approach to the planet surface, retro rockets blasting. Part of my mind calculated the power mods we were wasting, using thrusters to land without the assistance of a port's lifters.

But that was silly. We didn't need to conserve power for liftoff, we could all just stay here, on Nakana.

I didn't mind being tied up. I didn't care, I was going home.

Jamila had propped me up against a console next to Grim—unconscious and snoring.

She whispered to me, "Fight back, Patch. Whatever you're hearing, it's not for you."

I squirmed away from her. "You've been blind and deaf to the relic from the beginning. Balan and Deprata tried to tell you, but you dismissed them. You said they were deluded. You locked Suriel in a tiny case and kept it away from the only people who cared about it."

Come, beloved friends! The Sages' call was like the voice of Suriel, multiplied by hundreds. A community awaited us, a welcoming family ready to embrace us.

Jamila teared up and turned away. Perhaps she was beginning to regret her actions.

Kojo swept a hand over his eyes, his shoulders shaking.

Rachel fussed into the com node, "Danto, please listen. Some of the life on the planet could be dangerous." Ridiculous.

"Dr. Fiori, be quiet," he said.

I tried to soothe her. "Really, Rachel, you don't need to worry. We've been called. They are waiting for us. We'll be fine."

Rachel knelt at my side and looked in my eyes. "Patch, the Sages forced Gavorans into castes. They made you and your mother and all your mothers before her into slaves. Nakana is not peace and joy for you. It's slavery. Fight them!"

For a moment, the vision of peaceful animals slipped away and I saw instead the coursing of hot blood through their veins. It made me dizzy.

Kojo said, "You're Terran, Patch. Terran and free. Fight back."

I saw my brother as if he was a stranger. A brown Terran face showing hints of the wrinkles that age would bring. A man whose once-reliable charm had abandoned him. His clothes were worn and rumpled, the left sleeve torn away to accommodate the splint. His eyes—usually filled with humor—were ringed with pain. For a moment, I saw Papa's face in Kojo's, and the pain and hopelessness I'd seen in Papa's eyes during his last hours.

Poor Papa. Poor Kojo. Only Terrans, blind to the true beauty of the cosmos.

Sparrowhawk—I'd thought she was my home. She was nothing but a shabby old space hauler. A military cutter so obsolete the Selkids didn't care who owned her. A ragged vessel, barely ether-worthy, good only for carrying other people's castoffs from one poverty-stricken frontier planet to another, kept operating by substandard jump cells, massive amounts of Prestoseal, and sheer stubbornness.

Why had I fought so hard to keep her? Now I had a new home. A better home.

The ruined city below us filled the viewscreen. There was elegance in the massive blocks of stone hidden under the shroud of vegetation. It must have been magnificent.

We could make it so again.

"Don't worry, Kojo," I said. "I'm perfectly fine. Everything is fine."

His face crumpled, making him even uglier.

As *Sparrow* descended with blasting retros, a grazing herd scampered away. Their undulating, six-legged gait rippled as they ran. They were beautiful.

Come, beloved friends!

With a rattle and thump, *Sparrowhawk* came to rest on Nakana.

Mya appeared at the door to the cargo hold, Danto close behind her. She still clutched the relic to her breast. I could see from her paleness she'd been feeding it again and I burned with envy.

"Open the hatch," Mya said. "It is time to return Suriel to its home. It is time to meet the Sages."

Come, beloved friends!

"Don't open the hatch!" Rachel stood before Mya, blocking the way. "The beacon is affecting your judgment—please stop and think. We know the planet has large animals, they could be a danger. And we don't know what kind of other organisms exist here. Opening the hatch might expose us all to harm."

Mya looked at Rachel pityingly. "The Sages have called us. We will be perfectly safe."

"But will Nakana be safe from you?" Rachel voice was strident, annoying. "If you carry our microbes into the atmosphere, you could harm the life here."

Mya faltered. "No...we were called. The Sages want us here."

"I wasn't called," Kojo said. "And neither were the rest of us Terrans. What about our microbes? You never know what can happen when a new species comes to a planet."

"At least go through the airlock and use protective gear," Rachel urged. "I've already put two environment suits in the airlock."

I wiggled in my bonds. "Mya, take me with you, please. I've been called, too. I can help you." I wanted so badly to go. *Needed* to go.

Jamila covered her mouth with her hands.

Mya bent over me. "You are merely a slave. How could you be worthy of the Sages?"

"Please! I'll help you. I'll be *your* slave. Take me with you." Panic washed over me. Would she keep me away from my one true home?

Kojo made an odd coughing sound. He turned away, his eyes blinking.

Danto laid a hand on Mya's shoulder. "It might be wise to take precautions to protect both you and Nakana."

He pulled me to my feet. "Very well, slave. You will go with Mya and protect her from wild animals while I remain in control of the ship. If you allow anything to happen to her, I will destroy the Terrans on this ship. I will rip them apart, one by one."

"Thank you!" I cried. "I'll protect Mya."

Kojo wiped his sweaty face with his good hand, his shoulders shaking.

Rachel stared into the air, the fingers of one hand lightly tapping her hip. Her bruised face was lumpy, misshapen. "Mya, you should be careful…"

Danto casually reached out one of his long arms and swatted Rachel's head, sending her crashing to the deck.

"Now," he said, "into the airlock."

Mya and I shed our outer layers of clothing, down to leggings and undervests. We entered the airlock and sealed the door. "Quickly," Mya said. "They are waiting for us."

Crowded together, trembling with excitement, I helped Mya put on the enviro suit. For a moment while Mya dressed, I held Suriel in my own hands. Solid, cool, smooth—I hugged the relic to me, giddy as a schoolgirl.

Mya snatched it away, slipping it under her vest next to her skin. "Tie my belt over it to keep it in place," she said. "Suriel will be safe from the sterilizer within my suit."

I hurried into my own suit, double-checked the seals, and made sure our helmets were secured.

"Close your helmet visor, Mya," I said. "Initializing sterilization."

Through the eye-shielding visor, I dimly saw the bright blue sterilizing light. We turned and lifted our limbs to allow the light to bathe all surfaces.

When the light turned off, Danto said through the helmet mics, "Sterilization complete. You can open the outer doors. Blessings upon you, Mya."

In the background Kojo's voice called, "Patch, come back safe."

The place where *Sparrow* had landed seemed made for that purpose—a broad, flat hexagon near one of the wide avenues. I followed Mya out the hatch, marveling at the city, impressive and lovely even in its ruined state. Vines and shrubs shrouded the remains of long, low buildings, elegant in their simplicity. Horizontal ovals for doors and windows beckoned us to explore. Above us, clouds in a green sky glowed gold where the twin suns gilded them.

Home.

Nearby, a group of small furred creatures jostled one another, feeding in the brush. At our first steps on Nakana, they froze and silently watched us before rippling away with a collective twitch. Farther away, on the plain, a herd of the large hairy beasts steadfastly marched toward the distant mountains, snatching at grass as they passed.

I hugged myself with pleasure. It was all so beautiful.

The broad avenue led up a mild incline toward a dome amid the fallen buildings. "There," Mya said. "We must go there."

Come. Come, beloved friends! Here is the peace you seek.

With a small cry, Mya began to walk toward the dome.

"Tell us what is happening!" Danto demanded.

"We're being called to the dome," I said. "The Sages are waiting for us there."

Peace and joy. My feet seemed to move of their own volition up the path.

"Mya, slow down," Jamila called into the helmet mics. "Record everything you can. This is our first view of these ruins, we need as complete a record as possible."

Mya paused. "Yes, you are right. Our first expedition to Nakana. This is a historic moment."

"Pan your helmet imager over the buildings," Jamila said. "Look at the houses."

Walkways between the dwellings made the homes look light and pleasant.

"Let me see those columns." Lining the avenue were short plinths of gray stone, topped with shallow bowls.

Something flickered at the edge of my vision. I turned, awkward in the enviro suit, but there was nothing to see. The shrubs gently stirred.

Come, beloved friends!

Mya strode up the path. "We should go. The Sages are waiting."

Behind me, the brush rustled.

One of the hairy beasts wandered out of the vegetation, only steps behind me. Its back higher than my shoulder, it grazed along the path, head down, its mandible-like appendages twitching over the ground. Tails swished over its sides and its six feet scuffed up a cloud of dust.

Danto shouted into the mic, "What is that animal? Protect Mya."

"But the Sages call us…"

"*Protect her!* I will break Kojo's foot next."

"No! I'll do it."

I backed up the pathway behind Mya, keeping my eyes on the shaggy creature. On the plain outside the city were hundreds more, all moving purposefully toward a nearby range of hills, raising dust as they went. Perhaps this one was a rebellious soul, yearning for solitude or adventure.

Come beloved friends. This is your true home, a place of peace.

I backed farther up the path, eager to join Mya.

The huffing beast blundered forward, apparently oblivious to my presence, ponderously swinging its head as it snuffled for grass. Perhaps, somewhere in its dull brain, it dimly heard the call to the top of the hill.

"I'm sure it doesn't mean any harm." I made pushing motions with my hands. "Shoo, beastie. Go home."

Peace, the voices crooned. *Come, beloved friends.*

Sweet animal, lovely creature. No reason to fear it. I could almost feel the warmth of its flesh. My head swam with the thought of its blood pumping through its veins.

The animal veered into the brush, passing close enough to touch.

Beautiful beastie. As it passed, I reached out a gloved hand to stroke its long hair.

My hand came away covered with worms.

CHAPTER 30

The call of blood

I TRIED TO BRUSH the maggots off, but they stuck firmly to the enviro suit.

The beast stumbled. Its tails were, like me, frantically trying to dislodge the creatures. Seen closer, what I had taken for dense hair was a thick layer of the worms.

And that was no dust cloud following the beast—it was a swarm of tiny flying creatures.

The huge animal faltered and fell. The swarm immediately settled on it.

The emaciated animal kicked its six legs uselessly, struggling to get up, the maggots draining it while it was still alive.

Feeling sick, I backed away in disgust. Dozens of the maggots clung to my suit. I tried to pick them off one by one, but my gloves made me clumsy.

With a sudden surge of panic, I turned back toward the ship. The sterilizer would kill them.

Danto's voice sounded in my helmet mic. "Why do you delay? Stay with Mya. Make sure she comes to no harm."

Come! The voices of Nakana drew me upward, toward the ruined central dome.

Peace and joy. Come beloved friends.

The voices tugged at the core of my being. Veneration of the ancestors had been instilled in me since birth. All my life, the spirits had been with me, bolstering my courage and strength in hard times. I wanted only to obey and find the peace they promised.

From my helmet mic, I heard Rachel cry, "Patch, they're parasites! They're feeding on the animal's blood."

"Patch, get out—" Kojo's shout was followed by a grunt.

"Kojo?"

For a moment I turned, ready to run back to the ship, desperate to shut the voices out of my head.

Danto ordered, "Patch, your only concern is to protect Mya."

The power of the voices terrified me, luring me to surrender myself to Nakana's promise of peace. Inner horror urged me to escape back to the ship, to get off this planet.

Choosing was part of my life. Speak Gav or Terran? Gav robe or Terran jacket? Cut my hair short to look like a Gav pelt or let the Terran hair grow long? Hide under a hat or let everyone see my Gav brow? Never quite fitting in, never really at home. Only on *Sparrowhawk*, among Papa and Kojo and Hiram and even Archer, had I felt truly comfortable. Really able to be myself.

Fight back, Kojo had said. Like my mother, who had risked her life to send me to freedom. Like my father, who had smuggled me away to Terran worlds.

Above all, I had to keep my family safe. Abandoning Mya could mean Kojo's death.

I trod up the pathway toward the dome, panic alternating with despair.

Mya was far ahead, nearly to the dome.

"Mya, wait for me!" I called. I ran after her, tripping over vines encroaching on the broken stone pavement.

Come! Come, beloved friends! The voices were gentle, kind, generous.

Lies.

I silently prayed, *Ancestors, give me strength. I am free. I will fight back.*

As I stumbled up behind her, Mya reached the plaza. There, the dome, supported by thin columns, covered a broad plaza where six avenues converged. Where one of the columns had crumbled, the roof had dipped and cracked, leaving chunks strewn on the ground.

Mya paused, letting her helmet imager pan over the vine-covered, ruined city.

In the center of the plaza stood six low plinths, each topped with a broad, shallow bowl. Mya went to the closest, raised both hands, and began to recite a prayer to the Sages.

Come, beloved friends!

I waited nearby, silently adding my own prayer that she would dump the damned relic and get back to the ship quickly. I kept an eye out for any more of the wandering beasts, reflexively brushing the flying insect-creatures from my enviro suit.

I let my helmet imager play over the nearest plinth. The bowl was etched inside with six spokes, reflecting the layout of the city. Its metal rim curved inward at the top, remarkably clean and sharp.

Come, beloved friends! Prove your love! Feed us!

At a soft cry, I spun around. Mya had removed her helmet and was freeing her hands and arms from the enviro suit.

I ran to her, Danto frantically shouting in my ear.

The flying creatures buzzing about the plaza dashed to attack Mya. She thrashed at them with her hands.

"Put the helmet back on!" I cried.

Feed us!

I picked up her helmet and tried to cram it on her head. With surprising strength, she pushed me away and stepped out of her enviro suit.

Mya leaned over the bowl. With a quick outward movement of her arms, as if parting a curtain, she slashed both wrists on the sharp metal rim.

Blood spurted. She held her arms over the bowl and let her blood flow into the etched channels. Her lips still moved in her chanted prayer.

The insect-creatures swarmed to the scent of blood. They were all over the bowl, her arms, her back, her face.

The voices gave a collective sigh of satisfaction. *Thank you, beloved friends. You are the chosen ones. Bring your race to us and we will care for you and give you peace. You will know peace and joy.*

"It's a trap!" Danto shouted. "Bring her back! Bring Mya back now!"

I brushed as many of the creatures off her face as I could and jammed her helmet back onto her head. She swayed, nearly unconscious. I bent, put my shoulder under her and straightened, despite my aching abdomen.

Danto shouted nonstop.

Mya's legs hung before my one shoulder; her arms, still seeping blood and covered with hungry creatures, draped over the other. I had to hunch forward to keep her body from slipping back. As I hobbled down the slope toward the ship, her head bobbed with each step.

The voices sang in my head. *Come, beloved friends. Peace and joy.*

Lies.

My stunner-injured abdomen ached horribly. My back strained as I bent farther to keep her body from falling backward.

Something hard jabbed into my shoulder. *The relic.* She still carried it under her vest.

Mya began to struggle and squirm, screaming. "No! Let me go!" She ripped off her helmet and threw it into the brush.

I passed the place where the beast had fallen. It was nothing more than a dark mound, its outlines barely visible under a crawling covering of maggots and insects.

With a yell, Mya kicked her legs free and heaved herself off my shoulder. She landed on the broken pavement with a thump.

I straightened my back with relief. "The ship! Mya, run for the ship!"

Come, beloved friends.

Mya blundered off the avenue into the brush.

Damn her. She might want to stay here, but *I* didn't.

Danto's shout came through my helmet. "I will kill him, Patch! If you do not bring Mya to the ship, I will kill your brother!"

I went after her.

This time, I wasn't so gentle. The insects swarmed around us, seeking Mya's dripping wrists. I grabbed her arm and spun her toward me.

Maggots crawled on her face. Worms from the bushes clung to my suit, her clothes, and her skin.

I didn't bother to hit her in the head—Gavoran skulls are too thick. Instead, I punched her in her gut and slung her torso over my shoulder, holding onto her legs in front.

The voices urged me upward. Liars.

I took one step down the slope, then another, and another. I stumbled, but desperation kept me going. With every step, Mya bounced on my shoulder. Every time she began to struggle, I came down extra hard and knocked the breath out of her.

The door to the airlock yawned open. Ten more steps to go, then five, then three. Mya struggled weakly. I stumbled into the airlock and dumped Mya like a sack of turnips.

Hundreds of maggots clung to us. Half a swarm of flying creatures followed us in before I could shut the airlock outer doors. Immediately, they landed on Mya's skin and began to bite. Worms and insects fed on her face, in her nose and mouth and eyes and on every bit of exposed skin on her arms and her legs.

Peace and joy, the voices sang.

Ancestors, I prayed, *give me strength and courage. I pray I am making the right choice.*

I closed my visor and hit the sterilization control.

Confused cries came through my helmet receiver, but whatever was happening in the cargo hold was drowned out by Mya's screams as the burning, blinding blue light bathed her unprotected skin.

CHAPTER 31

The banshee's cry

IT TOOK A LONG TIME for the sterilization cycle to run. With my visor closed to block out the light, I blindly fought Mya's frantic blows as I tore off her clothing. She would be terribly burned, but even through my gloves, I could feel the maggots dotting her skin. They had crept in everywhere, burrowing into her clothes as they would burrow into the shaggy hair of one of the beasts of Nakana.

Peace and joy. Come, beloved friends.

"Quiet!" I sobbed. "Stop your lies."

Soon Mya's screams faded, and she slumped, whimpering raggedly in the killing blue light. I raised her limbs to ensure that every surface of her body was exposed to the light. I found the relic on the airlock floor, where it had fallen from Mya's vest, and exposed its surfaces to be sterilized.

Finally, the light faded out and the inner airlock doors opened.

Filled with fear, I pulled off my helmet.

Danto, roaring in fury, grabbed my arm and threw me to the other side of the hold. The relic slid from my arms and skittered across the deck.

"What have you done?" Danto shouted.

He leveled his pistol directly at my eyes. Somewhere to the side, Jamila screamed and Kojo yelled, "No!"

I shut my eyes. At least I'd die knowing Kojo was alive.

The voices would finally be silenced.

"Aieeeeeahhhh!" A heart-stopping scream echoed through the hold.

Zing. Instinctively, I dropped to the deck, my arms covering my head.

Zing. The stun pistol fired again.

Confused shouts swept over me: Danto, demanding; Kojo, filled with fear; Rachel, commanding and insistent; Jamila, pleading and near hysteria; Mya, moaning faintly; and over it all, some unidentifiable banshee's war cry. *Ey-ya-walla-walla-scree!*

None of it kept out the lying voices trying to lure me back to the ruins.

Thunk.

Sobbing, I opened my eyes.

Directly in front of me, Danto lay crumpled on the deck, his head seeping crimson.

Across the hold, Jamila knelt next to gray-faced Kojo. Grimbold lay unconscious nearby.

But near the door was Hiram, dressed in full mercenary regalia—chest armor, helmet, blade-resistant collar—grinning like a fool.

And next to Danto's prostrate body stood Archer, swamped in armor meant for a more powerful frame. In his hand was a huge steel wrench.

The wrench dripped blood.

Danto twitched.

Hiram shouted, "Look out, lad."

Archer brought the wrench down again with the full force of his wiry body. I turned my face away, not wanting to see Danto's head pulped.

But instead of the dull thud I expected, I heard a sharp crack. The wrench had connected with something much harder than a Gavoran skull.

The relic.

Again and again, Archer pounded the wrench onto the relic until, with a final crunch, it lay in shards.

Sweating and panting, Archer dropped the wrench and knelt beside me. He spared only a glance for Danto, now utterly still, eyes blank and wide.

"I was afraid he would hurt you." Archer looked around apologetically. "Hiram distracted him and I snuck in. Everyone forgets about me."

I buried my face in his shoulder. "I never forget about you," I whispered. "Thank you, Archer." He blushed and smiled shyly.

Hiram, still grinning, helped Kojo up. "Reminds me of the old days, it does. Like your pa used to say, brains can beat a stunner any day."

Archer kissed me, a real kiss on the lips. It made me dizzy, or maybe that was just exhaustion.

I sobbed against his chest.

Kojo limped over to hug me awkwardly, holding his splinted arm out of the way. "Thank Zub. Welcome home, Patch."

"Jamila," Rachel called from the airlock. "Help me with Mya. She's still alive."

"What about Danto?" Jamila asked, keeping her face turned away.

"Dead," Hiram said. "Archer's damn handy with a wrench."

"I still hear the voices," I said. "Please stop them."

Rachel's face tightened. "We will. Captain, get us away from here."

"Glad to," Kojo replied. "Hiram, clear to launch. Archer, man the thrusters. Get us off this burzing rock!"

"With pleasure, Captain!"

Hiram grinned and marched up the aft steps. Archer brushed his lips against my hair before striding, head up and lethal wrench on his shoulder, toward the engine room.

We cleared a table for Mya and rushed to follow Rachel's orders to treat her burns, wrist cuts, bites, and blood loss.

"The sooner we can get her to a medical center, the better," Rachel said.

"Hiram and Archer came just in time," Kojo said. "Danto would have killed you. He really loved Mya."

"I'm sorry," I said. "I couldn't stop Mya from taking off her suit. The voices were too strong." I shivered.

"Do you still hear them?" Rachel asked.

Come, friends. Peace and joy await.

"Yes. It's exhausting, having them in my head. We can't leave that beacon here. If any Gavorans were to follow us, they'd be drawn in like moths to a flame."

"I agree," Rachel said. "Patch, I know you're tired, but you need to prepare a new drone. This one must have grenades."

"Grenades?" Jamila asked. "Are you sure, Rachel? Wouldn't that violate the Settlement Authority's laws and regulations?"

Rachel smiled her feline smile. "Screw the laws and regs. I'm a commander, remember?"

Lifting off from the planet without the benefit of a port's lifters was rough, relying on just our thrusters to overcome gravity and winds. There were some unpleasant moments as the gales in the upper atmosphere threatened to topple *Sparrow* into the sea, but Archer hit the thrusters full bore and Hiram straightened us out.

As we reached orbit, Jamila helped me pull out a cargo drone. The voices battered at me, as insistent as waves on a beach. *Come, friends! Peace and joy!*

Terran, I told myself. *Free.*

As we stepped over the pile of rubble that once housed Suriel, Jamila cried out, "What's that?"

Something wriggled among the relic's remain.

Jamila backed away, hand over her mouth.

I froze in horror at the thought of something—Suriel—crawling out of the scraps.

In an orange-and-white flash, Tinker pounced, pawing at the shards.

"Tinker, no!"

She ran away with something wiggling in her mouth.

"Never mind," Rachel said. "We'll track her down. Put the remains in the drone. Valuable artifact or not, the relic is staying on Nakana."

Jamila looked ready to cry.

I swept up the gravel and shards trying not to see if anything was alive among them. I dumped them into the drone, along with the grenades set to detonate on impact. Shutting the payload hatch, I entered the coordinates for the beacon signal's location and pushed the drone into the airlock. Rachel keyed the launch herself.

Jamila sprayed Prestoscrub all over the deck where the relic had lain.

Peace. Joy. Come.

After we launched the drone, Hiram brought us into retrieval position for the last survey drone. With shaking hands, I maneuvered it into the airlock on the third try and let the sterilization cycle run.

Come, beloved—

Silence.

I fell back into my chair with a thump. "Oh."

Quiet. Pure blessed quiet. No voices from the planet. No voice from the relic. Nothing but my own thoughts.

It was wonderful.

"The drone has detonated," Rachel said quietly. "Are you all right, Patch?"

"Yes!" I took a deep breath. "The voices are gone. All of them."

"Then the drone hit the target." Rachel nodded with satisfaction. "Captain, we are clear to head for the nearest port."

CHAPTER 32

Science and belief and secrets to keep

WE MOVED MYA AND GRIM to the bunks in the large stateroom, where they could be strapped down during our return passage through the wall of energy and debris. Jamila volunteered to help Rachel care for them. I stayed in the engine room, shifting power mods as Archer babied our straining engines and kept our maneuvering rockets aligned.

Exiting the debris cloud was easier than entering, since we didn't have to fight against the outward expansion of the energy wave. Even so, we had hours of pressure waves and plasma discharges until *Sparrowhawk* battered her way through the energy wall. At one point, Archer put his arm around me and I wept into his shoulder out of sheer exhaustion. Then the helm called and, white-faced, he turned back to the console. I wiped my eyes and got back to work.

Finally, we burst past the cloud's energy and debris and once again faced the depressing prospect of the Gloom's dense ether.

I found Rachel in the stateroom, slumped in a chair.

"Grim is sedated," she said. "The turbulence exacerbated his concussion and I had to operate to relieve the pressure on his brain. I *think* he'll recover. I sent Jamila to get some sleep. She was a rock—helping me drill a hole in a man's skull while the ship is being battered to pieces is no mean feat."

"And Mya?" But a glance at her bunk told me her condition—the sheet was pulled over her face.

"Her injuries were too severe."

I sat at the watch station as Hiram patiently, methodically spiraled through the search pattern.

"We can't be too far off," he said, yawning. I pinged the locator codes again, peering into the scanner for a response from the buoy. "How's Kojo doing?"

"He's resting. Rachel shot him up with painkillers. She had to reset his arm—the thrust leaving the planet and the pummeling we took getting through the energy wall displaced his bones."

"Ah, I was afraid of that. He didn't say anything, but I could see he was hurtin'. He was real tore up over you, you know. When he saw you going off planetside, so happy to be ordered around by those damn Gavs, it shocked him silly."

I didn't want to think about it. "You and Archer made a great team, all tricked out in your mercenary gear, and Archer wearing Papa's old armor."

He chuckled. "The lad was all for charging in, armed with nothing but a spanner. I figured a little armor to fend off a stun shot wouldn't hurt."

"And some razzle-dazzle. What was that horrific yell?"

"Ah, hell. That's how my ma used to call me in for dinner."

Ping. Finally, an answer from the buoy.

We began the long limp homeward, backtracking through the dark.

Every two hours, I dragged myself to the drone console to pick up another buoy—we wanted no one following our breadcrumbs back to Nakana. The retrievals were so frequent, I didn't bother sleeping in my cabin, just nestled under a mound of blankets in the cargo hold with all the lights on and cuddling with Tinker, when she let me. Not that I slept much—every rustle and creak had me jumping up, shaking like a leaf, and madly brushing away imaginary worms. I spent as much time as I could in the engine room—spelling Archer so he could sleep, of course, but also because I didn't want to be alone.

"Couldn't we just stop for a bit?" Archer asked. "We all need rest."

I shook my head. "Some of the buoys have already drifted, just in the few days since we deployed them. We'll rest when we get to Kriti."

One buoy failed to answer at all. We quickly abandoned the effort to find it and ran toward the next one like children running past a graveyard on a dark night.

At some point, between buoys, Rachel certified Danto's and Mya's deaths and released their remains for disposal.

There wasn't much of a memorial, just me and Rachel at the recycle chute.

I couldn't bring myself to say a prayer. Rachel just said, "Rest in peace, Danto and Mya."

At least they were together.

Finally, we reached the last buoy and glimpsed a blur of light through ether haze. With a collective sigh of relief, we turned our backs on the Gloom and sailed toward Kriti.

That night, in the small hours while Rachel tended to Grim, Jamila slept, and Kojo managed the helm one-handed, Hiram and I silently resurrected the pieces of the synthreactor from their hiding places. I packed them into three drones, coded the locators and launched them into orbit around a tiny, inconspicuous moon. Rachel still had the hailer locked, but we had fifteen days to get to Kriti and contact Ordalo with the coordinates and retrieval codes.

Two days later, the Settlement Authority responded to Rachel's emergency hails by sending three ships to escort us the rest of the way to Kriti, where they imposed an in-orbit quarantine. Dour officers clad in protective suits came aboard to scan *Sparrow* for any lingering parasites. With the synthreactor gone, I didn't worry.

Grimbold—recovered enough to resume complaining—was moved to a med center and the rest of us were interrogated by humorless Settlement Authority officials.

Kojo argued bitterly against keeping us in orbit when we desperately needed rest and repair. Finally, they cleared *Sparrow* to dock at a secure facility on Kriti. Rachel and

Jamila left under Settlement Authority supervision, while *Sparrow*'s crew was kept aboard under house arrest.

I welcomed the chance to catch up on sleep. We had five days to get out of quarantine, contact Ordalo, and trade the synthreactor for the release of the mortgage on *Sparrowhawk* and the indentures over me and Kojo.

Two days later I was getting nervous, but Rachel had promised the quarantine would be lifted that day, subject to certain confidentiality agreements. She even brought a cask of ale to help us celebrate.

Archer filled tankards for me and him. "Here's to freedom," he said, hoisting one. He was his usual grubby self, cheered not only by the ale but by the fact that he'd had three full days to restore his engine room to sparkling condition.

Rachel smiled. "Kojo, how's your arm?"

He grimaced as he flexed the fingers of his left hand. "Better. The splint stays on for another two days. It will take a while to get the muscles back. Good thing I'm right-handed— it doesn't interfere with my drinking." He hefted his mug to demonstrate.

"Hear, hear," Hiram mumbled, already happily bleary.

"And, Patch, are you still having nightmares?" Rachel asked.

I scooched over so Archer could sit next to me. "Some. Not as many panic attacks." In fact, the night before, I had dreamed of Papa again. He hadn't issued any warnings, but had simply stood near as a reassuring presence. I'd felt overwhelmed with gratitude.

Rachel looked at the four of us in turn. "You understand, all of you are required to keep the location of Nakana secret. The Settlement Authority wants no pothunters looking for old tech, and maybe triggering another beacon."

"Fine with me," Kojo said, "I don't have any problem keeping quiet about that damn planet. That whole expedition was a burzing disaster."

I took a sip of ale. "I agree with Kojo. I don't really *want* to talk about it. But surely people will have questions? Danto and Lyden and Mya, Balan and that other woman Deprata—people will ask what happened to them. And Galactic and Rampart and the Cartel—they all know about the artifact. How is the Settlement Authority going to hush them up?"

"The Authority is not going to hush it up at all, just modify a few details. The main thing to remember is the place we went looking for the planet was not in the Gloom outside sector 377, but in sector 342, and the artifact turned out to be a hoax. The tablet and the rumors that it pointed the way to a Sage planet were planted by Galactic Conglomerate in order to distract their rival, Rampart Militech. It was all a lie."

"Sounds complicated," Kojo grumbled. "Why would Galactic go along with that?"

"They're getting a little something out of it." Rachel's eyes glinted over the rim of her mug.

Kojo and I looked at each other, puzzled.

Archer bounced on the couch. "The metal case!"

Rachel beamed. "Quite right, Virgil!" Archer blushed at his first name. "Gavoran scientists are eagerly studying the metal from the Cazar temple that shields against telepathic influences. Since the other races object to any enhancement of

Gavoran technological dominance, the Settlement Authority has given the metal samples from the case to Galactic and Rampart as well."

Archer giggled. "I predict we'll see rich Gavs wearing metal hats by next season."

"So," I said, twisting a lock of hair, "there was an expedition and a sixty-day charter, and everything happened as it did, except it was all a hoax and we never found Nakana."

"Right," Rachel said. "Jamila and Lyden were taken in by the fraudulent artifact and were convinced to search for a Sage planet. The haste in putting together the expedition was because outlaws had heard the rumors and were showing interest in stealing the artifact to find the planet first. The danger of piracy explains the attachment of a Corridor Patrol officer, and the uncharted location explains the participation of the Settlement Authority. All of which has the advantage of being, in a general way, true."

"Wait a minute," Kojo said. "Jamila's not going to let people think she was fooled."

"As it happens, Jamila Patil has a certain history of being associated with the black market in archeological objects. She's accepted a desk position with the Authority reviewing archeological survey reports while on probation—probation to be revoked if she becomes too talkative."

"So what did we find in sector 342?" Hiram asked.

"A planet that had conditions incompatible with life and no indication of technology. There was an emergency, a crash landing, and a fire. Mya was fatally injured. The whole expedition was a disaster, one death after another, all based on fraudulent information."

I nodded. "That's pretty close to truth. And Sergeant Danto?" I was suddenly trembling, remembering the seductive voices and the swarming parasites.

Archer put a comforting arm around my shoulder. He'd been doing that a lot lately. To my surprise, I rather liked it.

"Patch, are you all right?" Rachel asked quietly.

"I'm fine." I leaned into Archer's shoulder.

"The Gavoran clans have all been satisfied," Rachel said. "Danto died in a heroic attempt to rescue Mya. Deprata was a suicide over a love affair. Balan died courageously defending your ship against pirates. Lyden died of natural causes. To be honest, she never should have attempted the expedition."

"What about the burzing Patrol searching all those ships for treasure?" Hiram asked. "Every ship in the Selkid Trading Cartel knows about that."

"A cultural misunderstanding between the Gavoran and Terran members of the excavation team, now resolved, with apologies to the Corridor Patrol for their trouble."

Tinker jumped to my lap and settled in for a tongue bath. The cat seemed fine—Rachel had wormed her for any lingering parasites and had spayed her for good measure. No more yowling in the middle of the night.

"Don't you think anyone else will go looking for Nakana?" Kojo asked.

Rachel looked sternly at Kojo. "If they do, the Authority will have an excellent idea who told them where to look."

"Hell, I can keep a secret," Kojo protested.

Rachel switched her gaze to Hiram.

"Aw, don't worry about me," he said. "Nobody would believe me even if I *did* say something—everyone knows I drink a bit when I'm in port." He patted his tankard fondly, smiling at me and Kojo. "Besides, these youngsters will keep an eye on me."

"You're not joining the Cartel?" Archer asked.

"Nah. *Sparrow*'s in my blood. I won't jump ship just yet."

We all drank a toast to Hiram and *Sparrowhawk*.

"What about that snake Grimbold?" Kojo asked. "*He* won't stay quiet."

"As soon as he recovers, Grimbold will be spending the next year or three in a penal colony, clearing up certain outstanding warrants for fraud and theft. Frankly, he'll be safer there than walking around—Rampart Militech will be extremely angry that Grim lured them into chasing a hoax, resulting in the destruction of two of their vessels and the death and capture of their crews."

Tinker abandoned me and rubbed against Rachel's ankles. Rachel gave Tinker a little scratch behind the ears, eliciting a purr I could hear clear across the salon.

Kojo shifted uncomfortably. "Rachel, now the damn thing is gone, what *was* that relic? I know I saw Tinker get away with something. Was there really something alive in there?"

"Worms," Rachel replied.

I shuddered again. Archer held me close.

"The creatures within the relic were parasites," Rachel said. "I rescued a fragment from Tinker's scat. It may have been alive when she found it, but Tinker dispatched it very effectively."

Archer crooned, "Good kitty."

Rachel rubbed Tinker's spine, making her arch ecstatically. "The relic was a device, created to send telepathic messages to specific genetic populations. The worms were simply a biological switch, very efficient at breaking down blood. They excreted a specific chemical when they encountered a particular genetic marker in their food, a marker present in Gavoran blood."

Kojo glanced at me sideways. "Are all Gavs telepaths?"

Rachel shook her head. "Most Gavorans have a degree of telepathic receptivity, but they can't send telepathic messages. I suspect the Sages were a telepathic species. The best way for them to communicate with their allies, and control them, was to insert a gene that permitted this limited form of telepathy."

I nodded. "All Gavorans believe in spirits, whether it's ancestor spirits or Sage prophets. Maybe it's because for us, telepathy is real."

"The Sages may have selected Neanderthals to nurture because of their inherent telepathic abilities," Rachel said. "Or the Sages may have genetically modified the Neanderthal population on Gavora to be receptive. In either case, we can deduce that the Sages influenced Gavorans telepathically from the beginning."

The Sages, messing with Gav genetics, making us believe they were gods. Sentencing whole clans to slavery and implanting a religion to justify it. *Damn them all.*

Kojo asked, "Are you saying the worms were telepaths, telling the Gavs about Nakana, telling them when the relic needed blood?"

"It wasn't the worms issuing messages, it was the device inside the relic."

Archer nodded, tapping his foot. "I told you, Patch, remember? That if I were going to leave a map I would leave a machine, not an animal."

"It may have seemed like the relic was engaging in a conversation of sorts," Rachel said, "but it couldn't receive communication. The only changes to the content of the message came about in response to the worm's chemical excretions. The relic's primary message, its default activity, was a hunger call."

"For blood." I felt cold just thinking about it.

"Blood is the worm's natural food. During periods when they had no sustenance, the worms went into stasis, but the device continued to emit the hunger call, waiting for a person with the right telepathic receptiveness."

"So that was what lured Balan and Deprata to the relic in the first place," Archer said. "And once they fed the worms?"

"In the presence of food," Rachel said, "the worms awakened and reproduced. When the revived worms detected the genetic marker of an ally, the worms excreted a chemical trigger. That trigger caused the relic to reward whoever was touching it with a message that revealed the location of Nakana, and which simultaneously stimulated the pleasure centers of the brain."

"So, it *was* addictive," Kojo said.

"Exactly," Rachel agreed. "That kept the receptive person coming back. In addition, the trigger caused the device to change its general message from the hunger call to mental images that all members of the receptive species would receive—images of an idyllic, pastoral planet and promises of peace and joy."

"But it knew that Balan died," I said. "It started calling for blood again."

"The blood tie was supposed to be renewed periodically. When Balan failed to return and give additional blood, the worm's secretions reverted to its hunger mode, to find another donor."

"But why?" I asked. "Why leave the relic there at all?"

"A fail-safe device," Archer said.

Rachel smiled and nodded for him to continue.

Archer blushed, but carried on. "Suppose you're part of an advanced race in the middle of a war. You're worried you're about to lose a battle, maybe lose most of your forces. So, you hide some key resources somewhere no one knows about, so you can start again when things calm down. You create a device that will operate after a long time has passed, one that will show the map to the hidden fortress only to your allies, and you plant the device someplace out of the way, where it won't be destroyed in the battle."

"Very good, Virgil." Rachel beamed at him like a proud auntie. "You might leave it with some primitive people as caretakers by cultivating a myth that the device is sacred."

Kojo rubbed his jaw. "So, years or centuries later, when the device locates an ally, it gives them a map to the hidden fortress. It even helps them gather the rest of their people and bring them all to the fortress by promising good things. Bingo. Generations after some disaster has wiped out your forces, you have a ready-made army of willing recruits showing up at your fortress, ready to serve the old gods or, if needed, to fight another war. Very cute."

"The relic worked just like it was supposed to," I said. "It brought Gavorans to Nakana."

"When the relic got close enough to the planet," Rachel said, "it triggered the beacon in the ruined city. The beacon was another device, one that produced a stronger version of the telepathic call to come to the planet, designed to draw every ally within the planet's orbit to the central square. Mya couldn't resist the call. Even Patch and Danto were drawn to obey."

"But nobody was there," I said. "It was horrible."

"They probably intended for the device to be triggered millennia ago, but the destruction of the Cazar civilization meant there was no one in range to pick up the relic's call—not until Gavorans joined Jamila's archeology team. The people who originally lived on Nakana are long gone. The remaining animal life is infested by parasites—tormented, always moving, run to death. I don't know what happened on the planet to change its ecology. Perhaps some vital link in the plant or animal chain of interdependence was lost, some check on the parasites was allowed to die out."

"Do you think it was the Sages who lived there?" Kojo asked.

"I hope not." I shuddered again.

Rachel looked at me. "Why, Patch?"

"The bowls on those plinths—they had channels and pores, just like the relic. And they were rimmed with blades to draw blood."

Archer shrugged. "That makes sense. The residents would want any visitors to give a little blood, to test, like the relic, to make sure they're really allies."

"Maybe," I said. "But those bowls were awfully big, and there were a lot of them."

I tried to stop trembling. *It's over. The nightmare is over.*

"Suppose the reason *they*, the people who lived there, were so obsessed with blood is because they needed it? The place was filled with parasites that live on blood. Maybe the people who built the ruins..."

Rachel grinned. "You think the blessed Sages were highly evolved parasitic worms? Who wanted the Gavorans to come to Nakana as potential feedstock? It's possible. Theoretically, even a parasitic worm could evolve to become the apex predator. To develop reason and culture."

"And if it did," I said, "it would see a world filled with warm-blooded animals as a paradise, filled with peace and joy, just like it told us."

Archer jittered. "If that's true, they could still be there, in stasis like the relic worms, waiting for people to come and sacrifice enough blood to wake them up again."

"Let's hope not." The glint in Rachel's eyes told me she'd already worked out that possibility. No wonder she didn't want anyone snooping around Nakana.

We assured Rachel we'd keep all the secrets.

I didn't need the threat of drastic consequences to keep to the cover story; in fact, I was delighted with it. Since the Cartel knew we were carrying the synthreactor to Ordalo, we could make them understand that between running from the Rampart mercenaries and being commandeered by the Corridor Patrol to chase a hoax, we'd had no chance to turn the relic in to the Cartel. They might give us trouble, might even blackball us, but I was betting they wanted the synthreactor bad enough for Kojo and me to keep our freedom.

"Where will you go next?" Rachel asked.

"Ask Patch," Kojo said. "*She's* in charge of business." He winked at me.

I suppressed a smile. Kojo had lightly mentioned to me that once we were free of Ordalo's threats, he wouldn't mind staying on as *Sparrow*'s captain. At least for now, we were still partners.

"Once repairs are done," I said, "we'll look for some cargo to pick up and head back to our home sectors. It will be good to get back to trading again."

For once, I was hopeful about the future. Rachel had already approved the last installments of payment for the expedition. When we eventually reached our home port, I'd sell the premium brandy in the vault to favored trading partners—we'd been away for so long, I wanted to give them a reason to remember us. With the upgraded propulsion the Patrol had installed for the mission and the extended range scanner we'd taken from the Rampart harrier, we'd be able to take our pick of jobs. We'd be out of debt in no time.

First thing on my splurge list: go to a first-rate med center and get that damn skin graft fixed for good.

"There's one more thing," Rachel said, sipping her tea. "The microbial synthreactor."

Kojo's eyes widened. My stomach dropped.

"What?" Archer looked from me to Kojo in confusion.

Rachel smiled. "I tagged it with a locator before we even entered the Gloom, long before you dropped it off at that little moon. The Authority should have no trouble tracking it to its ultimate destination."

Kojo buried his face in his hands.

"A locator." My blood pounded in my ears. My worst nightmare was coming to life.

Rachel cocked her head like a curious robin. "Did you think all those scanners in your cargo hold were just for show? It took me half a day to trace the anomaly in my readings. I must say, I thought the grease on the bulkhead screws was a nice touch."

A rasping noise came from the corner. Hiram, now looking fully sober, was grinding his teeth.

Archer looked at me like I'd kicked a puppy.

Rachel settled more comfortably into the chair. "A Settlement Authority investigator will meet with you tomorrow at a safe location. If you want to stay out of prison on smuggling charges, you will provide her with every scrap of information you have about where you got the synthreactor and who the purchaser is. After that, you will proceed with whatever arrangements you've made to transfer the synthreactor. Thanks to you, the Authority will be able to close down an illegal terraforming operation and arrest that contraband ring."

Kojo muttered something unintelligible into his hands.

"You don't understand," I begged. "We were forced to carry that thing. If our contact suspects we've informed on him, that the goods are tagged...you have no idea what he'll do to us." Ordalo wouldn't be satisfied with our ship and our freedom, he'd want our blood, and prison walls wouldn't stop him.

"Something dire, I'm sure," Rachel said cheerfully. "But don't worry. The Settlement Authority has an interest in keeping your role secret—but *only* in return for your full cooperation in locating the wildcat terraforming operation."

Kojo raised his head, hope glimmering in his eyes.

Ancestors, give me strength.

"All right," I said. "You win. Whatever it takes to keep *Sparrowhawk* sailing."

Want to read more of *Sparrowhawk*'s adventures?

Ghost Ship

Sparrowhawk Book 2

PATCH AND KOJO are stuck in the frontier sectors bordering the Gloom, waiting for a sting operation to play out that will determine whether their future is freedom or prison.

When an old friend of Patch's father shows up begging for help, Patch and Kojo and the crew of *Sparrowhawk* take a side trip into uncharted space to salvage a valuable wrecked ship. The ship is there waiting for them—but so are the dangers of trackless space, pirate raids, warring worlds, and the menacing presence of the derelict ship's dead crew.

If you're a fan of *Firefly*, *Star Wars*, or *Battlestar Galactica*, or the books of Elizabeth Moon or J.N. Chaney, you'll enjoy the rough and tumble space adventures of Patch and the crew of *Sparrowhawk*.

Acknowledgements

WHILE ALL THE MISTAKES and draggy bits are mine and mine alone, I could never have brought a book to completion without the help of many others.

There is nothing like objective, constructive criticism to improve one's writing. I'm extremely grateful to my critique buddies at *Critiquecircle.com* for their support and suggestions, especially C.A. Collins, Allison Mulvihill, and Lizzie Newell.

Thanks to Shannon Roberts, Alana Joli Abbott, and Kelley Frodel for their editing expertise.

Most especially, a plethora of thanks to Douglas Phillips, author of the Quantum Series books, for his mentoring and inspiration and for helping bring the stories of Patch and her crew to life.

FINALLY, an infinity of thanks to my spouse Ari Patrinos for science consulting and his unflagging support, and to daughters Maritsa and Thalia for their support and patience with my technical questions.

ABOUT THE AUTHOR

KATHRYN HOFF has studied anthropology, manned the trenches on archeological digs, penetrated the mysteries of financial statements, and negotiated billion-dollar investments into developing countries. She has now graduated to making up stories. When not writing, she volunteers at a major zoo. Favorite animal: *Heterocephalus glaber*, the naked mole-rat.

Made in the USA
Middletown, DE
10 January 2020